I0544821

The de Chastelaine Chronicles

THE NILE PRIESTESS

CATHERINE CURZON & ELEANOR HARKSTEAD

The Nile Priestess
ISBN # 978-1-83943-768-7
©Copyright Catherine Curzon & Eleanor Harkstead 2022
Cover Art by Erin Dameron-Hill ©Copyright January 2022
Interior text design by Claire Siemaszkiewicz
Totally Bound Publishing

THE NILE PRIESTESS

Dedication

"To speak the name of the dead
is to make him live again."

Chapter One

Cecily leaned over the ship's railing, shielding her eyes from the hot Mediterranean sun with her hand. They'd travelled across Europe to get here, and now they were almost at their destination, a place Cecily had only ever dreamed of before.

"And tomorrow we'll see Egypt, just there on the horizon!" she excitedly said to Raf, her husband.

If only I could wish and wish and it'd appear there right away.

"And tomorrow night, we'll be snuggled in bed in the Rosetta of the Nile, counting the stars above Cairo." Raf beamed. He put his arm around Cecily's waist and said, "It's the perfect honeymoon, Sissy."

"It feels like a dream, Raf, like it's not quite real!" Cecily pictured pyramids and deserts, a world away from their home in Yorkshire or the places in Europe they had journeyed through. "We'll go everywhere by camel, of course, and eat nothing but dates."

"Just like we do in Yorkshire," he told her with a grin. Then he pecked a kiss to Cecily's cheek and asked, "Happy, Mrs de Chastelaine?"

"Oh, so happy I might go *pop*!" Cecily said excitedly. Then with affection, she added, "But then, I have been ever since I first met you, Raf."

Not so long ago Cecily would never have dreamed that she'd be married to a man—or *dhampir*, really— like Raf de Chastelaine, let alone be honeymooning in Egypt, but here she was. Her life had taken an unexpected turn and as she stood here beneath the sun, the botanical scent of Raf's homemade sun lotion mingling with the heat and sea salt, she'd never been happier.

A breeze rippled the brim of her sunhat, and Cecily turned to see another passenger lean against the railings a few feet away. Miss Mansour was a very glamorous Egyptian lady, who they'd sat with at the captain's table the night before, along with Miss Mansour's party of archaeologists. Cecily had been over the moon to sit at such an important table on her first long sea journey, and with a party who were travelling to Egypt to uncover its wonders, too.

But Miss Mansour seemed preoccupied and hadn't noticed them. Instead, she stared off towards the horizon.

Cecily's sixth sense, her ability to pick up on others' emotions, began to twitch.

She's homesick, Cecily thought, although she realised that was obvious.

"Raf," Cecily whispered, "let's say good afternoon."

Raf glanced towards the woman, then gave a nod. "Yeah, let's say how do," he decided.

Cecily moved along the salt-covered railing. "Good afternoon, Miss Mansour!" She smiled. "You must be very glad to be so close to home again."

Miss Mansour removed her sunglasses and smiled back, but there was something sad in her expression. "Oh, of course, if one has a happy home, then one is glad to return. I am thinking of all the work I must do when we arrive. Lord Bath has such great plans for his dig. I think we might uncover many wonderful things."

"It must be terribly exciting!" Cecily said. "All those treasures that haven't seen the light of day for years and years and years, and you brush away the sand, and there in your hand there's a little golden Anubis!"

"Lord Carnarvon hasn't put him off?" Raf asked. "If you believe the papers, pyramid-diving is a bad business. I don't know... I feel like perhaps English lords should leave Egyptian treasures in Egypt."

A flicker of amusement crossed Miss Mansour's face. She maybe didn't hear that sentiment often enough. But Raf's Romanian accent no doubt told her that he had no patience with the meddling of the English. "It is strange to me to think of my ancestors lying in museums across the world. I cannot think it was what they expected when they died — that one day their remains would travel the world, to be stared at."

"I heard that Lord Bath reckons he's found a tomb that nobody believed existed at all," Raf replied. "But legends sometimes turn out to be true, don't they?"

And Raf would know all about that, wouldn't he? Not many advertisements for family businesses that spanned the generations read, '*Ghosts need laying? Rates negotiable on application.*' Raf didn't work alone anymore though — Cecily was part of the family business, too.

But what fates had Raf's ancestors faced? His father might be human, but his late mother certainly hadn't been. After all, it wasn't many newlyweds who spent Christmas at a castle perched atop a precipice on the edge of the Carpathian Mountains. Cecily would never have guessed that vampires could be such generous and attentive hosts.

"The tomb of Menkare II," Miss Mansour replied, with a note of distaste. "He is sure that he has discovered it, even though the sands covered it from human sight longer ago than you can imagine. A pharaoh who has almost been entirely forgotten, but the legend of his missing tomb has persisted down the centuries. And now Lord Bath thinks he's found it."

Cecily shivered with delight at the thought. "Do you think we might come along to the dig and have a look? We won't touch anything. We'll be on our best behaviour. Won't we, Raf?"

"I don't want to touch anything that's been inside a forgotten tomb." Raf chuckled. "I've got an allergy to curses. I'd love to have a nose at the site, though...history's a bit of a hobby of mine. Along with gardening. And tinkering. I love tinkering."

Miss Mansour chuckled. Then she looked Raf and Cecily slowly up and down, as if she was assessing them. Cecily did her best to smile under her scrutiny. It felt as if Miss Mansour wasn't just looking *at* them, but *into* them. Although Cecily told herself she couldn't be. Then Miss Mansour nodded.

"Yes, why don't you come along? I believe I can trust you." Miss Mansour pointed to the jumble of necklaces and amulets around Raf's neck. "You're wearing a scarab, I see. And the Eye of Horus."

Raf nodded. "It's not my first time in Egypt," he admitted, almost bashfully. "And I like to pack on the protection. Whether it's from the sun, or...whatever else is floating about."

"You are very sensible to do so," Miss Mansour said. "Lord Bath scoffs at such ideas, of course. And I am told sometimes that I am too superstitious, but you never can be too careful. Especially not when you're robbing graves, even ancient ones." She paused for a moment, before adding, almost to herself, "*Especially* ancient ones."

"We're very careful about such things," Cecily said, knowing she couldn't go into detail with someone they'd not long met. "We always treat the dead with respect."

"They're people too," Raf pointed out, straight-faced. "Just like us."

"Oh, they are..." Miss Mansour glanced away for a moment, towards the southern horizon. Cecily sensed her homesickness again, a feeling of loss and loneliness. Then Miss Mansour turned back to face them. "You see, I knew I could trust you. There are not many people on this earth who share that sentiment, Mr de Chastelaine."

Raf smiled gently and admitted, "It's just something life's taught us." And he glanced towards Cecily, his eyes filled with love.

"Miss Mansour!" It was Lord Bath's braying voice, and it was coming closer from inside the ship. "I say, Miss Mansour, where are you hiding?"

Miss Mansour sighed. "I apologise. I must speak to Lord Bath." She raised her voice and replied, "I am out here on the deck, Lord Bath, taking the sea air."

"Dreaming of the old homeland, eh!" Lord Bath stepped out onto the deck. He put his hands on his hips and drew in a deep breath of sea air. "Good Lord, it's hotter than ever today!"

He was dressed in a linen suit, as most of the European men on the ship were. But Lord Bath's looked particularly expensive, cut to fit just right. His square jaw jutted out as he took the air, as though he was the master of all he surveyed. And the truth was, men like him were.

Not women like Cecily or Miss Mansour, not men like Raf. But wealthy English aristocrats in Jermyn Street linen suits ruled the world.

"This is not hot!" Miss Mansour chuckled. "You have the sea breeze here. But out in the desert, it doesn't matter how hot it gets, you hope the wind won't start up or a sandstorm might follow. But I will be glad to see my home again, yes. Are you not pleased to see yours when you return to England?"

"One has several, and one is *always* happy to see them. But the tomb of Menkare II is my life's work. I'll happily take a long-lost legendary treasure horde over even the nicest family pile in Bath." Bath guffawed. He lifted his Panama hat to Raf and Cecily. "Good afternoon, Mr and Mrs de Chastelaine. Egypt awaits, what!"

"Oh, it does!" Cecily replied. "You must be so excited about the dig. I know I am, and I'm not even digging anything. But then I've never been to Egypt before, and you're all experts on it. Miss Mansour especially."

Miss Mansour smiled wistfully. "Egypt and her myths and legends have been *my* life's work."

But it wouldn't be Miss Mansour's name connected with the find. Rather, the name of a man born in a country far away, in a land without a single desert to its name.

"I must confess this was a last throw of the dice," Bath admitted. "Seven failed digs over the years. But our Miss Mansour isn't only a dashed pretty face. She's got a very clever little brain in that head of hers!"

Little brain? Cecily had once been married to a man who spoke like that about women. She bristled on Miss Mansour's behalf.

"How kind of you to say so," Miss Mansour replied, acknowledging his backhanded compliment with a nod. "I have worked very hard — *studied* very hard — to acquire the knowledge I now have of my country's ancient past."

"And we're all terribly grateful," Bath assured her. "Miss Mansour was able to interpret the last clues to the location of the tomb. When the treasures of Menkare II are exhibited in London, I'm sure this young lady's beauty will dazzle almost as much as the pharaoh's gold."

Young lady's beauty?

Cecily bristled anew. She could sense that Miss Mansour didn't appreciate the way Lord Bath spoke about her either, but she didn't say anything.

"And everyone will want to talk to her to find out how she worked out the last clues," Cecily said.

Miss Mansour gave Cecily a smile, as if telling her that she appreciated her support. "I would be more than happy to."

Lord Bath met that with a bark of uproarious laughter. He clapped his hands together and exclaimed, "Quite so, Mrs de Chastelaine, quite so!" He wiped his eyes on a pristine white handkerchief. "And when one dines at the Ritz, one lauds the waitress for the chef's splendid work, eh?"

"But without Miss Mansour, you wouldn't have found the tomb," Raf pointed out, frowning. "Isn't that right?"

"And without *my* money to hire her, Miss Mansour wouldn't have been part of the party at all." Lord Bath's smile had become rather tight. Cecily could tell that he didn't take kindly to such ideas. "And she *certainly* wouldn't have had access to the tablets and *very* rare papyri that held the secrets of Menkare II's tomb. Believe me when I say that such treasures are highly prized and priced accordingly. Far beyond the reach of the Miss Mansours of the world."

Miss Mansour raised an eyebrow before putting her sunglasses back on. A chill breeze rose from the sea. "*That* is because the tablets and papyri I needed to study are held in a private collection in England."

"Guilty as charged." Bath chuckled. "And I may yet have one surprise left up my sleeve, madam. A little showmanship, if you will."

"Is that so?" Miss Mansour sounded like someone who was not easily surprised. She tapped her fingers against the ship's railing, her rings clanging on the metal. "I shall look forward to it."

"Well, you'll excuse me. I must dress for dinner." Bath gave a polite nod of farewell. "Miss Mansour, might I escort you to your state — cabin?"

No stateroom for the hired help then, no matter how valuable their knowledge.

"No, thank you, Lord Bath. I believe I can just about remember the way there. Good evening." And with that, Miss Mansour inclined her head, then turned and glided away along the deck.

Cecily glanced at Lord Bath, wondering if he had taken offence. But how else could Miss Mansour have reacted without any further dents to her dignity?

"She's homesick," Cecily told Lord Bath by way of explanation.

"Ah, England's green and pleasant land. We all miss her, of course," Bath replied, apparently untroubled by her departure. And somehow unaware that perhaps Miss Mansour, his Egyptian associate, might not consider England home, no matter how green or pleasant.

"Egypt," Raf said bluntly.

"Yes, she misses Egypt," Cecily prompted Lord Bath. "I think maybe she's glad not to be in England."

"Well, I certainly won't be asking her to come back to England if she prefers to remain in Egypt," the Earl of Bath replied with a magnanimous smile. "I shan't be requiring her expertise once the tomb is open. Miss Mansour can go wherever she might wish."

Raf frowned and asked, "You won't give her the credit for her work, then?" He added innocently, "I thought you said you couldn't have done it without her."

"She's terribly clever," Cecily added. "Just think of the number of languages she understands, modern and ancient ones. *And* she knows a terribly vast amount of things about the ancient world as well!"

"And dashed pretty too," the Earl of Bath replied. "Well, I shall take my leave. Good afternoon to you both!"

"We must go and dress for dinner. Good afternoon," Cecily responded, the words sticking in her throat. The earl gave another nod and retreated back towards the ship.

"Cheerio," Raf called, but Cecily knew that his bonhomie was an effort. He didn't like Lord Bath any more than she did. If the nobleman realised, of course, he didn't care. Instead he disappeared into the ship, whistling a cheery tune as he went.

Cecily waited until he had gone, then she whispered to Raf, "What a dreadful man, robbing Miss Mansour of her discovery. I really don't like him at all, Raf. But then, maybe I've known one too many men like him in my life."

Raf nodded. He put his arm around Cecily's shoulders and whispered, "Not my sort of bloke either. Do you want to head in and get ready to eat?" Raf kissed her cheek. "Do I have to wear shoes to dinner?"

"Oh, yes, let's go back to the cabin." Cecily chuckled. "Shoes? Well, if you don't wear shoes, we might not be invited to the captain's table tonight. But if the delightful Lord Bath's sitting there again, maybe that's a good thing."

"I'll put shoes on," Raf assured her. Then he added with a wink, "But I'll slip them off when I'm sitting down,"

Raf really didn't like shoes. He was happiest barefoot, wandering through the garden at home. Cecily smiled at him. "I'd expect nothing less, darling! Right, let's get ready for dinner."

Arm in arm, they strolled along the deck towards their cabin.

Chapter Two

Cecily dressed for dinner in a gown Raf had bought her during the week of their honeymoon that they'd spent in Paris. It was made from pink and grey silk, as soft as a whisper, and Cecily wore it with silver buckled shoes, a silver headband and a pink feathered fan. She felt very elegant and *à la mode*, and noticed the glances her chic outfit attracted as they sat at their table. For much of her life Cecily had missed out on wearing the latest fashions, and now that she could dress however she wished, she was like a child with a dressing-up box.

They hadn't been seated at the captain's table, but Cecily didn't mind, glad to be by the window where she could watch the sunset over the sea with Raf. Lord Bath's party were sitting with the captain again, but Miss Mansour seemed rather distant, eating her meal without much conversation with the others. She looked beautiful in a dark blue and gold dress, a peacock feather in her hairband.

Even in a dinner jacket and bow tie, Raf looked just like Raf always did. Cecily knew he'd brushed his hair, because she'd seen him, yet it was mussed before they even left the cabin. It was a miracle that his tie had remained tied, and she knew that under the table he'd be barefoot. Dinner suits just weren't Raf, and she loved him all the more for it.

"Last night at sea for a bit," Raf commented, gazing through the window at the setting sun. "It'll be nice to be back on dry land, won't it? I might live next to the sea, but I like solid ground under my feet…when I'm not in the air."

Cecily beamed at him. In Paris, they'd taken a moonlit walk to the Eiffel Tower, and Raf had transformed himself into a bat and fluttered around it, with some local Parisian bats. It really had been quite the show. And one that would remain a special, secret memory between them forever.

"It seems incredible that we're swapping endless sea for endless sand, doesn't it?" Cecily took Raf's hand. "I'm so enjoying this trip, you know!"

Cecily couldn't help her gaze wandering over to the captain's table again. The diners were almost all men, and beside Lord Bath, Cecily noticed Mr Snelling, his chief assistant. He laughed loudly at all of the earl's jokes, and each time, Miss Mansour flinched.

"Do you think Mr Snelling really finds all those jokes *that* amusing?" Cecily asked Raf.

"You're joking?" Raf grimaced and shook his head. "But Lord Stanhope pays his wages. So he laughs as loud as he can, to keep the wages coming!"

"And he makes himself look ridiculous in the process," Cecily observed, noticing Mr Snelling's habit of fiddling with his bow tie every few moments, as if he weren't entirely comfortable in it. "If Lord Bath had no title and only a farthing to his name, he'd never have all those people fawning over him, would he?"

Raf nodded. "But he's the almighty Julian Vane-Stanhope, third Earl of Bath," he reminded her. "And that, along with the bank balance and the old school tie, buys a man a lot of friends. Years' worth of fruitless digs in Egypt don't come cheap though." He dropped his voice even lower. "And he could've cursed Carnarvon himself. He beat Vane-Stanhope to the big discovery, after all."

"Tutankhamun!" Cecily breathed. The name was full of magic and wonder. She had poured over photographs of the find, and had never imagined she'd one day go on a dig in Egypt herself. "Gosh, I imagine he must've been furious to miss out on that. I tried very hard not to mention it last night at dinner, but you can't very well talk about the tombs of pharaohs without King Tut coming up once or twice."

"Carnarvon laughed at Vane-Stanhope, you know," Raf said. "He thought Vane-Stanhope was chasing a legend, a tomb that couldn't be found because it didn't even exist. But he found it. It cost the lives of some of his Egyptian diggers and a whole heap of cash, but he got there."

"A toast to the *late* fifth Earl of Carnarvon," Julian Vane-Stanhope exclaimed through a hollow laugh. He raised his glass and brayed, "I only wish you were here to see yourself proved so very, very wrong, Georgie!"

Miss Mansour smiled briefly before sipping her glass of water. But Mr Snelling laughed as if Lord Bath had told the joke of the century, and slapped the table with his hand.

"It's as well he's *not* here," he said, before shooting a brief but pointed glance at Miss Mansour. "Otherwise he'd be busy trying to claim your discovery as his own!"

"King Tut's curse got the blighter!" Bath laughed and around his table, polite laughter echoed his own. As it did, he straightened his face and added sombrely, "God rest his soul, of course."

"Of course," Mr Snelling said, all trace of his laughter gone now as he frowned with sadness at the thought of Carnarvon's death. "May he rest in peace. Well-deserved peace. Very well-deserved, poor chap."

"What a toady!" Cecily whispered to Raf.

"If I were him, I wouldn't be laughing," Raf replied. "If a tomb's been buried for three thousand years, there's usually a good reason for it. Leave well alone."

Cecily gasped. "I suppose you could have a point, Raf. If it's really true that there was a curse on Tutankhamun's tomb, then there's going to be one on Menkare II's as well. But I *am* excited about going to see the dig. If we stick with Miss Mansour, we should be all right, shouldn't we? She respects the tombs, after all."

"Does she?" Raf asked. "Why did she help Vane-Stanhope find it, in that case?" He glanced towards Miss Mansour, then ruffled his hand through his already disordered hair. "But we all have to eat, don't we? And pay our bills. I'm not about to condemn her because she's had to work with the likes of him."

Raf took Cecily's hand and brought it to his lips for a second before he spoke again.

"It's not easy to make a go of it as a woman alone," he concluded. "But she never looks too happy to me. That's probably the boss. I don't like him, for all his bonhomie."

"He's very rude about her talents," Cecily observed. "*Clever little brain,* indeed! He only says that because he resents the fact that all his money can't buy him knowledge — he can only rent out other people's."

"And nobody will know she even exists when he's soaking up the applause." Raf shook his head. "Times need to change, Sissy. It's the twentieth century!"

"They certainly do, and I'm certain they will," Cecily said. She had always liked the fact that Raf never spoke down to anyone, man and woman alike. "Isn't there someone we could talk to back home? Could we not find a journalist in England who'd want to interview Miss Mansour? That's if the tomb is where they think it is, of course."

Raf looked thoughtful, then nodded.

"If she wants it, there must be. But she looked so homesick for Egypt on deck, I wonder if she'll go back to England at all."

Cecily tipped her head to one side and looked over at the captain's table. Through her half-closed eyes, she could see the vibrations that each person gave out, like a quivering string on an instrument. It was a skill she had lately been refining. The vibrations were different sizes, different colours, and Cecily knew how to read them. Lord Bath's was thin and bright, agile and confident. Mr Snelling's fluctuated, sometimes much like Lord Bath's, but by turns rather slack and dull.

Miss Mansour's, however, stood out, a thick, grey vibration, and Cecily knew at once what it meant.

"It's not just homesickness," Cecily told Raf, clutching at her chest. "Poor thing. Miss Mansour's heart is broken."

Raf's frown deepened. He wouldn't question her, Cecily knew, and she loved him for it. Her husband knew that her gifts were a part of her, one of the things that made Cecily the woman he loved. And that made her feel special too.

"Do you think she needs a friend?" he whispered. "She's always alone. And there're no other women in that party. Just Miss Mansour and all those braying public schoolboys telling her she's a *pretty little thing*."

Cecily wrinkled her nose. "They're positively odious, aren't they? You know, I think you're right, she *does* need a friend. In fact, I prescribe *two* friends, a Raf *and* a Cec!"

At the captain's table, Lord Bath was leaning back in his chair. He clicked his fingers towards one of the waiters and called to him. "You there! Boy!"

The waiter, who was far from being a *boy* as silver flecked his dark hair at the temples, went over to the table and bowed from the waist.

"Yes, sir?" the waiter asked.

"I've left a box on the desk in my stateroom," Lord Bath told the waiter. "Go and get it, will you? Don't touch anything else. I shall know!"

"Of course, sir." The waiter bowed again, then he withdrew.

Miss Mansour had paused, watching their interaction, before returning to her dinner. She wasn't impressed by Lord Bath's behaviour.

A few minutes passed, and the waiter returned. Cecily felt uneasy as soon as he came back, and she reached for Raf's hand. The waiter was carrying a large silver box with a gold keyhole. The turrets at its four corners made it look for all the world like a portable temple.

Cecily looked away, her eyes closed. She heard a scream. Not a scream that anyone else could hear, but a portent that thrummed through her and told her that nothing good was inside that box.

The waiter handed the box to the Earl of Bath, who put it on the table in front of himself with so much care that it might have been made of fragile bone china. He laid the palms of his hands flat against its surface and looked at the faces of those who shared his table. As he did, Cecily saw Raf's nostrils twitch. What could he smell?

"Those of you who know my family know that my grandfather, the first Earl of Bath, was an explorer," Lord Bath announced to his table, but loudly enough to entertain the whole of the restaurant. "He went from the back of beyond to the last place God made, liberating the most beautiful treasures from the savages who held them and kept them from the eyes of learned gentlemen. Thanks to scholars like my grandfather, those treasures now reside in the finest institutions in London. We owe those gentlemen a debt of gratitude, for it is they who have made our sceptred isle the cultural jewel of the British empire."

Raf rolled his eyes and shook his head, but the captain's table erupted with applause.

"In other words, his rich grandad looted," he told Cecily in a whisper. "And probably did a fair bit of massacring too."

"I'll bet he did." Cecily sighed. *"Liberating from savages,* as if he had more right to the *treasure* than the people it belonged to."

Miss Mansour had put down her cutlery and was sitting upright in her chair, her gaze fixed on the box as if it had mesmerised her.

"This box is what set the Vane-Stanhope family on the road to this very voyage, all those years ago," Lord Bath went on. "It was acquired by my grandfather during his last expedition to Egypt, when a sandstorm swept the sands of Giza into a thick, suffocating cloud. The third earl, separated from his party, stumbled blindly into the sand. Hopeless and lost, he fell to his knees and there, beneath his desperate, clawing hands, he felt something in the sand."

Miss Mansour hadn't moved. It was almost as though she had turned into a statue.

"Do you think that's true?" Cecily whispered to Raf. "Or do you think he bought it in the souk?"

Raf opened his mouth to reply, but fell silent when Lord Bath went on.

"As the storm subsided, he saw this box, as though it had been waiting for him," the earl told his transfixed audience. "He dug it out with his bare hands and somehow stumbled back to camp. When his Egyptian servants saw this, they told him that he must never open it, that the sands of Giza would not give him a gift like this without exacting a terrible price."

Raf rolled his eyes again and whispered, "Not as terrible as his storytelling."

"Grandfather broke open the lock and found inside an ancient papyrus scroll," Lord Bath said. "One that might make the man who held it unstoppable. At the very least, it would clear his enemies and opponents from his path, for it provides him with an instrument of revenge that few could hope to oppose."

"He opened it?" Miss Mansour gasped in alarm. "No, he should not have done so!"

"Pipe down!" Mr Snelling snapped. "Lord Bath is speaking, not you."

"He opened it, madam," said Lord Bath, widening his eyes like an amateur theatrical in a melodrama. "And from within, a cobra with blood-red eyes reared up and bit his hand clean through!"

"No!" Miss Mansour shook her head, her eyes closed. "The cobra in the box in the sand, I have read of it. You must beware the cobra in the box in the sand!"

Cecily looked on in concern. Miss Mansour looked terrified, and her vibrations had changed from grey to red. She was frightened and angry.

"The cobra." He chuckled. "My grandfather snatched up his machete and cut the cobra in two. Then he cut off his own hand to stem the flow of the poison. *That* is the measure of the man! He lingered on the edge of death for weeks, wasting away. The earl barely opened his eyes when his wife had him brought back to England and called on every fine physician in London to treat him. All he could speak of was the box. In his few moments of wakefulness, he called for the box and the scroll within, one minute seized with the mania, the next plunged into oblivion again. But the strength of that remarkable man was in his survival, and six months to the day that the cobra bit him, he opened his eyes, took out the scroll and read it."

With that, Lord Bath opened the lid of the box. From within he produced a rolled scroll that looked more ancient than any paper or book Cecily had ever seen. As the earl lifted the lid, Raf took a deep sniff, then he grimaced and held his napkin over his nose.

"That smells like death to me," Raf whispered to Cecily. "Like a tomb."

Cecily shuddered with distaste. Raf had such a sensitive nose. She couldn't imagine how an ancient scroll from a tomb must smell to him.

Miss Mansour shook her head. "No, you must not, Lord Bath. Do you understand what that is?"

Mr Snelling shushed her, as if she was a difficult child. "He knows very well what it is. It's a scroll, for heaven's sake."

Lord Bath rose to his feet, the rolled papyrus in his pale hand.

"From the day he awoke, my grandfather dreamed of returning to Egypt to read the scroll once more. The words are ancient, and the power immense, but the scroll must be read in sight of the Egyptian shore if its magic is to take hold." He looked towards the captain. "Captain, I'm right in my belief that one can sight Egypt by the moon if one looks from the porthole tonight, yes?"

The captain nodded. "Yes, you can indeed."

"You mustn't do this!" Miss Mansour protested. She rose from her chair, pointing her finger towards Lord Bath. "I have warned you."

"What happened to your grandfather?" Raf called. He leaned back in his chair and blinked, waiting for the Earl of Bath to reply. For a moment the nobleman said nothing, then he gave a cool smile.

"On the eve of his planned return to Egypt, he was found dead in his rooms, this scroll in his one remaining hand," said Lord Bath. "According to his physician, he had been bitten by a cobra. In rural Somerset."

A shocked gasp ran through the room. The other diners were entranced by the story, but Miss Mansour looked suddenly weakened by it, and although she was still standing, she gripped the back of her chair.

"And you would read the scroll here, on this ship? In front of all these people?" Miss Mansour said. "You know it is dangerous. You must not read it. I forbid it!"

"You forbid it, madam?" Lord Bath laughed. "My father was a superstitious fool, too. He put this papyrus away and concentrated his efforts on the Raj, but Egypt has always been my particular passion. One might say I am my grandfather's boy at heart."

Lord Bath looked down at the scroll, then settled his gaze on Miss Mansour. His smile didn't falter, but his eyes flashed annoyance.

"I don't believe in magic, Miss Mansour. The scroll is theatre, nothing more," Lord Bath said. "Carnarvon was killed by a mosquito bite, my grandfather by a snake. But I owe it to his memory to read the scroll in the sight of the Egyptian shore, because it was the one thing he dreamed of, and the one thing he never achieved."

Miss Mansour shivered. "No, no, you must not!" For a moment she was rooted to the spot, then she ran at Lord Bath, a streak of blue and gold as she hurried towards him. "Stop, stop! Do not do this unholy thing!"

Mr Snelling intercepted her, roughly grabbing Miss Mansour's arm. Cecily winced.

"That'll do, Miss!" Mr Snelling chided. "Go back to your seat."

But Miss Mansour made no attempt to return to her chair. She scratched at the air with her free hand, trying to reach for Lord Bath or the scroll. Perhaps both, Cecily wasn't sure. She was muttering something in words Cecily didn't understand.

"I say, Captain," Lord Bath snapped. "Have this woman taken to her cabin. I believe she's drunk. Bally sorry show!"

"This isn't on," Raf whispered to Cecily as he rose to his feet. He turned to address the captain's table. "Miss Mansour isn't drunk, sir. She's simply asking you to respect the heritage of her country. Not every curse is a campfire story."

Mr Snelling was joined by another man from their party, who grabbed Miss Mansour's other arm.

"She's disturbing our evening enjoyment with her superstitious nonsense," Mr Snelling announced, trying to drag Miss Mansour away. She was still muttering, her gaze fixed on the scroll.

The captain pointed to two uniformed men who came over at once, grabbing Miss Mansour, who could not fight them off. The lights flickered as Miss Mansour was dragged towards the door.

"You must not do this!" Miss Mansour shouted across the room to Lord Bath. "I implore you not to! You have no *idea* what you are calling upon!"

But the four men took her away through the door, and Cecily was already out of her chair. "She needs us, Raf," she said.

"Don't manhandle her," Raf called after the men as he reached for Cecily's hand. He was still barefoot, she realised. "And if I were you, my so-called Lord, I wouldn't read that scroll here or anywhere. Your grandad might've been a fool, but that doesn't mean you have to be too!"

The Earl of Bath narrowed his eyes, then told Raf in a sneer, "Get off with you, you little foreign oik." He unrolled the scroll and cleared his throat. "No cobras, thank goodness, just an urchin from Lord knows where! The poorest end of the Russian Steppes, eh?"

And he laughed his braying laugh.

Cecily glared at him. "How dare you speak to my husband like that. Perhaps you ought to listen to those who know what they're talking about. If you're not careful, your arrogance will be your undoing." And with that, she and Raf left the dining room, hurrying in the wake of Miss Mansour.

Chapter Three

Cecily had seen Miss Mansour head into a cabin near the one she shared with Raf. But she could sense where Miss Mansour had gone, because her fear and anguish had left a discernible imprint on the air. And she knew that Raf could seek out the scent of Miss Mansour's perfume.

Cecily tapped on the door.

"Miss Mansour?" she called.

From inside the room, Cecily heard weeping. Then there were footsteps approaching the door. "Who is it? Is it you, Mrs de Chatelaine, and your husband too?"

"It's us," Raf replied, his voice gentle. "Are you all right, Miss?"

She sniffed before replying, "I am…a little shaken up."

"Would you like us to get you anything?" Cecily asked. "There's a doctor on board."

"No, no, you are very kind, but I do not need to see the doctor," Miss Mansour said. "Will you come in? I would appreciate your company."

Cecily glanced at Raf and nodded. "We'd be happy to."

Miss Mansour opened the door and stepped aside to let them in. She was still in her eveningwear, but looked rather unkempt, having been dragged through the ship.

Her cabin was much like Raf and Cecily's. Moonlight came in through the porthole window and Cecily remembered Lord Bath saying that the Egyptian coast would be visible out of their portholes tonight.

On the threshold of the cabin, Raf paused. He was already untying his bow tie, but he froze and stood there, still as a statue. A scudding cloud covered the full moon that illuminated the cabin, throwing a dark shadow across them all. After a moment in that passing darkness, Cecily saw a deep shiver run through her husband.

"I think he's reading his scroll," Raf said. "Are you getting anything?"

Cecily half-closed her eyes. Something was wrong. Miss Mansour had been right to be afraid, to try to stop him. Cecily couldn't quite explain what she felt, though. If Lord Bath had summoned a ghost or a demon, Cecily would have sensed it. She couldn't sense either, and yet... *Whatever is it?*

"I feel ever so uneasy," Cecily replied.

Miss Mansour ran her hand across her disordered hair. In a voice barely above a whisper, she told them, "He is playing dangerous parlour games with history."

Raf finally stepped into the cabin and closed the door. He cast his eyes up, as though listening for something, then reached for Cecily's hand.

"Something's off," he said. "I don't think I'd have read that, but...I'm me."

"You are quite right. He should not have done," Miss Mansour told them. "That scroll has great power, and it should not be in his hands. It is so kind of you both to speak up for me, and to come here to see me. Those brutes opened the cabin door and flung me in. They told me to sober up, but I was drinking only water! But you must not worry about me — look, through the porthole, it's Egypt. It's my home."

Cecily gasped. "Oh, Raf, let's look! My first view of Egypt!"

She led Raf over to the porthole and peered out across the perfect flat surface of the ocean. So flat that Cecily felt as if she could walk across it. And there, just at the horizon, she saw a narrow ribbon of land. Cecily's first sight of anywhere outside Europe.

"It's always something, seeing home," Raf said gently to Miss Mansour. Cecily recalled his own excitement at returning to that Carpathian castle where he had been born, and how his already exuberant joy had grown with every mile they travelled towards the borders of his Transylvanian birthplace. Now Miss Mansour was heading home too, but that sense of sadness somehow still remained. "Look at that, Sis. Egypt."

"I can't see any pyramids yet," Cecily said as she looked across at the distant land. "But I'm fairly sure I can see at least a couple of palm trees. And just think, we'll be there by morning and it'll be all hot and sunny again."

"It is very beautiful by moonlight, don't you think?" Miss Mansour's voice sounded very far away, as if she wasn't so much speaking her words aloud, but was remembering something from the past. "Do you know that the Ancient Greeks, who brought their beliefs to Egypt, thought that the moon was their goddess Selene, travelling across the sky in her chariot? It makes perfect sense when you see a sight like this."

Cecily glanced round at Miss Mansour. She was standing very still, silvered by the moonlight, her gaze fixed on the view beyond the porthole. Cecily had the strangest feeling, as if she weren't looking at a real flesh and blood woman, but an ancient statue.

I'm being silly. I'm just overawed at coming to Egypt and everything being so old.

She gently nudged Raf, wondering if he had noticed too. He replied with the slightest inclination of his head. It didn't surprise Cecily. It was part of what she loved about what they shared. Sometimes they seemed to even read each other's thoughts, in a funny sort of way.

After a moment, Miss Mansour moved, and Cecily jumped with surprise.

"Oh, I'm sorry, Miss Mansour!" Cecily said. "Only you were so still…"

Miss Mansour waved Cecily's worry away. "It is quite all right. I was lost in my thoughts. By the way, please, do not bother with all the *Miss Mansours*. Will you call me by my first name, Dina?"

"Of course, we'd be honoured to. I'm Cecily," Cecily replied.

"Raf." Her husband beamed. "Hello, Dina. I'm sorry about what happened just now. Does he carry on like that a lot?"

Raf's answer came with a furious knock at the door and the sound of Lord Bath's voice, raised in anger.

"Open this door, you bloody hussy! I'd like to hear what you've got to say for yourself, Miss!"

Dina muttered under her breath. "Must I answer to him? I suppose I must. He pays me, after all. But I hope he will behave better with you two being here." She sighed, then went over to the door and opened it. "There is no need to shout, Lord Bath."

"No need to shout," he bellowed. "No need to – ah, I see you have company. Mr and Mrs de Chastelaine, I can only apologise for Miss Mansour's ridiculous outburst upstairs, and for my own. Emotions are running high and all that."

He gave what was clearly supposed to be a self-deprecating chuckle, but anger was washing off him in waves. It was so intense that Cecily almost expected to be able to reach out and plunge her hand into it.

"Miss Mansour's entitled to her beliefs," Raf replied. "And after what happened to your grandad, can you blame her?"

"The natives are getting restless?" Lord Bath scoffed. "A man of superstition, Mr de Chastelaine? One is hardly surprised, you being a Russian and all."

"I'm a Transylvanian Yorkshireman," Raf corrected, his tone mild. "The best of both worlds."

Cecily grinned at Raf.

Dina stood very straight and told Lord Bath, "Even if you do not believe in the power the scroll contains, surely you must have some respect for its history? It is a rare and ancient artifact, a precious echo from ancient times. No ordinary scroll would have been placed in a casket like that. It must be properly cared for in the correct environment, not brought into dinner as a parlour trick. Once it is damaged, once it is destroyed, it is lost for all time."

Cecily noticed the shift in Dina's words. Gone was the fear of whatever the scroll contained. Now she appealed to Lord Bath as an antiquary.

He blinked, then cleared his throat. For a second Cecily thought he was about to apologise, but instead he said, "I am the third Earl of Bath, Miss Mansour, the

33

third generation of a noble family known and respected for our expeditionary and antiquarian zeal. I shall not take lessons on artifice preservation from a slip of a girl."

Dina pursed her lips for a moment, then said, "I am not a slip of a girl. If I was, would you want me to assist on your dig? I am an expert in Egyptian languages and history. But I suppose you will never understand. Even if one of my countrymen read from the pages of your Domesday Book, a mere baby of a text, over dinner, you would be furious, but still you would not understand that it goes the other way too."

"An Egyptian cobra." Raf let out a low whistle. "In rural Somerset."

Lord Bath shook his head.

"A frail, elderly man suffered a snake bite," he sneered. "And superstition."

"A man who had dabbled in something he did not understand," Dina retorted. "Or respect."

The anger coming from Lord Bath was still intense, and Cecily reached for Dina's arm. She was terrified that Dina would rile him. Not that she didn't have any right to be angry, but Cecily knew first-hand what happened to women who challenged the power of men.

"I think we should all be respectful towards everybody," Cecily said, hoping to dilute the tension a little. At her side, Raf nodded his agreement.

"You just remember who pays your wages, madam," Lord Bath said, pointing at Dina. "If you go bally native once you feel the sand beneath your feet, you can consider your expedition to Cairo over."

"Lord Bath," Raf chided. "Settle down. You're in Cairo, on the verge of seeing a tomb that's been legend for three thousand years. You ought to be chuffed, not taking on as though your horse came in last!"

"Raf — my husband's quite right," Cecily said placatingly. "Maybe it's the heat? Maybe the excitement? I know *I'm* terribly excited about the discovery, and it's not even mine. And Miss Mansour's excited too. Everyone is. Let's all calm down and be friends."

But Cecily wasn't sure that Dina *was* excited. Homesick and desolate seemed more the case, and Cecily wondered who was waiting for Dina at home.

"I am grateful to you for funding the dig, Lord Bath," Dina said quietly, with a dip of her head.

"We'll say no more about it, my dear. Women do have their odd ways, after all," Lord Bath said, suddenly the very image of avuncular benevolence. Or so he thought. Cecily had known his kind before, and she could still sense his animosity despite his smile. He stepped away and opened the cabin door. "Well, good evening, Miss Mansour, Mr and Mrs de Chastelaine."

"Good evening," Dina said, following him to the door. Once Lord Bath had stepped outside, Dina closed the door behind him. "I am sorry that you have witnessed these hot-tempered episodes."

"Don't apologise," Cecily said. "Lord Bath's terribly unthoughtful. And he really ought to have taken more care with the scroll." That sense of darkness and cold came back to her, a coldness like a tomb, and Cecily shivered.

"I've met his type before," Raf assured her. "They think they own the world and everybody in it, and woe betide anybody who doesn't agree. He must be a right pain in the neck to work for."

"He's dreadful," Dina admitted. "But what choice do I have? Men like him run the digs, and with my expertise, I cannot easily do anything else besides take tourists around the sites as a guide."

"I should imagine you're wonderful at that!" Cecily said keenly. "I should love you to give *us* a tour, if you weren't already busy, of course."

Raf nodded. "And if you ever come to Yorkshire, we'll return the favour. Not so many pyramids, though."

Dina nodded. "I have been to Yorkshire. I was looking at some artifacts at someone's stately home up there. I didn't get the chance to see very much of it, but I should very much like to take you up on your offer some day. Thank you."

"Oh, really, we'd be happy to," Cecily said, glad that they had made a friend. Especially someone like Dina, who seemed to be in need of friendship.

Raf smiled. "Come and visit us in Acaster Garrow," he said. "It's a long, long way from Bath."

Dina chuckled for the first time that evening. "I'm very glad to hear it! Well, I shall wish you good night. I've taken up enough of your time. I really do appreciate you coming to see me. You have reminded me that people still care."

"Honestly, any time," Cecily said. "We're just along the corridor, in cabin number twenty-two."

With a very courtly bow of goodbye, Raf said, "Cheerio, Dina. Sleep well. You'll be home tomorrow."

"I will indeed," Dina said gently, as if her homecoming would not promise her joy. "Goodnight, both of you." She raised her hand towards them and uttered something under her breath.

Cecily felt a strange tingling, as if tiny, invisible grains of sand had rained down on them. She was surprised when she couldn't see any on her clothes.

"You mustn't mind me," Dina said. "It's a blessing, to see you through the night."

A protection spell. Cecily knew about those, Raf having introduced them to her. Her husband met Dina's admission with a beaming smile and said, "You can't have too many blessings. Sleep tight, Dina."

With that he opened the door and escorted Cecily out of the cabin.

Cecily heard the door close behind them. The ship's engines hummed in the background, and the sea lapped at the hull. It all seemed very normal, but it felt as if they were on a different ship from the one they had boarded in Venice.

"I'll be glad to get to shore," Cecily whispered as they reached the door of their own cabin. Raf opened it and stood back to let her go inside first.

"Yeah, me too," he admitted. "I'm not made for the nautical life!"

Cecily went inside the room and put down her fan and her handbag. Once Raf had closed the door, Cecily turned to Raf and put her arms around him.

"Whatever have we walked into, darling?" she whispered, as if the very walls would hear her.

"Trouble." Raf put his arms around Cecily's waist and gave a carefree shrug. "Happy honeymoon anyway!"

If Raf's unafraid, then so am I.

And with that, Cecily brought her lips to Raf's in a kiss.

Chapter Four

Cecily was awoken the next morning by the ship arriving in Alexandria. The ship's horn released an almighty blast, and chains rattled as men on the deck and on dry land called to one another. She hopped out of bed in her nightdress to see, and looked out of the porthole at Egypt. It wasn't quite palm trees and pyramids yet, but the dusty harbour under a relentless sun was quite different to what Cecily was used to.

They had a last breakfast on board ship, then arm in arm, she and Raf were jostled along the gangplank by the other passengers, heading into the cavernous barn where they'd go through customs. Cecily took in everything, watching the passengers and the Egyptian locals. She wondered what it was like to be Egyptian, to live in a land where your ancestors' faces from four thousand years ago were still carved in stone.

After the whirlwind of customs, Cecily and Raf met their luggage again, but only for as long as it took a porter to load it onto a trolley. The porter hurtled away towards the train that would take them to Cairo. Cecily thought she saw Dina on the hectic platform, but only for a fleeting moment as the crowd separated them.

They were squashed into a carriage with other European tourists, in a flurry of fans and maps and sunhats. The train pulled out of the station, and it wasn't long before a huge river appeared beside the track.

"It's the Nile, Raf! Look, there it is!" Cecily pointed. "The very river that Cleopatra sailed along in her perfumed barge, and everybody fell in love with her."

"You're prettier." He smiled. "Is this something? Me and you, in Egypt! And married!"

And so happy, it felt almost unbelievable.

Cecily tapped her fingertip against the end of Raf's nose. "I'm really having the most marvellous time, you know. Even with all that other business yesterday, I just can't believe I'm here at last. It's so magical, isn't it? It's so old... I just can't get my head round quite how old it all is."

"About as old as it gets." Raf chuckled. "And hot as it gets too. I'll go through the sun lotion...but it's worth it. Egypt with my wife!"

"Don't worry, I'll help you put it on." Cecily giggled. "You won't get the chance to be sunburned at all."

The train carried them farther south. It seemed to get hotter by the minute, and Cecily wasn't sure if it was because the day was advancing or because they were heading nearer to the equator. Perhaps it was both.

They arrived in Cairo into rush and hurry. Cecily wondered if they'd ever see their luggage again. The platform was so busy with people that it was hard to get down from the train, and everywhere were people selling something—enormous pieces of fruit, necklaces bearing little Tutankhamen heads and sphinxes, hats, linen blouses, toy camels, fresh dates and syrupy little pastries dotted with green pistachios. One day, maybe, they'd be selling souvenirs of Menkare II.

Cecily wanted to stop and look at everything that the vendors had for sale, but her feet barely touched the ground as she and Raf plunged through the crowd towards the exit. Once outside the station, they climbed into a little horse-drawn carriage decorated with brightly coloured pompoms.

It wasn't quite a camel, but it was close enough.

"To the Rosetta of the Nile!" Cecily said to the man who held the reins.

As the carriage made its way through the densely packed streets, Cecily almost had to pinch herself to be sure that she wasn't dreaming. A year ago she had been so unhappy, trapped in a marriage to a man who had never loved her, hardly able to imagine a life beyond the walls of the ancient boarding school where her late husband had been master. Few people had the fortune to be given a second chance, but on the day that Raf wandered into her life in the middle of a séance, Cecily had been. And she had seized the opportunity for escape, and for love, with both hands.

And this was the result. A honeymoon that was taking them across the world, to places she had only ever seen in books and had never even dared dream she might one day visit.

The carriage brought them out into a grand square filled with palm trees and the striped awnings of market stalls. Elegant buildings which could almost have come from Paris stood around it, but taking up almost one side of the square was the imposing frontage of the Rosetta of the Nile hotel.

It had only recently been built, and was designed to emulate the architecture of Ancient Egypt. The stone front tapered up to the roof, like photographs Cecily had seen of the pylon gates at the Philae Temple, and was carved all over with Ancient Egyptian figures and hieroglyphics. Two sphinxes flanked the vast steps that led to the front door, and stone columns, stylised to look like palm trees, rose up the front of the building.

"Oh, my word, well, we're certainly in the best hotel in town, aren't we?" Cecily giggled. "What a splendid place!"

Cecily handed a fistful of coins to their driver and, with a bright smile of thanks, he climbed down from the carriage and took Cecily's hand to escort her down too. As they disembarked, Cecily noticed a small legion of porters ferrying a pile of trunks into the hotel and she recognised them at once.

So too, it seemed, did Raf.

"Looks like the Earl of Arse is staying here too," he said, his voice filled with mischief. "Lucky old us!"

"The Earl of Arse!" Cecily spluttered with laughter. "Goodness me, whatever does he have in all those trunks? Yet more silver caskets and ancient scrolls, or has he brought his entire sock collection with him?"

It felt good to mock such a rude, pompous man.

Among the porters, Cecily spotted Mr Snelling, wagging his finger and striding about delivering orders.

"Come along, Snelling!" The Earl of Bath strode out of the hotel, trailing his entourage in his wake. "Leave the bags to the servants. The dig site awaits!"

The dig site? They don't waste a moment.

Mr Snelling brushed his hands together. "Of course, your lordship. Right away." Mr Snelling grabbed a knapsack and a Gladstone bag from a passing trolley just as a large car drew up outside the hotel. Snelling shouldered the knapsack, then opened the car door, nodding towards Lord Bath.

"We should pity Lord Bath, you know," Cecily joked to Raf. "He doesn't even know how to open a car door!"

"*My Lord*," the earl corrected, his gaze withering. He climbed into the car. "Snelling, at the double! The rest of you, follow along once everything is unpacked. Snelling!"

"All that money," Raf grinned, "and no lessons in car doors."

The car roared into life and shoved and tooted its way through the crowds of pedestrians in the square.

Cecily chuckled. "Gosh, he's so rude to everyone. Even his *car's* rude to everyone. At least he's gone for the day. I wonder if Dina made her own way to the dig? But I suppose we should unpack, then see the sights."

"Only the very best for my missus." Raf took Cecily's hand and together they strolled past the remainder of the earl's party and bags and up the steps towards the hotel. "That's why we've got the honeymoon suite. You can see the pyramids out on the horizon, they tell me."

"You can?" Cecily breathed in awe. "It must be one of the best views from any hotel anywhere!"

The inside of the hotel was stone just like the outside, but here the figures and hieroglyphics were tricked out in gold, blue and red. There were real palm trees inside the foyer, in large brass pots, and to one side of the room was a huge fountain with water gushing from the mouth of a Sphinx.

Once Cecily and Raf had collected their keys, they were whizzed up through the building in a lift made from brass and mirrors. They arrived at their floor and walked along a thick red carpet through a white-painted corridor filled with statues of pharaohs and Ancient Egyptian deities to their door.

The honeymoon suite was dominated by an enormous bed. Cecily blushed to see it. But then grabbed Raf's hand and rushed to the window with him.

"I'll always remember the first time I see the pyramids," she told him with excitement. Then she looked outside, across the roofs of Cairo, and there, trembling in the heat haze as if they were nothing more substantial than a mirage, were the pyramids. They stood, silent and still on the edge of a noisy, busy city, staring out across the desert as they had done for millennia. Cecily was awestruck.

"I know you dreamed of this." Raf rested his head on Cecily's shoulder. "Thanks for coming out to meet my folks before you got to have your dream come true, Sissy. You're the best there is."

"I wouldn't have missed meeting them for the world," Cecily assured him. "Family comes first, before holidays. And we'll go and see them on the way back, won't we? I'll buy them lots of lovely things from the souk. Thank you for bringing me here, Raf. I never thought I'd ever see this place."

"This is what we do. We see amazing places, and we cuddle a lot." He lifted his head and kissed Cecily's cheek. "And sometimes we save the world. And plant nice flowers, obviously."

"But of course." Cecily kissed him in return. "I do hope we get to see the sights, darling. It's just that with all that strangeness on the ship, it had me worried that our services would be called upon. But now we're here, nothing seems all that untoward."

"We're going to see everything," Raf assured her. "Don't you worry about that."

"Oh, I'm so glad!" Cecily kissed him softly. "Let's go for a walk. I'd love to see what they're selling in the market, and later we can put on our best things and have dinner in the hotel!"

Chapter Five

Cecily and Raf had a wonderful day exploring the city. Cecily had tried to keep to the old, narrow streets so that Raf could walk in the shade and get some relief from the relentless sun.

Seemingly everywhere they went in Cairo, there was talk of Lord Bath's discovery. At every stall and shop, Cecily and Raf were asked if they were in Egypt to see the tomb of Menkare II. The people of Egypt believed that Lord Bath had found it. Perhaps he had. Although Cecily and Raf knew that the discovery was really Dina's.

Cecily and Raf returned to their room with all manner of trinkets and gifts that they'd bought in the markets. After taking a rest in the only way that newlyweds can, they freshened up, before going down to the hotel bar for the cocktail hour. Cecily felt very glamorous wearing another of her dresses from Paris, and Raf was in his tuxedo.

Happy and relaxed, lounging with her new husband, Cecily sipped her gin fizz as the hotel band played. But she had heard about the tomb of Menkare II so much that the name repeated and repeated in Cecily's mind. She wondered if Lord Bath and Snelling had discovered anything out in the desert at the dig that day while she and Raf had been enjoying the city. As each guest arrived in the bar, Cecily looked up in case Lord Bath or someone from his party should arrive.

At Cecily's side, Raf tapped his foot in time with the music. He held her hand in his own and now and then, whenever the band played a slower tune, he settled his head on Cecily's shoulder and they listened together, needing no words to express their feelings.

What a place to be on honeymoon.

"I wonder where Dina went off to," Raf murmured. He picked up his glass and took a sip. "I hope she's all right. The way he pushed her around...it made me think of you and that rotten old husband of yours."

"It did me as well," Cecily admitted. "I saw her on the platform at Alexandria, but it was so busy I lost sight of her. I suppose she's gone to stay with her family somewhere in Cairo. And once the dig's finished, then perhaps she won't bother with that horrible man anymore. I just wonder how they got on today, at the site."

"I wish they'd leave things where they find them." Raf sighed. "Sometimes when rich men open sealed places, things come out. And not only angry cobras."

"Ghosts and demons?" Cecily whispered. She knew a lot about *them*. "Very *old* ghosts and demons, at that."

"And bad-tempered too," he reminded her. "For every mischievous goblin or saucy fairy, there's half a dozen grumpy ghouls waiting to make trouble."

"I'm not surprised they're bad-tempered," Cecily remarked. "*I* wouldn't be very happy either if I'd been woken up after sleeping for thousands of years in my casket."

There was laughter at the next table, and Cecily overheard an Englishman say, "I wonder how wrinkly this old Menkare will be when they unwrap him?"

Cecily glanced at Raf. "Seems *everyone's* talking about the find."

"A wrinkled king is still a king," laughed an elderly Englishwoman at the table opposite, overhearing the man's comment. The diamonds around her wrist glittered in the glow of the ornate chandeliers as she picked up her wineglass. "If this were London, he'd already have a queue of debs at the door of the tomb!"

"Good old Lord Bath," brayed her companion. "It's only taken three generations, eh?"

"Imagine cutting off your own hand!" a young woman at another table exclaimed. Then she leant across to the elderly woman and shared her gossip rather loudly. "You know, I overheard someone from his party earlier. They said they were staying out in the desert to work through the night, because they're very, very close to finding the entrance. How thrilling!"

Cecily felt Raf tense.

"Maybe we ought to go out and take a look?" the Englishman suggested. "Borrow one of the hotel charabancs? We could be there when they open the tomb and reveal the wrinkly king! That'd be quite something to write on a postcard home, wouldn't it?"

"I say," called an American from the bar, where he was downing the contents of his cocktail glass. "We're taking a few cars over there. They say it's not just a tomb — it's a *pyramid*! Join us, the more the merrier!"

Raf frowned and whispered, "A pyramid? In the sand?"

"So it's bigger than they expected?" Cecily breathed in awe. "It'll be the find of the century."

The Englishman got up from his table. "Well, I say we tell the kitchens to halt dinner. We'll all go out to the dig site right away, what?"

Everyone at his table nodded, and the other guests did too. Cecily felt a rush of excitement, but at the same time a cold breeze cut through the bar and it gave her pause. None of the other guests seemed to notice though.

"Raf, I think we ought to go with them," Cecily whispered, concerned.

"Then we go," he replied, squeezing her hand. More guests were already rising from their seats, a buzz of excited conversation running around the room. "Have you got your *cocosul*, just in case?"

Cecily took the piece of stone from inside the neck of her dress and showed it to Raf. He had painted the protective cockerel onto it and added its length of leather with his mother, when he was a child.

"I never go anywhere without it." Then Cecily took his hand as they rose from their seats. Together they followed the growing crowd that was heading towards the lobby, but Cecily didn't share their jubilant excitement. Instead she felt a sense of deep unease, as though something was shifting again, out in the desert. Raf was right. The tomb had been hidden for three thousand years and whatever it contained, perhaps it was better left in peace.

A line of cars was drawn up outside the hotel, and Raf and Cecily climbed into one of the charabancs that had *Rosetta of the Nile* written along its side. The Englishman from the bar had opened his wallet, and was handing a banknote to the Egyptian driver.

"Look, I know it's not usual to take the guests out on an evening excursion, but here's an Egyptian pound note to make it up to you. How's that, my dear fellow?"

"Thank you very much," the driver said, but Cecily heard a note of nervousness in his voice. Could he too sense that something out in the desert wasn't quite right?

More guests poured from the hotel and climbed into the vehicles awaiting them. There was even a motorbike and sidecar. A few more minutes passed, and finally their convoy was off, heading out to the desert among peals of laughter and song.

"They're behaving like it's a Sunday School outing," Cecily whispered to Raf. He nodded, then leant forwards to address the driver.

"Pardon me, mate," Raf said in his friendly way, "does this sort of thing happen a lot? Daytrip — night trips, really — to the necropolis?"

The driver shook his head. "No, sir, it is quite uncommon indeed. There is nothing to see in the necropolis at night. It is not a place to go after dark. But everyone has heard about your Lord Bath and what he has discovered out there. It is the next tomb of Tutankhamen, so they say."

"Look how that ended up." Raf sighed. He sat back and told Cecily, "Maybe it'll come to nothing. Just the sort of big folly that costs rich men their hands."

"Maybe so." Cecily shivered. The evening was still warm, but a cold breeze cut through it. She leaned forwards and asked the driver, "Excuse me, what have people been saying about Menkare's tomb?"

The driver glanced round at her quickly with a proud grin, then returned to focus on the road ahead. They were travelling through the city but the desert wasn't far away.

"Ah, I have heard of nothing but *Menkare, Menkare* for months from my nephew. He's working at the site," he explained. "He studies at the university here, and was hired by Lord Bath. We are all very proud of Abasi. He is very excited by the find, but equally...he says it is very unusual."

Unusual? As in...haunted?

"Unusual?" Raf asked. "That's how we make a living. What does Abasi think?"

"Menkare II isn't the sort of pharaoh you want to wake up," the driver replied. "Abasi says that he's noticed strange things around the site. He said the earth is not still there. It is alive."

Cecily shuddered at the thought. But then...maybe the mighty Nile made the land unstable, as its levels rose and fell. But she knew only too well that science didn't have an answer for everything.

The convoy emerged from the city and struck out across the moonlit desert. Cecily saw the serene pyramids at Giza, silver against the dark blue sky. Cecily gazed at them as they drove past. She had longed to visit them, but now something more pressing was at hand than sightseeing.

They drove on. After cresting a hill of sand, a huge valley opened up before them, with a huddle of tents lying ahead.

"There, that's the camp," the driver told them.

As they drew nearer, Cecily saw a huge number of people labouring under arc lamps. Buckets of sand were being carried away from a central point, and soon Cecily realised that she was looking at a pyramid, one that was a few yards tall.

"That's it," Cecily said. "That's his tomb."

And as she looked at it, Cecily felt no awe, only fear. Her previous excitement and anticipation had gone. Something evil was here. She could hear Raf muttering something under his breath, and though she couldn't hear the words, Cecily knew that it would be one of the charms of protection that had kept them safe on their adventures. He raised her hand to his lips and kissed it.

"I don't like it here," he whispered. "Not *here*. Just here. This dig."

"I don't either," Cecily said. "It feels as if something very bad is trying to get out."

And it was strange, because the pyramids of the Giza necropolis had looked so peaceful. It wasn't only because of the frantic work afoot here. Something was waiting.

The convoy came to a halt, and Cecily and Raf climbed down from the charabanc. The desert night was far colder than Cecily had expected.

A young man in khaki-coloured work clothes strode up to the driver of the charabanc and excitedly shook his hand, speaking to him in what Cecily thought was Egyptian Arabic. He had a spade in his other hand and had evidently been at work on the dig.

The driver turned to Cecily and Raf. "Please, this is my nephew, Abasi."

Abasi waved to them. "We weren't expecting visitors! But news travels fast."

Raf waved a greeting to the young man. He said to the driver, "Do you think he'll have time to talk? I know Lord Bath can be a bit of a tartar. I've seen it first-hand."

"He can talk, but not for long. Like you say." The driver gestured, and grimaced.

Not a fan of Lord Bath either, then.

"I must get back to work in a minute or two," Abasi told them. "But you must be curious about the dig, to come out here in the evening? What would you like to know?"

"Raf and Cecily." Raf took the young man's hand and shook it. "I've got to be honest, I wasn't expecting a mini-pyramid. I mean, it must be a small one, mustn't it?"

"What you can see at the moment isn't the full story," Abasi explained. He pointed towards the point of stone rising up through the sand. "It goes deeper into the sand. Our expert, Miss Mansour, told us that the pyramid had been buried in a sandstorm. But we don't think it can be as tall as the Great Pyramid. If it is, Lord Bath will need more people to come and dig! As it is, the workers on the site have been here all day, and Lord Bath won't hear of anyone going home. He's certain we're close to finding the entrance."

"Tonight?" Raf sounded surprised. "What's the rush? It's not going to turn into a pumpkin at midnight!"

Abasi shrugged. "Lord Bath is keen. He keeps tapping his watch and saying, '*Money is time, time is –* '"

Cecily grabbed for Raf. She nearly lost her balance as the ground shuddered beneath her feet. "Whatever was that?" she gasped.

"Earth trem –" The ground shifted again, more violently this time. In the area lit by the glow of the arc lights, Cecily heard voices raised in panic. Long shadows fell across the moonlit sands as tools were thrown down and the workers began to scrabble away from the site of the dig.

One of the arc lights tottered before keeling over with a groan, expiring in a burst of sparks.

"Everybody get back!" Raf shouted, stumbling back towards the vehicles and pulling Cecily with him. "It's a landslide!"

"Where the hell do you think you're going?" Snelling shouted through a megaphone. "Get back to work, you lazy shower!"

But the workers ignored him, running past Snelling over the shuddering ground as he roared into his megaphone again. "Get back to work!"

"What do we do, Raf? Is there time to drive away?" Cecily was terrified. She hadn't factored a landslide into their honeymoon. Were they going to make it home? She was starting to wish she'd never insisted on coming to Egypt.

They were in the desert. There was no shelter, no high ground, just the vast expanse of sand, so they couldn't even run. Raf and Cecily looked back towards the charabanc and he told her, "There's no time to —"

The sand around the exposed pyramid was moving, rippling like a vast wave. The site was abandoned, with even Snelling making a run for it with the rest of the workers, and it seemed as though they'd made their escape just in time. The whole ground undulated, and patterns formed and changed in the sand around the structure, like waves sweeping over the surface of the ocean.

And there in the moonlight a little distance from the pyramid, apparently oblivious to the scenes that were erupting, Cecily saw the figure of Julian Vane-Stanhope, third Earl of Bath. He held the unfurled scroll before him, and his lips were moving silently as he read it again.

"He's doing this!" Cecily exclaimed, clinging on to Raf. "It's what's in the scroll, it must be! Can't anybody stop him?"

Several other figures came to shelter by the bulk of the charabanc, and Cecily recognised Dina. She was wearing a desert outfit of a long skirt, a khaki jacket and a scarf tied around her neck that flowed on the cold breeze.

"Dina, it's us, Cecily and Raf!" Cecily called, and Dina turned towards her, looking as dazed as someone woken from a dream.

"The desert speaks. The desert will yield up its secrets," Dina whispered.

"I wish it wouldn't," Raf replied. The air was filled with a roaring that seemed to come from the bowels of the earth itself. That almighty noise drowned out the panicked voices of the hotel guests and the workers, and Raf drew Cecily to him, holding her tight.

She closed her eyes, but she desperately wanted to see what was going on. Around the edge of the charabanc, she saw the sand seemingly come alive before her eyes. It rushed away from the pyramid and Cecily stared in amazement and horror as the pyramid grew taller and taller, revealing its depths, which had been buried in the sand. It would've taken months, if not years, to dig away the quantity of sand that was hurrying away from the pyramid's sloped sides.

The air was filled with the escaping sand, rasping Cecily's skin. She closed her eyes again and pressed her mouth to Raf's shoulder, fighting to keep out the grit.

"Oh God!" the American woman with the glittering diamonds screamed. "It'll suck us right down with it!"

Cecily dared another look, relying on her eyelashes to catch the sand. The landscape had completely changed in moments. Where there had been a small pyramid on a flat area of sand, there was now a huge pyramid inside a hole. And the charabanc was teetering right on its very edge.

But as Cecily watched, the sand settled, no longer scouring the air as it escaped. Instead, everything was still again under the bright African moon, as if the pyramid had been sitting just like that forever.

Chapter Six

"Raf, it's stopped," Cecily whispered, and around them the others stirred, evidently sensing that the worst of the danger had passed. The air had suddenly turned very cold and Raf took off his dinner jacket even as a shudder ran through him. He wrapped the jacket around Cecily's shoulders and together they peered at the newly revealed pyramid, its silent stone surface revealed to the cool night air for the first time in three millennia.

It didn't look worn like the other pyramids that Cecily had seen in photographs. The sand had protected it through the years.

How strange that something so old can look so new.

Dina brushed the sand from her face and stepped around the edge of the charabanc to look at the pyramid before them.

"Just as the legends said," she murmured. "Lost in the sand, the tomb of Menkare II. But now it is lost no more."

"My God." The awestruck whisper was Lord Bath's. He was making his way towards the edge of the pit, the casket containing that ancient scroll tucked safely beneath one arm. He paused on the lip of the hole, then began to hurry down towards the newly revealed pyramid, sliding and stumbling on the shallow incline.

Snelling followed him, skidding on the sand as he went. "My lord, they'll be toasting you from here to London! It's truly the discovery of the century!"

Dina sighed and leant against the side of the charabanc as if she was exhausted.

"It's immense," Bath gasped. He stopped his descent halfway down, bracing one hand against the sloping sand to steady himself. "Look at it. Hidden, all these years... And they laughed at my grandfather. They laughed at *me*!"

Snelling slid to a halt beside him. "Well, they're laughing on the other side of their faces now! It's huge! And just imagine what treasures there must be inside it."

"And they're not yours," Cecily whispered, so that only Raf could hear. She felt sick at the thought of Lord Bath and Snelling plundering a resting place that had been hidden for so many years.

"Miss Mansour," Lord Bath called as he continued his descent. "Come down here!"

Dina pushed herself away from the charabanc and stood tall, her head held high. She said something under her breath before heading down the sandy slope towards the pyramid. Unlike Lord Bath and Snelling, she didn't lose any of her poise. She walked on the shifting sand as if it were hard as concrete.

And as Cecily watched her progress, she spotted something on the face of the pyramid. "Is that the door, Raf? That big slab? It's covered in hieroglyphics!"

Raf nodded and murmured, "That's it." He drew in a deep breath, then grimaced and took out a little bottle. "The air's foul."

With that, Raf uncapped the bottle and held it under his nose for a few moments. Cecily sniffed, but couldn't smell anything besides the gritty sand and the cold night. But then, she didn't have Raf's sensitive nose.

"How many mummies do you think might be in there, Raf?" Cecily asked him. Dina had arrived at the bottom of the hole where the pyramid stood. She was statue-like again and didn't move. "Fifty? Hundreds?"

"They're pungent, however many it is. But this isn't like the smell I'd expect, it's just...bad," he replied. "According to the legend, there were a hundred people buried under the sand when the tomb was lost. If the pyramid's now uncovered, I suppose that means they're under this sand somewhere too."

Cecily blinked at Raf in alarm. "A hundred people? Just...lying under the sand here? And they must've come to a horrible end. No wonder it smells bad with that many people left here in the desert, and not only because of those mummies. I've been so carried away with my excitement, and then the ground fell in. I need to listen, I need to feel."

Cecily half-closed her eyes, trying to clear her mind of all the noise inside it. Now that she was tuning in to the realm of shadows, she was aware of anger and grief. Cecily steeled herself against it, because it was so intense that it threatened to overwhelm her. Was it from the dead whose lives had been suddenly cut short here? Or did it emanate from the mummies inside the enormous pyramid?

Raf held his arm around Cecily's shoulders, his jacket keeping her warm against the desert night. If people were moving around her now, or even speaking, Cecily was barely aware of them. Instead she focussed on the feelings that assailed her, and the misery that seemed to tinge every one of them.

She saw a crowd of people, men in armour that reflected the bright sunlight, standing in front of people whose attention was fixed on a brightly painted sarcophagus that was being carried into the pyramid. And standing between the men in armour, she saw a figure in chains.

The image left Cecily so uneasy that she pulled away from it at once. Why was there someone in chains at a funeral? Had they been they placed into the pyramid too, as a living sacrifice?

"Oh, Raf, something dark and horrible happened here," Cecily told him. "I saw someone in chains."

Raf nodded and asked gently, "A woman?"

"I…I think so. I'm not sure," Cecily replied. "I had to retreat, I couldn't keep looking. There was so much grief, so much anger."

Dina awoke from her trance. "This is the tomb of Menkare II," she told Lord Bath as she pointed to the hieroglyphics on the door. "That slab gives his names, and invokes a curse on anyone who would wake him."

"The tomb of Menkare II," he repeated, his voice filled with triumph. "My grandfather dedicated his life to discovering this place, and I took up the cudgels on his behalf. Oh, my father said it was all a legend, but he was wrong!" He turned and placed the palms of his hands flat against the carved stone slab that towered over him. "The lost tomb of legend."

Cecily couldn't help but feel aggrieved anew for Dina. It should've been her triumph, but Lord Bath had taken it from her. Abasi went over to Dina and they spoke together, pointing and gesturing at the slab.

Snelling strode over to them. "Speak English, and only English," he warned them. "You've been told before. This isn't a time for your lot to start acting up."

"He's talking to them like they're children," Cecily whispered to Raf. "How rude!"

"What do the hieroglyphics say?" Lord Bath asked Dina urgently. "Is this the entrance to the pyramid? I've never seen symbols like these. What do they actually *say*, woman?"

Dina spoke, and although Cecily didn't understand the words, a shiver went through her. Because it was a language she'd never heard before—until she had been shown the image of what had happened here at the funeral. Dina was speaking in Ancient Egyptian.

"And in English," Dina now said, "it reads Horus Great Bull, He of the Two Ladies ruler of the Nile, Horus of Gold conqueror of nations, He of the Sedge and the Bee, Son of Ra, Menkare, noblest of men. Then after his name, it says, *He who would disturb this king from his slumbers will call down the wrath of Apophis and Ammit.* A god of chaos and a demon. Are you sure you want to proceed?"

"Why can't I read this?" the nobleman asked, his tone accusing. Apparently the wrath of demons wasn't enough to stop him, but Cecily knew better. She'd seen enough to heed such warnings when given. He stabbed his finger towards the symbols. "I've never seen anything like this before. Have you ever seen the like?"

"No, I haven't," Snelling said. "Are you making it up, woman?"

"No, I am not," Dina retorted. "But it is written in an unusual script, devised for casting enchantment. It was used by priests and priestesses along the Nile. You are fortunate to see it here."

"That slab'll be worth a damned fortune, then!" Snelling said, smiling gladly at Lord Bath. "A rare script, indeed, My Lord!"

"Rare and welcome," the earl chuckled. He ran his fingers down the edge of the slab, where it was seemingly sealed against the edges of the pyramid, tracing its shape. "We'll have to pry it, Snelling. Unless our so-called enchantment offers any clues, Miss Mansour? It'll be worth that much more undamaged."

Raf shook his head and whispered, "They should leave it as it is. There's a reason it was hidden away."

"I should imagine so!" Cecily replied.

"It was closed by the sweat of Menkare's slaves," Dina told Lord Bath. "No spell or charm will open it."

There was a disturbance in the crowd standing at the edge of the hole, and a group of workers rushed forwards, running and skidding down the side before bowling Lord Bath out of the way. They were wielding chisels and mallets, and aimed them at the edges of the priceless tomb door. It must've been an exciting moment for the Egyptian people, the untouched tomb of a long-dead pharaoh coming to light as it had. And it seemed that they wanted to be the first people to go inside it.

"What the—Get away from there!" Lord Bath bellowed. "You'll damage it, you ignorant savages."

From beneath his linen jacket he drew a pistol. He held it above his head and fired two shots into the air.

The crowd flinched and drew back, although Cecily noticed some of the hotel guests giving Lord Bath a round of applause. Whether for the entertainment value, or the fact that he'd drawn a firearm on a group of people in their own country, Cecily wasn't sure.

All but one of the workers retreated, and the sound of his chisel ringing against the ancient stone with each fall of his mallet cut through the night.

Lord Bath seized hold of the back of the worker's neck and wrenched him away from the tomb. The man fell back into the sand and as he went, the earl stood over him, red-faced as he screamed, "I told you to get back, you ignorant bloody peasant! How dare you disobey your betters? How bloody dare you?"

"You shouldn't carry on like this," Raf called. "Don't talk to people that way!"

Abasi and Dina hurried to the man's side, helping him up, talking to him in their own language.

"In English!" Snelling bellowed.

"He doesn't speak English," Dina replied defiantly. She glanced up at Raf and nodded to him, seemingly acknowledging his words.

"Then it's time the bloody imbecile learned!" Lord Bath holstered his revolver and told Raf, "As for you, sir, I'll thank you to keep your opinions to yourself. I pay these peasants to obey my instructions, and obey them they will."

"They are not peasants," Dina replied. "They are hard-working men who have sweated under the sun to dig out this tomb. If they are excited about it appearing, then why should you blame them? Why *shouldn't* they want to enter the tomb first?"

Lord Bath fixed her with a cold, angry stare. Then he gave a sharp nod and said, "Tell them, Miss Mansour, that any such disobedience will be met with the strongest possible sanctions. Tell them also that their positions here and their wages are entirely dependent on my kindness. Furthermore, make sure they know that there is only one pharaoh they need fear at the tomb of Menkare II, and his name is Julian Vane-Stanhope, third Earl of Bath. Is that quite clear?"

"I'm not sure all of that will exactly translate," Dina said, her eyebrow quirked. Then she turned to the workers and spoke to them in a flow of Egyptian Arabic. Although Cecily had no idea what Dina was saying, she wouldn't have been surprised if the workers were receiving an embellished version of what Lord Bath had said, with added insults about the monstrously egotistical earl who claimed to be a pharaoh.

The workers responded with dismissive hand gestures in Lord Bath's direction. They didn't seem to care that while Lord Bath might not understand their words, their body language spoke loud and clear.

"They have said they will follow your orders," Dina translated for Lord Bath. "And they are of course very sorry for any offence they may have caused by trying to unseal the tomb for you."

"They may go for the night," Lord Bath said with a dismissive wave of his hand. "We've lost the lights and most of the bloody equipment. Tomorrow they can start on digging them out again while we work on getting the tomb open, Miss Mansour. Snelling, if the legends are correct there should be a fortune in treasure out here on the skeletons of those who were buried in the first sandstorm. At first light, marshal a team and start digging. We want to find *everything*, understood? Both inside the tomb and out."

"Understood, My Lord," Snelling replied. "We'll be out here at first light, and the whole lot will be dug out—equipment, dead Egyptians, the whole lot."

Dina shuddered. "You must take care."

"It's not really a grave after all that many years, though, is it?" Snelling replied insolently. "Take care? Maybe they should've taken care and they wouldn't have ended up buried in all this sand!"

"Friends!" Lord Bath looked up towards the edge of the pit, where the excited crowd of tourists had gathered to watch the display. "Come down and see the legendary tomb. I ask only that you don't touch it. After all"—and at this, he laughed—"we wouldn't want to upset any demonic gods now, would we?"

The hotel guests laughed as they descended into the hole. As they drew nearer, they pointed in and gasped in awe. It certainly was an impressive sight, but one that was too ominous for Cecily to enjoy as she once might have done. Everything felt very wrong indeed, like a cloud scudding over the sun.

Chapter Seven

"Who was this chap, then?" one of the guests asked aloud. "There's a little pyramid at Giza for Menkare. Is this fellow his son, or one of his cousins?"

"A cousin, as far as we can tell. Records of his origin are scant to say the least." As Lord Bath was speaking, he reached back and rested his palm against the slab again. "But he was a powerful man. A warlord who was feared as far as word could spread. Menkare II was a conqueror of men and the land, and even at the time, the legends that were attached to him spoke of dark magic."

A ripple of interest went through the hotel guests. Dina folded her arms.

"Dark magic?" a woman said. "I'll be standing well back when you open it, then!"

"And so you should, madam," he told her. The anger was gone now as the earl revelled in being the centre of admiring attention. "Menkare's court was known for being a place of enchantment, but despite all his priests and magic workers, there was one who eluded him. No amount of money or promise of favour could buy the loyalty of the priestess Selene, who dwelt on the banks of the mighty Nile. It was said that she possessed a magic more powerful than any that had ever been practised in Egypt, and Menkare wanted that magic for himself."

"They always do," Raf murmured.

If Lord Bath had heard, he gave no indication. He went on, "Menkare became obsessed with her resistance. After all, what if she shared her favours with one of his foes instead? The mightiest pharaoh in the land might prove no match for the most powerful magic, and Menkare II knew it. But how to secure her loyalty when she resisted his every gift and entreaty?"

The hotel guests gasped.

Dina shook her head. "And why should she have given her magic to Menkare II? It was hers, to bestow as she chose."

"Well said," Cecily whispered.

"But she had one weakness. Love," Lord Bath said with a sly smile. "The Nile priestess, so untouchable, so proud, had a secret lover. *Ido*, the captain of the pharaoh's guard. But they didn't keep their secret quite as well as they hoped, and when Menkare II learned of their attachment, he knew that he had finally found the one thing that would give him control over Selene."

"Typical rich bloke," Raf tutted.

"He had Ido and Selene brought before him in chains and gave the haughty madam a choice," said Lord Bath. "If she would marry him and accept his love and all the riches and privilege that he would bestow on her, then Ido — who was, let us not forget, a traitor to his master — would be exiled. If Selene chose to stay with her poor soldier, he would have Ido executed. Now, we mustn't be tempted to view Menkare II as the villain of this particular piece. Let's not forget that he offered Selene a life beyond her wildest dreams...no shack by the Nile. And Ido *had* betrayed his master. In doing so, he had betrayed the gods themselves."

"Isn't that just like a woman?" laughed an American gentleman. "You offer her a prince or a *bad boy*, she always goes with the bad boy! Typical gal!"

"Oh, but I feel sorry for them," a young woman said. "Selene and Ido should've been allowed to live together in peace."

Dina turned to smile at the woman, then covered her mouth with her hand as if she hadn't wanted anyone to notice her reaction.

"Chains..." Cecily murmured. "That must be what I saw, the woman in chains. I saw Selene. And I felt her pain, her anger and grief. No wonder those feelings are still here!"

"She chose to save her lover," Raf said under his breath. "But Menkare didn't keep his word."

"Well, of course, she followed the money and submitted to the will of the pharaoh," brayed Lord Bath. "But one of Menkare's seers warned the king that there was still a cloud of betrayal over him. Ido was his one bargaining chip, so he threw the traitor into the cells and assured him that once Selene had given herself freely as a wife should to a husband, then and only then would Ido be freed into exile. Menkare II didn't tell Selene this, of course, because he had a sneaking little suspicion that his self-regarding priestess might just try to deny him his husbandly rights."

Cecily shuddered with disgust. She'd been married to a man who had demanded *'husbandly rights'*. The entitled cruelty she had suffered under was the same as Selene had been forced to endure.

"Oh, Raf, why must he speak in this horrible way?" Cecily said. "I can only imagine that Lord Bath's never been in love with anyone, except himself and his title."

"What choice did she have?" Dina shook her head. "She would lose the only man she had ever loved, all because the pharaoh must have what he wanted. Marry Menkare II and Ido would live, even though Selene would never see him again, in that life at least. And refuse? No, she could *not* refuse, because she loved him, and she would not see him executed. But what did that matter to a man like Menkare II? He cared nothing for Selene's sacrifice because he cared nothing for *her* — only for her power."

"But, madam, wasn't Menkare proved right?" Lord Bath challenged. "For she *did* resist. She refused to grant him those rights that were his by marriage and when he tried to claim them, she threatened him with the magic she was said to possess. What was he to do? A king must have an heir, and a queen must fulfil her duties."

"What choice did *she* have?" Dina repeated, more forcefully this time. "History is written by men, and few if any ever stop to think, as women would, *What if she didn't want to? What if she made her choice to keep another human being from execution, only to realise once she was Menkare's wife, that she didn't want to be?* And what, Lord Bath, did the other people in Menkare II's realm think of what he had done? I suppose some might have thought him formidable, a man not to be crossed. But there were people — and I have seen the evidence — who pitied Selene."

"Other *women*, no doubt," Lord Bath sneered. "Well, Menkare had his bargaining chip, didn't he? If the hussy wanted her palace guard, then she would have him. *Eternally*. Even in death, he would be a servant to the pharaoh whom he had betrayed."

Lord Bath turned and looked up at the towering pyramid and the full moon that glowed above it. When he turned back, his eyes were alight with glee.

"He had his priests wrap the prisoner from head to toe, a living mummy, and had Selene clapped in irons. A funeral procession was held, as grand as any king's, and Ido was brought here to this tomb, enclosed in a sarcophagus of unmarked stone, and sealed up whilst his unapologetic *slut* watched it happen." He settled his gaze on Dina and said, "Then he gave her one last chance. She was to submit and become his servant, or she too would be sealed inside the tomb, where she would submit to him in the life that follows this life. No matter how she resisted on this side of the veil, they would meet again on the other. Unless her much-vaunted magic included immortality!"

Dina stood taller and raised her chin as imperiously as any queen. "And what happened then, Lord Bath, after Menkare had committed that despicable act against a blameless, living human being? A young man in the prime of life, wrapped in bandages and put into a sarcophagus?"

"A traitor," Lord Bath corrected, "who had betrayed his king, and the hussy who had joined him in doing so."

"There's only one villain in this story," Raf said. "You can try and spin it any way you like, but only one bloke buried another alive and forced a girl to marry him. Not much of a Prince Charming, if you ask me."

"Hear, hear!" some of the hotel guests chimed in.

"I'm glad his pyramid got covered up like it did," a woman in the crowd remarked. "What a nasty little tyrant! It's not enough for some men to be a king, is it? They have to have everything else they want, like a spoiled little child demanding every toy in the shop."

The earl's eyes narrowed as he told them, "This woman was wicked. She doesn't deserve your pity. Here on these very sands, she was so full of rage that by the sheer force of her will, she stopped her husband's heart stone dead. The very memory of the terror on his face as he died caused such horror amongst the priests that the holy ceremonies of his burial were carried out with undue haste. Once his body was prepared, he was placed in the burial chamber beside the sarcophagus of the traitorous Ido. They had barely sealed the tomb when the sandstorm blew in. It buried the pyramid of Menkare II and his entire court, who had gathered here for his funeral, for two centuries. Beneath this sand, still in chains, lies the body of his faithless bride."

"He deserved to die after what he had done to Selene and Ido," Dina replied. "And all the other cruelties he had inflicted during his reign. Indeed, I wonder if the priests buried him so quickly because of that look of horror you describe, or because he was so thoroughly bad and twisted, they could not wait to have him put away for good."

"I wish she *had* lived forever," said a woman. "Then she could've escaped him in the afterlife too. Poor Ido, still having to serve him even after death!"

Cecily looked over to the carved slab door to the tomb, and pitied poor Selene and Ido. What a horrible way for Ido to die, starving and thirsty inside a casket, while the woman he loved was in chains outside.

"This could get messy..." Raf murmured. "In all sorts of ways."

"Should we offer our services to Lord Bath?" Cecily suggested, though it seemed hopeless. "He needs to know that he's playing with fire. Or at least, with an ancient mummy."

"Maybe we should," he said. "He might not know what he's getting into."

Cecily took Raf's hand and they approached Lord Bath. Her heart leapt with trepidation, but if they walked away now just as something awful was unleashed, Cecily knew that she and Raf could never forgive themselves.

"Excuse me, Lord Bath." Cecily did her best to offer him a smile. "I believe you may be in need of certain services that my husband and I can offer."

The earl narrowed his eyes. "What's that?" he asked. "*Services*?"

Cecily nodded. "Services, yes. Of a supernatural nature. It seems you've woken something from the past that you might need some help dealing with. My husband and I are experienced dealing with ghosts, demons, vampires and wraiths, both friendly and otherwise, *and* we have a great many protection spells that you might think it wise to avail yourself of too. And we're very reasonably priced, too."

"Negotiable," Raf told him. "On application."

"Ghosts and Who put you up to this?" Lord Bath began to laugh. "Was it Pongo Featherstonehaugh? Or Beefy Potter? Those bally jesters!"

Cecily stared at him in surprise.

He thinks we're joking! This isn't going to go well.

She shook her head. "Oh, no, we're deadly serious. You really don't want to fall foul of an ancient curse, *or* have a mummy running after you! Well, not run exactly. More of a shuffle. But even so..."

"You read that scroll and the sands receded," Raf pointed out. "When your grandfather discovered it, it killed him. Why take the risk?"

"I'm *in* bongo-bongo land, but I'm not *from* bongo-bongo land," Lord Bath snapped. "So don't try to sell me your blood snake oil! Not one conman, but a conman and his conwoman!"

"Now just a minute," Raf warned. "Don't you speak to my wife like that. If you don't believe it, why did you read the scroll? Why not just leave it at home?"

Cecily held Raf's hand tighter. He never let anyone disrespect her.

Not even an earl.

"Deep down, you know that scroll has power, don't you?" Cecily said. "We're not conning you, we're trying to protect you. And not *just* you, but the innocent people who may well end up in the line of fire."

But even as she said it, Cecily knew there was no point appealing to Lord Bath's altruistic side. Men like him didn't have one.

"But if the scroll has power, then that power is all with the man who holds the papyrus." Lord Bath regarded them both with a look of superiority, as though he had somehow outwitted them. "If Ido is to become the servant of the possessor of the scroll, then what fear could I possibly have of him? He would be *my* servant to command."

Raf winced and shook his head.

"That's what we in the trade call famous last words," he told the earl. "These sorts of things…scrolls, spells, enchanted bits and bobs and mystical this and that… Power comes at a price. And one day, if this scroll does have the power it claims to, you'll be the one who has to pay the piper."

Cecily nodded. "You really don't know what you're dabbling in. I knew a man once…" She drew in a steadying breath, preparing to dive into her unhappy past. "He thought he was favoured by the spirit of a man who had once known great power. But in the end, he was used as his puppet. And it sent him to his doom."

And through the sadness and tension in the air, she felt that familiar wave of love from Raf. It enveloped her like a hug, as it always had and always would.

"Then he must have been a weak man indeed," was Lord Bath's conclusion. "I fancy I have rather more mental stamina than that. This tomb has been nothing but a fiction for millennia and yet, thanks to me, here we stand before it. I'm the sort of chap who makes things happen. Do you follow? This isn't the place for cheap parlour tricks."

Raf shook his head.

"Look, you know where to find us when you need us." He quirked one eyebrow. "And you *will* need us, if our experience is anything to go by."

Cecily realised that Dina had been listening to them. She turned and Dina looked away.

Lord Bath might not be the only person who needs our services.

"Of course, we might get booked up quite quickly, and there's only so many cases we can take on at a time," Cecily told him. "And we do charge more for emergency call-outs, you know."

"And all of this must come at a price." Raf gestured around at the remains of the dig site. "But we'll leave it with you. Just keep it in mind."

Cecily and Raf walked back up the slope, away from Lord Bath and the pyramid. "Let's go back to the hotel, Raf. I think we'll be needing our sleep."

"He's made his bed," Raf replied. "But let's hope it's not innocent folk who have to lie in it."

Chapter Eight

The next morning, Cecily and Raf went out onto their balcony to have breakfast. The awning was pulled over to shade them from the sun that was bright even first thing in the morning. She'd already helped Raf to slather on his lotion to keep the rays of the sun from his skin. Even half-vampires had to be careful.

The table was laid out with baskets of pastries, fruit and tea and coffee. Cecily was pleased to see such a lovely spread, with a gorgeous view as well. The pyramids of Giza looked different in the morning from how they had when they'd arrived, and again when she'd seen them the evening before.

"It's funny how the pyramids keep looking different, even though they haven't changed for thousands of years," Cecily observed as she took her seat beside Raf. She kissed his cheek and ruffled his hair affectionately.

"When you look at them and think about what they've seen..." Raf reached out and picked up the teapot. He filled their cups as he went on, "And there they sit, unchanged but still different every time you look at them. I can't believe something the size of Menkare's pyramid was just *lost*. That thing's immense. There's no way it was just bad weather that covered it in sand."

Cecily had already guessed as much. Even the worst sandstorm she could imagine didn't seem like it would be able to bury a structure that seemed even taller than the Great Pyramid that now sat before them, immovable and silent against the bustle of Cairo. Was it really possible that a woman's broken heart could have done it? The same outpouring of anguish that had left her tyrant husband dead?

Cecily sipped her tea, then said, "I could feel something in the sand, as if each grain held an echo of the emotions that had been felt there. And I wonder, could that be because it was Selene's emotions that moved the sand over Menkare II's pyramid? If she was such a powerful priestess, then it wouldn't surprise me at all if it were true."

"So there're two ways of looking at this." Raf picked up a pastry and took a bite. He chewed thoughtfully and swallowed before going on. "First, the scroll's of a lot of archaeological importance, but that's as far as it goes. Or…when Vane-Stanhope read that scroll, he stirred something up. And you and I know, things do get stirred up from time to time."

"Don't they just!" Cecily took a spoonful of ruby-red jam for her toast. "We both certainly felt something, didn't we, on the ship, when Lord Bath read the scroll? Even though we were in Dina's cabin, we both felt a shift. A coldness. And it would've been at just the moment that Vane-Stanhope read the scroll out. Then he was reading from it again yesterday evening, and what happens? Well, what *didn't* happen? Thousands of tonnes of sand moved by themselves, and suddenly, there's the rest of the enormous pyramid, including a door with Menkare II's name on it!"

"And that stink." Raf grimaced. "Ancient bones...there's nothing like it. And it's not the same as the bones buried in the sand. It's mustier, a cooped-up sort of stink. If I could smell it, then there's air blowing through that pyramid. It's not as sealed as it looks."

Cecily blinked at Raf in surprise. The thought hadn't occurred to her.

"So it's unsealed. After centuries, it's open again." She shuddered. "I dread to think what might be coming out of it, and not just a bad smell!"

"Life's never dull!" Raf reached out and patted Cecily's knee. "We could just...do nothing. Let whatever's going to happen, just happen. But we both know we won't."

Cecily nodded. "We could say *Leave Lord Bath to it*. And it's not as if he's hired us anyway. But it feels like something malevolent's in the air. Something that might do a lot of damage — and we might be able to stop it."

"And it's not only Lord Bath who might run into trouble," Raf agreed. "That's the thing about undead armies, or mummies or even bad-tempered dead kings... They're not always picky about who they rip limb from limb."

Cecily grimaced. She knew exactly what it was like to be in the sights of a creature that was powered only by evil. "And Lord Bath isn't the kind of chap to care a straw about anyone else being hurt by his actions. But if something bad *has* got out, and we did nothing while it ran riot... I couldn't live with myself, Raf."

"Yeah, I feel the same," he admitted. "Let's get this breakfast down us, then we'll maybe saddle up a couple of camels and mosey out to the dig. How does that sound?"

Camels!

"Oh, well, seeing as you've said *camels!*" Cecily beamed at him. She'd bent Raf's ear so often about the prospect of riding a camel. "We *do* need to make sure we still have a holiday, even if we have to go and sort out whatever it is that Lord Bath has unleashed."

"Just me and my girl and a couple of camels," Raf said, his gaze twinkling with mischief. "What more could a bloke ask for?"

"A very big bed?" Cecily nodded towards their bedroom. "Oh, we already have one of those!" She took his hand in hers, and gently kissed him on his lips.

* * * *

They took a taxi to the pyramids at Giza, then swapped motorised transport for a camel each. Despite the excitement of their holiday having been dented thanks to Lord Bath, climbing up onto the huge creature filled Cecily with glee.

"I can see so far from up here, Raf. It's amazing!" Cecily called.

"Isn't it brilliant?" Raf beamed from beneath the shadow of his hat's wide brim. "It's the only way to travel in Egypt!"

The camels grunted as they started their trek across the sand. Cecily looked over to the pyramids and couldn't quite believe that she was achieving one of her life's dreams. There had been a time in her life when dreams had appeared to be all that she would ever know. But that had all changed when Raf had arrived.

Cecily was enjoying the camel ride so much that by the time they reached Lord Bath's dig, she'd almost forgotten that she and Raf were working. The sensations of anger and grief that she had picked up on the evening before were there again, but they felt different. No longer the ancient emotions lodged in the sand, they were now something altogether fresher.

The workers' tents stood far enough from the pyramid that they were still standing, despite the sand having swallowed the dig's equipment when Menkare II's last resting place had risen. She noticed figures by the tents, sitting next to their campfires, where tin pots were on the boil.

And when she glanced over to the pyramid, everything seemed unchanged from how they had left it the night before. The workers were already toiling, loading sacks and baskets with sand as they cleared away the space around the huge edifice.

"It's very quiet, isn't it?" Cecily remarked to Raf once they had climbed down from their camels. His nose was twitching again, and he lifted his head to sniff the air before he said one word.

"Blood."

Some other tents stood a little distance from the workers' tents, with vehicles parked up nearby. Cecily hadn't seen them there the evening before, and supposed they belonged to officials who needed to come and see the newly revealed pyramid.

She wasn't surprised when some men in uniform, wearing hats that looked like fezzes to Cecily, appeared from a large tent. When she spotted handcuffs dangling from the belt of one of them, she realised they were police.

"Coppers," Cecily observed to Raf.

Suddenly, Cecily coughed. She couldn't catch her breath. Maybe it was the sand? But with dread, she realised it wasn't as she coughed again. Limp in every bone, she grabbed for Raf.

He caught his arm about her waist and stopped her before she fell.

"What is it?"

"I can't... I can't breathe," Cecily rasped. "It's tight, tight around my neck. It's like someone's trying to choke me!"

"Focus on me," Raf told her as he helped her stand straight. "Come on, Sis, look at me. Focus on where you are right now."

Cecily swallowed and fixed her eyes on Raf. They were in the desert. It was hot. The sun was like needles on her skin. And there was no hand around her neck. She could feel it, but it wasn't real.

It's not there.

A shadow darted by where no shadows could be, and another, and another, sending a wave of sadness over Cecily.

At last, Cecily knew what was happening.

She sagged against Raf, the choking sensation gone. She took a deep breath.

"Raf, people died here. And their shadows are fresh." She gestured towards the place that the shadows had run to, but there was nothing there now. "I don't think it's anything to do with the people buried under the sand, Raf. There were deaths in the camp last night. It's why the coppers are here. The life was choked out of them, I'm sure of it."

"Well, of course it's a sorry business," an Englishman was saying as he followed the policemen from the tent. He looked absurdly incongruous in a dark business suit, beads of sweat collecting on his balding head. "And if we can be of any assistance, please don't hesitate to get in touch. The High Commissioner has told us to place all our resources at your disposal."

"Of course, Mr Ellenby," said an Egyptian policeman with an impressive moustache. "We would like to close down the site for our investigations. Can you not convince the earl that we must?"

Close down the site?

Cecily couldn't imagine Lord Bath closing his site for a moment.

Mr Ellenby shook his head. He took out a handkerchief and dabbed it against his forehead as he said, "He won't hear of it. Tomb robbers... So unlucky. One has to be so careful these days!"

"Do the lives of Egyptian men not matter to the earl?" the policeman asked. The mournful tone in his voice told Cecily that he already knew the answer to that.

The earl couldn't care less.

"They *were* attempting to rob the tomb," Ellenby pointed out carefully. "And heavily armed too. What happened was terribly unfortunate, but let's not forget that they had no business here. Lord Bath has all the necessary permits."

"But somebody killed them, Mr Ellenby," the policeman reminded him. "It could be the local workers in the camp, it could be one of the Englishmen. But *somebody* killed them."

"Lord Bath is happy to cooperate," said Ellenby, with a raised eyebrow. Cecily knew what that meant. Money talked, especially when the victims were criminals to start with. "And always happy to support local officers. I'm sure you understand."

The policeman didn't reply at once and stroked his moustache. He was evidently thinking over Ellenby's words. Then he smiled as he replied, "I see. In that case, then, I can see no reason why the dig cannot continue as planned."

And Cecily realised that meant the police would drop the case, or at least pursue it with little enthusiasm. They could easily claim that a fight among the thieves had got out of hand. But then, was the murderer a living, breathing person who they could put into handcuffs? Cecily had her doubts, and as she glanced at Raf, she got the feeling that he was thinking the same thing.

"The smell's stronger than ever," Raf told her. He lifted his hand and shielded his eyes as he looked towards the pyramid. Cecily had expected to find it bustling but it seemed to inhabit its own space, silent and foreboding. "If they've had tomb robbers…"

"I wonder if we could find out exactly what the scroll says?" Cecily wondered.

Raf sighed. "There's no way Lord Bath'll give up that scroll. Not a chance."

Cecily had an idea. "We could ask Dina! Do you think she'd tell us?"

"That's an interesting one, actually," Raf mused. "Because she seemed to know what was in it, but Lord B said it'd been in his family for three generations. Before that, it was in the desert."

Cecily gasped. "I hadn't thought of that. How very peculiar. But then she does know a great deal about Ancient Egyptian history, doesn't she? Maybe she'd read about it somewhere?"

"And she's travelling with him," Raf observed. "So maybe she snuck a gleg when his lordship wasn't around."

"Well, wouldn't you have a peek if you could?" Cecily said. "I know I would."

"I would, but I don't know if I'd understand it." He chuckled. "I wonder if word blindness extends to ancient hieroglyphics too. Luckily I've never fancied controlling a mummified murder victim."

"Thank you, gentlemen, thank you." Ellenby closed the door of the spluttering black car into which the Egyptian police had squeezed. A second car sat beside it, this one bearing the small diplomatic flag of Great Britain. It was considerably newer and shinier than that of the Egyptian visitors, Cecily noticed. Ellenby dabbed his handkerchief to his perspiring brow again, then lifted the square of white cotton and waved it after the departing vehicle, like a princess seeing off her champion. "Much obliged!"

"And off they go, back to Cairo, to forget about the people who were killed out here," Cecily remarked as the car drove away, churning dust and sand into the air.

"What's to do?" Raf called to Ellenby. "Trouble at t'mill?"

The Englishman frowned, either at the juxtaposition of Raf's Romanian accent and his words, or simply at his unashamed approach. Not for Raf to try to winkle out clues with professional politicians and their ilk — he preferred the more direct approach.

"Tomb robbers." Ellenby opened the rear door of the car with the diplomatic flag. In the driver's seat, the peak-capped chauffeur glanced in his mirror. "They descend like flies. It's not often they're swatted quite so comprehensively."

"How'd you mean?" Raf asked, all innocence. Ellenby glanced back towards the tents then rubbed his hands together, evidently relishing the chance to share some gossip.

"Six of them," he whispered. "And every neck snapped in half. I've never seen the like. If you fancy a quick look — good story for the bar at the Rosetta, eh — they're piled high behind the earl's tent. Better hurry though, the truck's on its way."

Necks snapped in half?

Cecily recoiled in horror.

"And…and you think they were killed by other robbers, I suppose?" Cecily said, trying not to appear too shocked at Ellenby's suggestion that they should include corpses of the recently dead in their sightseeing.

"Oh, without a doubt," Ellenby breezed. "They're savages, you know. *I* was on Major-General Stack's civilian staff. They don't know any way but violence and thievery."

Cecily had read about Stack's assassination. He'd been shot in his car as he was driven through Cairo. Someone like Ellenby wouldn't forget about *that* in a hurry.

"I'm sure not everyone in Egypt is bad," Cecily said. "Of course, thieves and assassins *are* bad, but that's the case wherever in the world they may be."

Raf nodded. "We even have them in Yorkshire sometimes."

"Yorkshire?" Ellenby exclaimed, surprised. "I certainly would never have guessed. Well, if you'd like to see the miscreants, do it with as much subtlety as you can. The labourers are rather worked up about it, and we don't want to upset the natives, what!"

Cecily turned slowly to look at the workers by their tents. She realised that they were sitting in such ways as to avoid looking at Lord Bath's tent, as if trying not to catch sight of the bodies.

"It must've been unnerving," Cecily said. "Who found the bodies?"

"That's the queerest thing," Ellenby said. "Lord Bath arrived at dawn and found these chappies dead and his security men nowhere to be seen. They'd abandoned their posts, it seemed, telling tales of strange lights in the sky and sounds from within the tomb." He lowered his voice and confided, "Rubbish, of course. The thieves no doubt paid them to look the other way and they were happy to oblige."

"Strange lights...sounds..."

Despite the heat of the day, Cecily shivered. "I'm not so sure, Mr Ellenby. If tonnes of sand can move by itself, then why couldn't there have been strange lights and sounds?"

"Superstition. Sir, might I ask where your accent hails from?"

"Transylvania," Raf told him with a grin that showed off the little fangs that he was so proud of.

Ellenby chuckled and said, "And there we have it. After all, you're a Transylvanian gentleman and you have considerable canines, but I'm sure you're not constantly seeing vampires!"

"Only at family reunions." Raf laughed.

Ellenby doesn't have a clue, does he?

Cecily smiled politely at him, but she wondered what on earth he'd say if she and Raf were to tell them that an earl had roused a cursed mummy from its ancient sleep.

"And they're all very well-behaved vampires, too," Cecily explained. "They won't try to nibble you if you're family."

Ellenby guffawed at the very idea of it and told them, "What a tonic after a difficult morning! Well, I shall bid you good day and good sightseeing. One mustn't tarry." He climbed into the car and, as he closed the door, told the chauffeur, "Drop me at my club, Osaze. An early start calls for a Bloody Mary."

The chauffeur gave a smart nod, then the car pulled away and began its journey across the desert, back to Cairo.

Cecily watched him go, dust billowing behind him. "And he thinks we're teasing."

Chapter Nine

Raf laughed and put his arm around his wife. He gave her a squeeze, then pecked a playful kiss to her cheek.

"Booze at this time in the morning." He winced. "You can tell Ellenby's in the civil service."

"And it's not even time for elevenses yet," Cecily remarked. "Raf, I wonder if we should speak to the workers, ask them what they saw. But I think we might need an interpreter."

"I'm going to have a look at the bodies too," Raf said. "Just to see if there're any clues. Do you want to wait here?"

Cecily shook her head. "I don't want to see the bodies... You're very brave, Raf." But it was typical of Raf, to shoulder horrible things to try to protect Cecily. Because he loved her.

And she thought of Selene and Ido.

How cruel that Menkare II had torn them apart.

"I won't be more than a minute." Raf kissed her cheek. As he approached the tent, he was already taking the little bottle of scented botanicals from his pocket.

Seeing the dead was bad enough, but Cecily dreaded to think how strongly those corpses would smell to a man like Raf with such a sensitive nose. She hung back, awkwardly kicking a pebble across the ground.

It caught the sun, and Cecily realised that it wasn't a pebble at all, but a piece of gold. She bent to pick it up and was momentarily stunned.

It must be thousands of years old.

Cecily was holding a long-necked Egyptian cat god. She held it on her palm, marvelling at it. Where on earth had it come from?

She glanced up and saw Menkare II's pyramid, and the gold figure strained towards it, like iron filings towards a magnet.

"That's where you belong, isn't it?" Cecily held her hand out so that the figure could see the pyramid more clearly. As it fidgeted on her palm, Cecily felt a sensation of longing and loss deep inside her, so intense that she dropped to her knees on the ground and sobbed.

A hand was laid on Cecily's shoulder and she jolted as she turned to look up. It was Dina.

"I did not know you were here," Dina said. "Are you quite all right? Is your husband here?"

Dina helped Cecily up to her feet.

"He's gone over to the tent," Cecily told her, wiping her eyes on her sleeve.

"Let's go and see him," Dina said gently. "But not—"

Cecily was sure Dina had seen what was lying on her palm. But Dina didn't say anything. Instead, she put her arm around Cecily's shoulder and guided her over the tent. They stopped before they reached the back of the tent where the bodies lay. Cecily turned her head away. Dina whispered something in a language Cecily didn't understand, but it had the effect of calming her.

A moment later Raf was there beside them. He couldn't have heard Dina's whispered charm, but somehow he seemed to know that Cecily needed him. He always did. Without a word he took Cecily's hand and held it, a wave of serenity sweeping over them just as a wave of fear had on the previous evening.

"I found a little gold cat," Cecily told them.

Dina closed her eyes for a moment before glancing back at Cecily. "Bastet, that's who you found."

"Is that a good sign?" Raf whispered, brushing his fingertips against the tangle of charms he wore around his neck.

Cecily held the ancient gold figure out for Raf and Dina to see.

"She protects," Dina explained. "And the size of this figure tells me that she was inside the wrappings of a mummy." Then, speaking quickly, she said, "But the desert is full of strange and marvellous things. It could have fallen out of wrappings many, many years ago after a tomb was disturbed."

But Cecily knew where the figure had come from. She was certain it had come from Menkare II's pyramid.

"What should we do with—" Raf held his fingertip to his lips as a car engine drew closer. The engine idled, then fell silent.

"About bloody time!" Lord Bath bellowed from inside the tent. "Where the devil have you been, Snelling?"

A car door slammed and footsteps crunched across the sand.

"My Lord, I'm sorry I'm so late this morning," Snelling said. Cecily heard the fabric of the tent slap in the breeze as Snelling went inside.

"You've heard what happened? Or perhaps you haven't, since you were lolling in your pit until the middle of the morning!"

"Some dead fellows turned up, that's what I heard," Snelling replied. "Tomb robbers, isn't that right?"

"Dead fellows?" But something in the Earl of Bath's tone had changed. The anger was ebbing in favour of something rather more self-satisfied. "*Six* dead fellows to be precise, the neck of each snapped like a matchstick."

"Half a dozen of them?" Snelling gasped. "Bound to have been other robbers who did them in, no doubt. Cairo's full of talk about the new pyramid, after all, and rogues with a nose for treasure would hear about it easily enough and come out here like a shot." He emitted a whistle of disbelief. "Six dead... Someone wants this treasure badly, don't they?"

And not just Lord Bath.

"Our security chaps were nowhere to be seen," Lord Bath said. "Tales of phantoms or some such. We'll need a fresh complement of guards, Snelling. I'll leave that to you. Perhaps cut the pay a little, eh? Ten percent less? We need to keep costs down."

Raf raised an eyebrow, but said nothing.

"Of course, my Lord," Snelling said, obsequious as ever. "But...may I be so bold as to say that I don't think reducing the pay will help with recruitment? If news has got back to Cairo about the murders, which I suspect it might if the guards ran home, then I'll have a dashed hard time trying to convince the superstitious natives to come out here."

"Have you ever heard such nonsense?" Lord Bath scoffed. "Howling wolves and crying women. Ghost lights in the sky. This tomb comes with a heady tale, I know that of course, but a tale is all it is. Go into the city and rally double the security. If I have to pay, then pay I shall. I hardly—"

There came a shout then, the voice of one of the workers calling urgently, "Sir! Sir! Miss Mansour!"

Dina nodded to Cecily and Raf. "I'm sorry, please excuse me."

The man was labouring up the sloping side of the pit towards the lip, his face slick with sweat. At the pyramid the workers were crowded around the entrance slab, but they were standing back from it, as though afraid to go any closer. The man who had shouted reached the top of the incline, panting for breath as he called to Dina again. She hurried over to him, speaking in their own language.

"I wonder what he's found?" Cecily whispered to Raf, as the golden Bastet figure twitched in her hand. She held it up again to show Raf.

"We'll talk to Dina about this little bloke," Raf decided. "She'll know what's best for him. Don't let on to Lord B that we've got him, or I've a feeling we won't have him much longer."

"He might think I'm one of the tomb robbers," Cecily whispered. The worker looked spooked, and Cecily said to Raf, "We ought to find out what that worker's discovered."

Hand in hand, Cecily and Raf went over to speak to Dina and the worker on the edge of the pit. As they drew closer to the edge, the figure of Bastet twitched and jumped in Cecily's closed hand.

"What's all the commo—back again, Mr and Mrs de Chastelaine?" Lord Bath had emerged from the tent and stood now on its threshold. He held one narrow, pale hand above his eyes to shield them from the sun, whilst the spidery fingers of the other held a cigarette. "You've heard we had trouble, I assume? One simply can't get the manpower, you know. Superstitious bunch, these Egyptian fellows. Unless the money doubles, then their superstitions disappear like smoke on the wind."

Cecily tried to look casual as she shifted her hands behind her back, hoping Lord Bath wouldn't notice.

"Yes, we heard about the tomb robbers," Cecily replied. "It's spooky work out here for the guards and the workers, I should imagine, especially at night!"

"*Especially* at night," Dina said. "Lord Bath, something unexpected has happened. Not only this…" Her arm described the broad arc of the pit, hollowed out by the movement of tonnes of sand. "It would seem, from what this man says, that the tomb is unsealed."

Cecily glanced at Raf. That was exactly what he'd detected with his keen sense of smell.

"Impossible," Lord Bath replied, but there was the slightest hint of something in the tightening of his jaw. Cecily had grown used to reading such subtle clues when she had been married to a brute, and she knew better than anyone how the slightest twitch of an eyebrow, or wrinkle of a nose, could indicate the approach of a maelstrom. In front of her was a pillar of the establishment, but his placid expression belied something more. He took a draw on his cigarette and called into the tent, "Snelling!"

Snelling emerged. "My Lord, I heard all of Miss Mansour's nonsense. It's superstition, that's all!"

Cecily tensed, her focus on Lord Bath. She feared for Dina and the worker who'd brought her the news.

Dina stood straight and calm as she addressed the doubting Lord Bath and Snelling. "Lateef is a very experienced archaeologist, and he knows an unsealed tomb when he sees one."

"The odour is unmistakable," Lateef said. "You can smell the air seeping out."

Raf touched Cecily's hand and murmured, "He's right there."

With a heavy sigh Lord Bath said, "I'm sure the robbers didn't breach the seal, I would've noticed if they had." He threw down his cigarette and extinguished it with the heel of one polished boot. "Very well. Let's go and see this supposedly unsealed tomb, shall we?"

With that, he set off towards the pit.

Snelling strode after him, the smoke from his pipe trailing on the breeze, and Dina and the worker followed.

Cecily and Raf weren't far behind. As they negotiated the steep, gritty side of the pit, the Bastet figure fidgeted and shifted in Cecily's hand with more energy than ever. She held it tighter, hoping it wouldn't leap free of her hand.

"It feels like Bastet's dancing a jig," Cecily whispered to Raf. In reply, he closed his fingers around Cecily's free hand, holding on to it reassuringly. Then he took out a handkerchief and pressed it to his nose.

"The air stinks," he murmured. "Be glad you can't smell it."

Bastet twitched even more until finally they made it to the bottom of the pit. It stopped moving, but now leant towards the pyramid at an angle, like a plant reaching for the light.

Dina was standing at the door of the pyramid. She brushed her fingertips against the engraved stone, her eyes closed. She appeared to be in a trance again.

Then she opened her eyes and intoned, as repeating a spell, "The sepulchre is open."

Lord Bath ran his fingers around the edge of the vast stone slab, shaking his head as he did so. After a few seconds he told them, "Nonsense. It's sealed tight."

"If you please, sir," Lateef said carefully. "You can't smell it?"

Now that she was by the door, Cecily realised she could smell it too. A musty, ancient smell that took her back to the chapel at the school she had once lived at. But it was more intense than that, older, and tinged with a darkness that Cecily recognised as the shadow of death.

She gulped and took a step back. "It's *awful*," Cecily said. "Can you really not smell it, Lord Bath?"

"I can smell the sun baking stone that hasn't seen daylight in three thousand years," the earl replied. "Believe me, I wish it *were* unsealed. It would certainly save this expedition a pretty penny."

Dina ran her hand around the stone and shook her head. "It *is* sealed. But then how can the smell escape?" She looked up at the enormous structure that towered above them, perhaps looking for a gap between the stones.

Raf looked up too, shielding his eyes from the sun with his hand. After a few seconds he whispered to

Cecily, "You think it's worth me having a fly around? See if there's anything we're missing?"

Cecily nodded. If there was something to be found, then Raf, as a tiny, high-flying bat, would find it. "Oh, you certainly should, darling. As long as you feel safe to do it under this hot sun."

"It's still early, so it's only going to get hotter." He gave a nod. "I can do it, but I'll be quick. And I'll come back after dark too, just in case there's some truth to those lights in the sky."

"Oh, we *must*," Cecily replied earnestly. They hadn't been hired by anyone, and yet they were trying to solve the mystery anyway. "I'll look after your clothes while you fly."

As the party at the tomb continued their fingertip investigation of the unyielding stone, Raf and Cecily slipped away from the group. They climbed the edge of the pit and headed back to the tents and the shelter they offered.

Cecily glanced around. The workers who had been sitting by the tents had all begun work. The camp was empty.

She looped her arms around his neck and kissed him. Cecily's heart thudded at the thought of the risk that her husband was taking.

"Good luck," she whispered. A moment later Raf's clothes and charms dropped to the ground and a tiny bat rose up from them. He touched Cecily's cheek with the tip of one wing, then flew up into the sky and away.

Bastet struggled in Cecily's hand but she barely noticed it now. She watched Raf go from under the shade of her sunhat. He flew across to the tip of the pyramid, then made his way down in a spiral. He perched occasionally, and Cecily wondered if he'd found something, but then he was off again.

A couple of the workers spotted Raf, although to them he was merely a bat who was out at the wrong time of day. They raised their spades and pickaxes, perhaps thinking it was another sign that something was amiss at the pyramid site. But fortunately Raf was flying too high, and was too quick for them.

Eventually Raf took wing again and soared away from the pyramid, heading back towards the shelter of the tents. To Cecily's surprise though, he didn't come straight to her, but instead disappeared into Lord Bath's private tent.

She hoped he wouldn't accidentally turn back to a man before he'd had time to leave the tent. Cecily wasn't quite sure what Lord Bath would make of finding a naked man in his tent.

She was on tenterhooks, wondering what on earth he might find.

"That chest he had on the boat is in here," Raf whispered through the canvas side of the tent. "Bloody empty."

"Oh, what a pity," Cecily replied. She put Bastet in her pocket, then gathered up Raf's clothes. Cecily glanced down at the pit, seeing Lord Bath and the others busy at the sealed door to the tomb. "Do you want to get dressed in the tent? They're all busy down by the pyramid at the moment."

"Yeah, better had," Raf decided. Then he gave a low whistle and told her, "For a bloke who doesn't listen to superstition, our Lord Vane-Stanhope of Bath has certainly got a hell of a collection of magical this and thats. Come and have a nose."

Cecily stepped inside the tent. It took a moment for her eyes to adjust to the shade, but once they had, she stared in surprise at what looked like a makeshift altar. Lord Bath had set up a table covered in a linen cloth that was printed around its edges with a design of hieroglyphics. A metal ankh stood on it, in the same way as a cross might stand on a church altar. On one side of the ankh was a bowl of spices, and on the other, a brass plate stacked with large, pointed teeth. Standing around like miniature sentinels, Cecily saw more little figures of Ancient Egyptian deities in metal and stone.

Bastet had stopped moving.

"Gosh, is this where he says his prayers?" Cecily wondered. "And are those crocodile teeth?"

"Looks like it." Raf took his clothes and began to dress as Cecily looked around at the unexpected scene. "This isn't an antiquarian's collection, is it? This is a working altar. What does our new mate Bastet have to say?"

"Bastet's gone very still," Cecily replied. She glanced quickly at her undressed husband, then took Bastet from her pocket. The figure was unmoving, until Cecily stood it on the altar. Then it started to move again, shuffling over the cloth as it made its way across the altar towards the ankh as if it were drawn by a magnet. "Look at it, Raf! It's sentient, somehow."

The figure kept moving, then it stopped, standing in front of the ankh.

"Look at that…" Raf was dressed now. He peered at Bastet, watching the now unmoving figure. "Are you picking anything up, Sis?"

"Bastet's looking for something," Cecily said. "I feel this *pull*. Dina said it came from a mummy's wrappings. I wonder if the figure is trying to get back to the mummy? The mummy got out of the pyramid, attacked the tomb robbers, and went back inside — but Bastet dropped out. The ankh has calmed it just now."

"There's nothing about the pyramid that looks amiss," Raf told her. "But the stink's all around it. And whatever — or whoever — killed those tomb robbers, there was a hell of a strength behind it. I don't really believe any human could overpower six men and break their necks without any of them getting away or fighting back. But whoever killed them did just that."

"And yet a mummy could?" Cecily asked. She knew full well that the world was stranger than anyone could imagine. "I've never met one outside of a picture in a book. Could a mummy be strong enough, even though it's so old and dried up?"

Raf shook his head and admitted, "I don't know. I suppose... Well, if Menkare II intended to reanimate him and return him to duty as a bodyguard just to mess with Selene, maybe *anything* can happen? I mean, how many Transylvanian Yorkshiremen can transform into a bat?"

"Not many," Cecily replied. "Other than you and your brother, I'd be surprised if there were any others. Raf... Ido was one of the palace guards. It would stand to reason that he'd attack robbers, wouldn't it? He'd merely be doing what he did in life."

Raf nodded. He picked up a sheaf of papers and began leafing through them, then admitted, "Word blindness makes this side of investigating a pain." Raf held out the papers. "Bills, right? Being a noble tomb robber instead of a *peasant* tomb robber's a dear business! The only difference is one of them has permits, the other gets his neck broke."

Cecily went over to look. It was a bewildering collection. "Bills, final demands...so much red ink. That one's for equipment by the looks of it, that's for a tailor, then there's one here from a security contractor. This is from a university department. And the Rosetta of the Nile are demanding payment too! But then maybe it's his policy to only pay when he gets the final demand? Unless his funds are running down and he's told them he'll pay once he's got inside the tomb."

"He's spent his life chasing this," Raf said. "Half a dozen failed digs before this one...it's got to stretch even a bloke with his sort of money. But this is payday, isn't it? He's found a tomb that nobody believed existed, and it's a bloody great big pyramid! This is his name made, and probably his fortune too."

"No more worrying about paying the bills." Cecily glanced around the tent. It was basic, but even so there were expensive flourishes that showed Lord Bath hadn't economised. The travelling trunks were unbattered and well-varnished, the lamps were new and the floor was covered in thick Turkish carpets with elaborate designs. Lord Bath's shoes and boots didn't look worn down, and his field glasses, hanging on a hook on one of the tent poles, looked new and were an expensive brand. "And anyone looking on wouldn't see a poor man. Not with all these things. But they're for show. He's saying, *I'm not skint, honestly!*"

"—a problem from here on in," Lord Bath's voice said, coming closer to the tent. "I intend to stay here at the site overnight for the majority of the time. I'll personally command the security arrangements, and I doubt we'll see any more trouble."

He'll find us!

"Oh, heck!" Cecily grabbed Bastet and put it in her pocket, where it awoke and twitched. She looked around for somewhere to hide. "Under the bed?" Lord Bath hadn't settled for a small, ordinary sort of camp bed, which was just as well.

Raf grabbed Cecily's hand and bundled her under the bed before scrambling beneath it beside her. There was a breeze as the tent flap opened, then Lord Bath's polished boots strode across the richly patterned rug and he murmured, "Bloody peasants."

A pair of canvas boots followed.

"A nice reviving cup of tea, My Lord?" Snelling asked. "If only Miss Mansour and Abasi were stricter. They're too bally soft with the workers. And to be honest, I'm not sure about Miss Mansour. She's very distracted. Must be some sort of…" —he lowered his voice as if he was uttering something shocking— "*woman problem.*"

"I think when we sail for England, we'll leave Miss Mansour here," Lord Bath decided. "But we need her here to decode the hieroglyphics we'll find. Nobody understands Menkare's ridiculous pidgin Egyptian better than her."

Snelling sighed. "More's the pity. Well, as long as she focuses on the job in the hand. She went very silly over the scroll. It's embarrassing. If only Menkare II had used proper Egyptian!"

"But that would've been too easy!" Lord Bath sounded utterly exasperated. "Go into Cairo, Snelling. Have them come and get these damnable corpses while I round up more chaps to stand security. We begin work on opening the tomb at midday… I foresee a long, late night."

At the words "*opening the tomb*", Raf winced.

"Right you are, my Lord," Snelling replied. He rubbed his hands together. "I'll head off at once. Can't wait to jemmy open that door and take a peek inside."

"Come along." Lord Bath opened the tent flap and as they left, he chuckled coldly and told his companion, "And if those thieves are still stacked up at supper time, I'll use them as fuel for my campfire!"

Snelling laughed along with him. "Oh, very good, sir, most witty!"

Then all Cecily heard were their retreating footsteps crunching on the sand.

Cecily waited a moment, making sure they were both gone, before saying to Raf, "Thank goodness they didn't hang around for a cup of tea! Should they *really* be opening the pyramid? But Lord Bath's not about to stop, is he?"

"Life's work." Raf crawled out from under the bed, then offered his hand to Cecily. "There's no way he's leaving Egypt without cracking that pyramid and letting out whoever's inside. Mind you, whoever that is, he's already been out once, hasn't he?"

Cecily took his hand and wriggled out. She got to her feet and brushed down her dress. "Exactly — it can get out whether that door is closed or not. What a horrible thought! I hope it doesn't come after us. Imagine waking up in the night, and it's just *there*, standing at the foot of the bed, *staring*."

"He'd better not. I'll unravel his bandages if he tries it." Still holding Cecily's hand, Raf crept on his bare feet to the tent flap and peered out. "Everyone's still crowded around the pyramid. Let's get out while nobody's watching."

Catherine Curzon & Eleanor Harkstead

Cecily nodded, and she and Raf headed outside, back into the searing sunlight. It had got hotter even in the time they'd been inside the tent.

"Is the sun too much for you, darling?" Cecily asked Raf. He glanced towards the pyramid, as though weighing up whether to stay or go. Eventually he seemed to decide, and gave a nod.

"Let's head back, if that's all right?" Raf asked. "I don't think we'll miss much here. That slab's going nowhere without some serious kit." He pecked a gentle kiss to Cecily's cheek. "And it *is* our honeymoon, after all."

Chapter Ten

Once Cecily and Raf had returned to Cairo, she locked Bastet in her jewellery box and put it in the safe in their room. While it seemed mean to imprison it, it was too precious to risk losing, dropping from her pocket in the souk. It rattled inside the box for a few moments, then fell still.

Cecily and Raf spent the day exploring more of the city, and returned loaded with even more presents. Lamps with coloured glass, hand-stitched leather slippers, beaded lace and miniature pyramids and sphinxes. Everywhere in the city there was talk of the newly uncovered pyramid, and even if Cecily couldn't understand Egyptian Arabic, she could pick out the name *Menkare* on many people's lips. There was a certain awe in people's voices, and she wondered if the news of the murdered guards was spreading through the city, and not just the discovery of the enormous pyramid.

Cecily found a lockable wooden box in the shape of a pyramid, which she bought for the Bastet figure.

It'll be far more at home in that.

They returned to the hotel, and Cecily took Bastet from the jewellery box. She could almost have sworn that it blinked as it came out of the darkness.

"Look, I found you a new home," Cecily said, lifting Bastet so it could see the wooden pyramid. "I think it's far more your thing than a jewellery box."

A vibration went through Cecily's hand, like a cat's purr, and it surprised her so much she nearly dropped the figure. She carefully laid it on the box's velvet lining, and stroked the figure just as she would any cat, before closing the lid again.

"You have a nice nap," she whispered, then stood the pyramid box on a sideboard by the window, affording it a marvellous view of Giza.

The Bastet apparently content in its new abode, Cecily and Raf sat on the hotel's shady terrace to enjoy a late afternoon tea. It was wonderful to behave like tourists, just any other couple on their honeymoon, rather two investigators of the paranormal. Inevitably, they would have to return to the site, but at that moment Cecily was content to sit with her husband and nibble honey cake.

"It's nice being married," Raf said presently as he took a sip of tea. "But that's because I'm married to you, I reckon."

"I'm glad to hear I pass muster as a wife." Cecily chuckled. She lazily drew a circle on the back of Raf's hand with her fingertip. "And you're quite the perfect husband."

"You only want me for my wings." He turned his hand over and twined his fingers with Cecily's. "Love you, Sis. I'm having the time of my life on this honeymoon, because I'm sharing it with you."

"Your dear little leathery wings," Cecily replied. She thought back to the time when she had found a tiny pipistrelle bat on her windowsill and, not knowing it was Raf, had tickled its furry stomach. It still made her laugh when she thought about it. "But I'm not tickling your tum on the terrace! I'll save that for later. Besides, I'm having a fabulous time as well. There's so much to see, and Cairo's like somewhere from a storybook. But it's better than that, because it's real."

Raf nodded, then said with a smile, "And you rode on a camel! One of my girl's dreams coming true."

"I did! Wasn't it funny how they grunted, as if they were in an awfully bad mood?" Cecily laughed. "But they soon cheered up, didn't they, and enjoyed their stroll into the desert. I wonder…do they have a terribly sharp sense of smell? Maybe they noticed that pong at Menkare II's tomb."

"Maybe they did," Raf murmured, thoughtful again. "They do have a sixth sense. They know when something's up."

"It must be quite exhausting being a camel around here, then," Cecily observed. "Not only do they have to keep ferrying tourists about, but their sixth sense is constantly being jangled each time some archaeologist discovers a new tomb! And it must've been *really* jangled by that vast pyramid suddenly appearing like that."

"I've seen some things. You *know* I've seen some things," Raf chuckled and ruffled one hand back through his tousled hair. "But that's got to be a first. And a first like that can't be good news. They won't bother to investigate those six tomb robbers either, you know. That's done with."

Catherine Curzon & Eleanor Harkstead

"I know…" Cecily sighed. "Not that I'm going to claim that tomb robbers are all sweetness and light, but they were human beings who were alive yesterday morning and never got to live to see today. And I think that not trying to find out what happened to them leaves the way open for more bad things to occur."

Raf nodded. "Someone whose family won't see them again."

And Cecily couldn't imagine that, now she had Raf. They were a little family, just the two of them…and the shades of her brother and Raf's late mum. And all those de Chastelaines of times gone by who occasionally pottered through the garden in Yorkshire, pausing to inhale the scent of the blooms.

Cecily loved every one of them, phantom or not.

"But we'll find out what happened, won't we?" Cecily said. "And that makes a difference, doesn't it? I know men like Lord Bath couldn't care a fig, but we do."

"He's just looking for the jackpot. He wants the prize, and he doesn't care who he tramples on to win it."

"Men like him never do," Cecily replied. "They think they rule the world, and to be honest, I suppose they do."

Cecily sensed someone approaching, and turned to see one of the hotel staff heading towards them with an envelope on a salver. He leaned in and held it out to them. "A message for Mr and Mrs de Chastelaine," he said.

"Cheers, mate." Raf beamed as he took the envelope and passed it to Cecily.

She didn't recognise the writing on it, but she knew who it was from.

"It's from Dina, I'm sure of it," Cecily said as she opened the envelope. She unfolded the note inside and read aloud, "*Dear Raf and Cecily, Could I trouble you with an invitation to my home this evening? I should very much like to speak with you on an urgent matter. You may find me at home for the rest of the day. Your friend, Dina Mansour.*" Her address followed. Cecily looked up at Raf. "Gosh. I suppose we ought to go and see her."

"I'm game." Her husband smiled. "Sounds like she needs a mate."

"She really does." Cecily drained her teacup. "Let's go and get Bastet. I think she'll appreciate a trip after being shut up all day, don't you?"

Raf gave a firm nod. "I'll bet. And that's after a few thousand years in a pyramid!"

Chapter Eleven

Cecily and Raf rode through Cairo in a taxi, the wooden pyramid rattling on Cecily's knee as Bastet fidgeted about. After a couple of streets, she opened the box so that Bastet could see out, and this seemed to calm the figure, who watched Cairo go by quite happily then.

The taxi stopped at the top of an old, narrow, cobbled street. He could take them no farther because his car wouldn't have fitted. So Cecily and Raf climbed out, and at once Bastet strained against Cecily's hand like a dog pulling at its leash.

"Raf, look," Cecily whispered as they made their way along the narrow street, past tall frontages closed away behind their shutters. Raf watched the little figure as they walked, Bastet's upturned face pointing the way towards Dina's home.

"Do you know where you are?" Raf asked Bastet in a whisper. "Or you know something, don't you?"

Thoughts formed in Cecily's mind but each time she tried to grasp one, it flitted away like a fish through reeds.

"Perhaps Bastet knows that Dina understands her origins," Cecily suggested. "She knows, better than anyone else alive, what life was like before Bastet ended up in that pyramid. But that seems a little vague, doesn't it?"

Dina had added to her address the fact that two blue pots stood at either side of her front door. Cecily was glad she had, because not all the houses were numbered, and those that were used Arabic numbers, which Cecily couldn't decipher as easily as she'd hoped.

"That must be Dina's house," Cecily said as she spotted the two pots. Small wooden balconies leaned into the street, heading up the four stories of the house. The building was so old that it looked as if it had grown from the rock in a time before human hands could have shaped it.

They reached the large wooden front door, and Cecily pulled the chain fitted into the wall. She heard it echo into the distance.

"I hope Dina's all right," Cecily whispered as Bastet strained even harder.

"There's a question I want to ask our hostess," Raf decided as they waited. "But maybe I won't need to."

Cecily glanced at Raf, wondering what that question might be. But before she could ask him, she heard footsteps approaching from inside the house, and finally the door creaked open. Dina stood before them in a long linen dress, a wide necklace sparkling at her neck and bangles on her wrists, her hair loose. Cecily was surprised, because for a moment she hadn't been in a street in Cairo, but standing in a temple by the Nile.

"Thank you so much, both of you, for coming," Dina said, and beckoned them into the cool shade of her home. Raf stood back to let Cecily enter first, then followed her through the door and out of the sunshine.

"This is a peaceful part of town," he told Dina with a smile. "Thanks for inviting us over."

"It's lovely, isn't it? You can barely hear any traffic!" Dina said. "I'm sorry, I should have warned you that the road is too narrow for cars to come all the way to my door."

She led them through the hallway, which was plainly decorated apart from its colourful floor, tiled in geometric patterns. They went through a door and along a corridor with prints and photographs of Egyptian views on the walls. Very old pieces of furniture stood along the corridor, with ornaments sitting on them. Despite their age, all the furnishings seemed unused. Cecily sensed the same about the house. It *felt* very old, but at the same time, unlived-in.

Bastet was still straining, and Cecily wondered what it was that Bastet sensed.

"This looks like a lovely place to call home," Raf said casually. "D'you live in London too? When I was a lad, we were half Yorkshire, half Transylvania. Covered lots of miles in a year!"

Dina nodded. "Oh, I have to travel a lot in my work. The papers that I need for my research are scattered all over the world. But Cairo is home."

Cecily wondered if the house seemed to be unoccupied because Dina wasn't here very often. But as she looked at the ornaments and furniture, Cecily had the oddest impression, as if she were in a museum.

Bastet suddenly shot out of Cecily's hand. The gold cat goddess flew through the air and Cecily tried to grab it. The light from the cast-iron filigree lamp above picked out the bright gold figure, and Cecily was surprised to see the figure was emitting that vibration again that seemed so much like a cat's purr as it rubbed itself against a brass shield with a scarab on it.

"Bastet's taken a shine to your shield!" Cecily said.

A cloud crossed Dina's expression for a moment, then she bent and picked up the figure.

"Come with me, Bastet, come along now," she crooned, and the figure went on purring as Dina led them farther into the house.

Cecily glanced back at the shield and wondered if Raf was just as puzzled as she was. What was so pleasing to Bastet about it?

Finally, Dina opened a door, and led Cecily and Raf out into a courtyard. It was open to the sky, with a fountain bubbling at its heart. The upper floors of Dina's house reached up on all four sides and vines climbed up the walls, throwing forth bright flowers. Pots in various sizes stood here and there, filled with herbs and flowers.

Dina gestured to a metal table and chairs, which looked as if they'd just arrived from a pavement café in Paris. "Please, take a seat, won't you?"

Once again Raf waited for his wife to settle before he took a seat. Then he reached out and patted Cecily's hand as he took a deep breath. Raf's eyes closed and Cecily knew that he would be able to identify every scent in this floral, aromatic courtyard. He looked utterly at home outside, in the fresh, shaded air.

"I'd never have guessed the courtyard was here from outside," Cecily said, in awe. "What a beautiful place, Dina. It's like an oasis in the desert, but here in the middle of the city."

"It is my own little paradise," Dina told them, pouring tea into glasses. "You do like mint tea, I hope? And I have some *basbousa*, too. Help yourselves."

Squares of sugared semolina cake sat on a plate, and Cecily gladly took a piece. As she bit into it, she reminded herself that she and Raf weren't here on a social call. At least, not wholly.

"Dina, something's troubling you, isn't it?" Cecily asked her. "Raf and I came as soon as we received your message."

Dina handed them their glasses, then she sipped her own tea, before saying, "I want to hire your services."

Raf cocked his head to one side and watched her through his bright eyes. A few seconds passed before he said in a kind voice, "Tell us the problem and we'll see what we can do." He squeezed Cecily's hand. "So long as Mrs de Chastelaine agrees. It's her honeymoon, too."

"I overheard you talking to Lord Bath yesterday, offering your services to him," Dina admitted. "And, yes, I was interested. You see, he has awoken something… An ancient power he does not respect. And when I found out about those murders" — she tutted, shaking her head — "I knew I must hire you. I know, I know, you're on your honeymoon, and you want to enjoy yourselves, but I would consider it a great favour if you would permit me to hire you. I would ensure you are paid for your time. Raf, you said you know about protective spells. That is what I need from you — because otherwise, I fear for what Lord Bath is capable of with a mummy in his control."

"So you think that scroll's the real thing?" Raf asked. "That intrigues me, because we meet a lot of academics and antiquarians and experts, and virtually none of them believe their charms or spell books actually have any power. They're nearly always wrong, of course, which is *why* we end up meeting them." He gave a laugh and confessed, "But the fact you didn't bat an eyelid when Bastet went for a fly should've been the first clue. You really believe Lord B's in control of an ancient Egyptian mummy?"

Dina glanced at the figure, which she had sat on the table. Bastet was still purring, apparently very happy to be with Dina in her home.

"I have worked long enough among the remnants of my country's past to know that the old ways must be treated with respect," Dina told them. She knitted her fingers as she leant against the table. "That scroll is indeed the real thing. I knew it as soon as I saw it. A silver coffer such as the one it was found in is not an everyday way of storing scrolls. Only the most important, and the most powerful, would be kept like that. I admit, I had already looked at it. I'd seen it on Lord Bath's desk in his house in London. I thought he had forgotten to show it to me, so I looked. I had read about it and I knew what it was at once — Menkare II's scroll, to control that poor murdered man, Ido."

Dina's voice quavered as she spoke, and she quickly sipped her tea. Cecily glanced at Raf. The story of the mummy evidently saddened Dina.

"And this is your life's work?" Raf asked. "Just like it's Lord Bath's. Or maybe not *just* like him."

"Not entirely like him, no," Dina replied. "Because I am Egyptian, it means more to me, do you understand? For instance, when he told that story about Menkare II, he was so wrong to speak about Selene as he did. As an Egyptian woman, I felt honour bound to protest his twisted interpretation."

"His interpretation was rubbish." Cecily heard the uncharacteristic anger in her husband's voice, and she knew precisely where it had come from. She had been yoked to a monster once too, just like Selene and the pharaoh. "His life's work and that's the best he could do? No wonder he's single."

Cecily couldn't help but laugh. "He's not exactly impressing any ladies behaving like he does."

"He was so wrong… Selene did not want to marry him." Dina shook her head. "She made what she thought was the best choice. She took the path that would protect Ido. He would live. And yet…and yet, Menkare II, a pharaoh who truly is best forgotten, decided that he would kill the poor man anyway. A man who had risked his life, his safety, as the palace guard. A man who had done no wrong, and who should have been thanked by Menkare II. Not murdered by him, and certainly not in such a vile way. Bound and buried alive, because he was loved by Selene. You can well imagine her despair, I'm sure, for she felt as if she was to blame for his death, though it was not her fault at all."

Dina brushed a tear from her eye. Cecily wondered why Dina took the story so personally. Perhaps there was a lost lover in her past somewhere. And in the story of Selene and Ido, Dina saw a kindred spirit. That had to be it.

"And Ido doesn't even get his rest now, thanks to Menkare II and the Earl of Bath." Raf sighed. "Can the spell be undone?"

Dina nodded. "It can be, but only with a spell from another scroll. And it can only be read inside the burial chamber of the pyramid. It is not specifically to remove control of a mummy, but to grant eternal rest to the dead. It must be used wisely, or…"

"Or the ghosts you consider to be your friends would vanish into the ether forever," Cecily said. And the thought filled her with sadness, because she had always welcomed visits from the dead.

Raf glanced towards Cecily with an affectionate look, then asked Dina, "Do you know where the second scroll is?"

"Yes," Dina said, smiling to herself. "*I* have it. Not Lord Bath, not some other earl… *I* have it. And I could use it to end Ido's servitude, but only if I can get inside the burial chamber with it."

Raf nodded, slowly at first, then a little faster.

"Got it." He took a sip of mint tea. "The reanimating spell works outside the pyramid, because Menkare II would use it while he was alive. Once he died and needed his bodyguard in the afterlife, somebody — one of those hanger-on priests, I suppose — would read the release scroll and send his spirit on. To rest, I hope, because I'd hate to think of him serving that rotten old bast — So-and-so in the afterlife too."

"That's exactly it," Dina replied. "Ido needs to be set free, otherwise Lord Bath will control him for the rest of his days. And more people will die. But until I can get into the burial chamber…and bearing in mind that the door is stuck fast, no matter how hard Lord Bath makes people work…I need you to cast protective spells. I have cast my own, but I want to make sure we have done all that we can."

"We can do that." Raf glanced at Cecily again. "But we make decisions on cases as a team."

"Of course we can help, Dina," Cecily assured her. "Raf's the one who knows the spells. I'm learning! But if you've cast spells, and Raf and I do too, then that must make some sort of difference, don't you think?"

Dina nodded, then she glanced at the Bastet figure. "Do you mind if I borrow this lady? I think she might help with the spells. She was put in a mummy's wrappings for protection and if, as I think, this fell from Ido, then it gives us a connection with him. It might help us to reach his conscious mind, which might still be there beyond Lord Bath's control."

"If it'll help, then of course," Cecily said.

"I'm a bit rusty on ancient Egyptian lore," Raf admitted. "But when Menkare II gets into the underworld, am I right that the gods weigh his heart? To make sure he's worthy of his place in paradise?"

"Yes, that is right," Dina said, evidently pleased that Raf knew about Egyptian beliefs. "Anubis, the jackal-headed god, weighs the heart, and if it is heavier than the feather of truth, the soul is devoured by the goddess Ammit and is destroyed forever. It is possible, if there is any truth in it, that Menkare II's soul was heavy. Far heavier than the feather. And so Ido, condemned to be his servant in death, has lain in the pyramid without a master for millennia. Until…until Lord Bath read that scroll."

Raf nodded again, more slowly this time.

"And there under the sand where they fell," he murmured, "all the court, buried by the storm."

Dina nodded. Her gaze was far away, as if she was remembering something. Cecily wondered if her family had been lost to some tragedy. It would explain why Dina's house felt so empty.

"Selene was a good woman, a powerful, gifted priestess," Dina told them. "She would never have deliberately set out to hurt *anybody*. You must understand that. All those people died, and it was her fault. I can only imagine it weighed heavily on her...as she died, too, under the sand."

"But it wasn't her fault," Cecily insisted. "It was all the doing of Menkare II. All the rage and grief that caused the sand to blast in — she only felt like that because of what Menkare II had done to her."

"That story he told, all that bunk about the wronged husband..." Raf shook his head and tightened his grip on Cecily's hand. "I met a man like that once. A *wronged husband*. He was the most wicked creature I've had the misfortune to come up against. They get hold of something precious and they try to crush the life out of it."

Cecily smiled gently at Raf. She knew exactly who he was talking about, the woman she had once been, a bullied, unloved drudge.

"But he met a nasty end, just like Menkare II," Cecily said.

"Good." Dina nodded. "You know, there is a shelter in the city for women who end up under the sway of bad husbands. I help out there whenever I am here. It seems the best thing I can do, because not everyone can stop their husband's heart."

"Men like that hardly have a heart to start with." Raf took a deep breath, calming himself. "Dina...you're the expert here and I know this might sound like I'm a daft romantic — " He paused, laughing at his own words. "I *am* a daft romantic. But, if we can get you into the burial

chamber and you read the scroll, and Ido passes over…
D'you reckon there's any chance he'll find Selene
waiting on the other side?"

Cecily watched Dina's expression. She was looking
at Bastet, then she lifted her head. "As long as her
disobedience as a wife is not considered a sin, as long
as the deaths of the court by the pyramid are not either,
then she would not be consumed by Ammit.
Then…yes, they *could* meet again."

"I'm sure they will! Poor Selene, she's been waiting
for such a long time," Cecily said.

"She has. But if she and Ido do meet, then all of those
years will pass" —Dina clicked her fingers—"in the
blink of an eye."

"From what I read in the legends of Menkare II, the
court was a bit of a magnet for the worst of humanity.
The bloke and his pals made Caligula look like Father
Christmas," Raf said. "Priests devoted to black magic,
sacrifice, all that business. Not the sort of pharaoh who
really endeared himself to the gods. No wonder they
buried him quick. They must've realised a reckoning
was on the way. Just seems unfair to me that Selene was
lost in the storm along with her husband's rotten
hangers-on."

Dina nodded. "It is a very sad tale. And for all that
they were evil, Selene still felt guilt at those deaths. And
poor Ido, he worked for Menkare's father, a good, kind,
honourable man who was much mourned on his death.
He knew Menkare II was not a worthy successor, that
he was a spoiled child who had turned into a despotic
man. And he knew he had to rescue Selene from him."

Cecily listened, fascinated. How wonderful that
Dina knew so much about that long-lost period, and

could speak about it with such feeling, as if it had only happened last week.

"I want to send that bloke to his rest. And to find his girl." Raf looked at Cecily. "We'll take the job, right?"

Cecily nodded. "Right. Definitely. We'd love to, Dina."

Dina gasped with joy, then she leapt from her chair and hugged first Cecily, then Raf.

"You cannot imagine how glad I am to have met you," Dina told them. "The treasure hunters want only gold, and the scholars only the history. But you two, you think of the past as I do. That those lives, those beliefs, are as worthy of respect as our own."

Raf met Cecily's gaze and raised his eyebrow. She knew what it meant, because she'd seen it before when they dealt with a bad-tempered poltergeist in Mr Beesom's farm on the edge of their village just before they'd left for their honeymoon.

Let's do this one on the house. A favour for a pal.

And he was waiting for her to give the nod... How unlike her old life being married to Raf was.

Cecily grinned at him. "Oh, you're quite right, darling." She squeezed Raf's hand as she turned to Dina. "We're not going to charge you a penny, Dina. Think of us as your friends—your like-minded friends."

"Oh, are you sure?" Dina wiped her fingers against her eyes. "I'm going to cry! You're so kind. I know what I shall do—I will donate your fee to the shelter. If you do not mind?"

"I don't mind one little bit," Cecily replied. "That sounds perfect to me. And, Raf, what do you think to that?"

"What d'you think I think?" Raf beamed. "It's a cracking idea."

Dina smiled broadly. "Well, it is all arranged. Now, you must tell me if you need anything for your spells. My garden here is well-equipped with plants and herbs."

"You know, I'd love a tour of the garden if it's not too much trouble," Raf said.

That didn't surprise Cecily at all. In fact, as soon as she'd seen her husband draw in that first deep, happy breath, she'd known that he was in his element. It was amazing that he still had his shoes on really.

"You're a gardener, aren't you?" Dina clapped her hands. She rose to her feet and said, "Come, I will show you. See the mint, growing just there?" She pointed to an earthenware pot with a lizard painted on it. "You drank some of that earlier! Fresh, beautiful mint."

"The first thing I ever grew," he reminisced. "When I was just a weeny. Mum and Dad always reckoned I had a little mint crop on my bedroom windowsill before I could really talk!"

"How wonderful! You can use it in so many things, and once you have the knack, it will grow and grow and grow," Dins said. She led them over to the pot and snapped off a stalk, holding it out to Raf. "Here, crush the leaves and smell that beautiful scent."

Raf did as she had asked and offered his hand to Cecily, so she could inhale the aroma.

"This is my sort of magic." He beamed.

The scent was intense, and Cecily wondered how strong it was to Raf.

"And here is lavender, too," Dina said, gesturing to the next plant. The silver-leaved plant looked very happy in its home near the desert. It was dotted all over with tiny green leaves where it was putting out new growth.

"Does someone care for them while you're travelling?" Raf asked. "Or is there a little bit of magic in it?"

Dina winked at him. "Oh, just a sprinkle. It so happens that a cloud forms over the yard each morning, before the sun gets too hot, and waters the garden."

Dina crumbled some lavender leaves between her fingers and wafted the scent towards them. It smelt strong to Cecily, and she and Dina both laughed at Raf's reaction to it.

"Oh, will you just smell that!" Raf closed his eyes and breathed in so deep that Cecily thought that he might almost take off as he rose up onto his toes. "That's heaven, that. Reminds me of Mum's corner in the garden at home."

"We planted a cutting there," Cecily explained to Dina. "And it's grown, and grown, and grown. Dina, you *have* to come and see it when you're next in England."

Dina smiled. "I should like that very much." She led them past a thorny plant, without passing comment, then showed them a wall of pots that worked their way up the wall, full of springy green plants. "Thyme, six different kinds!"

Raf glanced back at the plant she had missed and Cecily knew that he'd recognised it, but he said nothing. Instead he let Dina continue with her tour, and as she did, her cares seemed to melt away.

Thanks to the little rain cloud that fell only on her garden, Dina had been able to grow a wonderful oasis in the narrow, old streets of Cairo. The day was wearing away, the sun fading from the sky, by the time she finished her tour. Cicadas sang and a lizard scuttled across a wall and away into its hiding place behind a pot of feathery white cumin.

"I call him Sobek, after the god of crocodiles," Dina explained. "He wanted to say hello."

"How do, Sobek." Raf beamed after the departing lizard. "Good job keeping an eye on your domain for our pal Dina."

Cecily wondered if Raf had hit on something there. What if Sobek could transform himself into a crocodile and scare away anyone who would threaten Dina's idyll while she was absent?

For a moment she caught herself wondering if that was silly, but after seeing all that sand move, perhaps it wasn't such a daft idea after all.

"I've taken up enough of your time," Dina said. "Thank you so much for coming, and for agreeing to help. It means more to me than I can ever express."

"We'll sort it," Raf promised. His evening was only just beginning, of course, since he intended to soar over the dig site again once night fell. "Don't you worry."

"Thank you for having us," Cecily said. She wasn't just rattling off her thanks, she meant it. Cecily wasn't sure that Dina had many visitors.

"While you are in Cairo, you are welcome to come by whenever you like, when I'm not at the dig site," Dina said. "I'm back there tomorrow of course. Early. That door is being *very* stubborn."

"You poor thing," Cecily said. "Lord Bath's having you work very hard. Look…would you mind me staying a little while this evening, as long as you're sure I won't get under your feet? Only Raf's…got an errand to run."

Dina smiled knowingly. "Of course you can stay. And, Raf, is this an errand you can share with me, or something you wish to keep secret?"

"I fancy having a bit of a look at the dig site." *From above*, though of course he wouldn't mention that. "Nothing too exciting. Just being nosy."

"And see if it looks different at night?" Dina raised an eyebrow. "If what the guards say is true, then it must. Cecily and I will prepare a feast for you that we can *all* enjoy once you get back. How does that sound?"

"I'd love to cook with you," Cecily said to Dina. "Doesn't that sound delicious, Raf? And you'll certainly be hungry once you get back." He always worked up an appetite during a flight.

"I'd be chuffed with that," Raf assured them. "And I'll be famished too. Thanks, Dina, that's really kind."

"Not at all," Dina said. "It's so nice to have guests. I don't often have people come round."

Cecily had intuited correctly, it seemed. But tonight would be different, because she and Dina would keep each other company and cement their burgeoning friendship as Raf soared and swooped above Menkare II's silent tomb.

The last of the day bled from the sky.

"It is time to light the lamps now that the sun has set," Dina told them. "Please excuse me."

She took a long taper from a small cupboard and went round the courtyard lighting lamps and candles. Cecily watched in awe as the place was lit up, seemingly glowing. Beside her Raf watched for a few seconds, then decided, "I'd better head off and see what's what. I shouldn't be too long. I'll be back before you know it."

Cecily kissed him goodbye. "Good luck, darling. I'll see you really soon." It wasn't safe out there for a little bat, but Raf wasn't an ordinary pipistrelle.

"Dina, I know this might sound like a weird question," Raf said, "but have you got a room with a window where I can leave my stuff while I'm gone?"

Because what bat needs clothes?

Dina blinked at him, then she smiled. She had evidently heard stranger things in her time than that.

"Of course. Would you like to use one of the bedrooms?" she asked him.

"Are there any on the top floor?" Cecily asked.

Dina nodded. "Yes, come this way." And with that, Dina led the way out of the courtyard and up a flight of stone stairs with a carved banister. Higher and higher they went, until they came out on a flat roof covered in yet more plants. A door led off it into a sparsely furnished bedroom. "Is this room to your liking, Raf?" Dina asked him.

"Perfect," Raf told her with a smile. "Thanks, Dina. You're a mate."

"I imagine you will find your way back into the house when you return," Dina said. She opened the shutters and let in the night air. "I don't ask questions, you know."

Chapter Twelve

Cecily tried not to worry about Raf, but the thought of him flying across the city, and out across the desert and back again—and around the pyramid where those men had been killed—kept preying on her mind.

But I mustn't think about it. He knows what he's doing.

Dina seemed to intuit that Cecily was fretting, so she involved her in the preparation of their feast, enthusing over every piece of food. They picked herbs from the courtyard as well as lemons from the tree there. Cecily helped to scrape the seeds out of ripe pomegranates and crushed chickpeas to make hummus. Then she sliced rumi cheese and pickled cheese while Dina prepared stuffed vine leaves. Cecily was surprised that the kitchen was so full of food when Dina lived in the house all alone.

"There, it is all ready for when Raf returns," Dina assured her. As she spoke, Cecily sensed a certain change in the ether, a wave of affection that told her that her husband had returned. It was like the clearing of the air after a storm.

"He's here," Cecily said, then she left the kitchen, heading out into the courtyard. She wondered if she would see him flying over, or if he was already upstairs in the bedroom, returning to human form.

As Cecily looked up into the dark sky, she saw a tiny figure flit through the moonlight. Raf swooped down low enough to ruffle his wife's hair with his wing before he banked upwards and headed for the room that Dina had assigned for his use.

Cecily smiled.

He's safe. Thank heavens, he's safe.

Dina appeared in the courtyard, bringing the food out on a tray.

"Oh, let me do that, Dina, please," Cecily said. She so easily switched back into her servile mode.

"No, you must sit and enjoy my hospitality," Dina said. "You and your husband are my guests. Helping to prepare the food is one thing, but bringing it to the table? No, I won't hear of it."

From above came the sound of Raf whistling a merry tune, letting their hostess know that he had returned. Thank goodness that Dina didn't ask difficult questions.

And thank goodness Raf hadn't turned back into human form in the courtyard before he'd been able to get upstairs to the room where he'd left his clothes.

"He sounds happy," Dina observed as she unloaded her tray. "I hope that means it all went well."

Cecily hoped so too. She took a seat at the table again, and glanced at the door that led upstairs, wondering what Raf had seen at the site.

"Vane-Stanhope was as good as his word," Raf was already saying as he strolled barefoot into the courtyard. He stooped to kiss Cecily's cheek and told the women, "He's moved into that tent. He's living at the pyramid."

Dina rolled her eyes. "As long as he does not expect everyone else to do so too," she said. "And what was he doing? If you tell me he was *still* trying to open the door of the pyramid, I would not be surprised at all."

Cecily shivered, even though the night was warm. Lord Bath's determination to get inside the pyramid had become an obsession.

"That's a tale," Raf told them with a sigh. "Dinner smells really special. I could smell it on the other side of town!"

Dina laughed. "Thank goodness it smells nice! Let me go and get the rest of the food." She went back into the house.

Cecily took Raf's hand. "Oh, thank heavens you're all in one piece. You know what you're doing, and it's so silly of me to worry, but you know how much I do."

"I'll always come home if you're waiting there," Raf told her. He tapped his thumb against her gold wedding band. "You're my girl."

Cecily gently kissed him on the lips. "And you're my chap," she told him.

Dina appeared in the doorway with another tray loaded with food. Cecily was still wondering where it all could've come from because her kitchen had seemed as unused as everywhere else in the house.

"I'm so pleased to see you back, Raf, although not as pleased as Cecily, of course!" Dina said. She came over to the table and put down the tray, unloading bowls of olives and pitta breads, tomatoes and peppers.

"Look at this!" Raf rubbed his hands together. "You're coming to Yorkshire, Miss Dina Mansour, and we're going to spoil you rotten."

Dina chuckled as she took her seat at the table. "I should very much like that, as long as everything goes well here."

"Raf has some Egyptian pieces at home," Cecily told her. "And all manner of amazing things from around the world. You'll love it. And the garden. I promise you, Yorkshire is smashing!"

"And the pieces I've got were given as gifts," Raf assured Dina. "By the Egyptian people who owned them. No tomb diving for us!"

"I should hope so too!" Dina said. "And besides, you are both sensitives in your own way, and you would not be happy if you had stolen grave-goods in your home. You would *feel* it most intensely. It is not a good thing at all."

"Oh, no, I shouldn't like *that*!" Cecily shivered. "It all gives off feelings of…contentment, I'd say."

"Then I am happy." Dina started to serve up the different dishes she had prepared with Cecily. "Raf, Cecily is a natural with Egyptian food. You will have to eat like this at home as often as you can. Then you will always remember Egypt. And maybe you will remember me too."

Raf beamed and assured her, "That sounds good to me." He cast his gaze over the food, then closed his eyes and inhaled the aromas again. "I know, I know, you both want to know what's to do, but this is too good!'

"All the herbs are from the garden, and we used a lemon from the lemon tree too!" Cecily told him.

"So many people think of Egypt as just endless desert dotted with the occasional tomb," Dina said, drizzling olive oil from the bottle over her meal, "but there would have been no great tombs if it wasn't for the fact that this country can produce such wonderful food. I am very proud of it."

"I grew up in the Carpathians." Raf pressed his hand to his hand. "Bram Stoker's got a lot to answer for!"

"He does have a habit of...how can I put it?" Dina tapped her fingernails against the table as she sought the right word. "Making our countries seem rather more over-the-top than they are. I should point out, it's not every day that tonnes of sand move by themselves..."

Raf nodded and told them, "It's not every day that a slab of stone refuses to be moved too, but this one has."

"Do you think it's being stubborn, because it knows Lord Bath is desperate to get inside?" Cecily dipped some pitta bread in the hummus. "If a block of stone could be sentient enough to decide such a thing?"

"Perhaps..." Dina considered. She speared an olive with a fork, then said, "Or something inside the pyramid doesn't want the door to open. It will hold it closed for as long as it pleases."

"But if he does have control of Ido, and Ido killed those tomb robbers..." Raf shook his head. "The tomb's *been* open. That's why Lateef could feel the air and I could smell it. It's been open, and now it's closed again."

"Been open...?" Dina laid down her fork for a moment. "Yes, of course, it must've been, in order for the mummy to escape. And now he is back inside and he has sealed himself up. Until he emerges again."

Raf nodded and asked, "So Lord Bath can control Ido, and he could read the scroll, but not the hieroglyphics on the slab. Why was that, Dina? A different form of language?"

Dina nodded. "Yes, that's quite right. Menkare II's court used a slightly different language, one that was more potent with magic. And they used it for ill, of course—apart from women like Selene, and men like Ido. It's a very rare sort of Ancient Egyptian language. There are very few examples of it about, and as a result few scholars nowadays understand it. It's always been seen as rather a footnote, so never attracts much serious study. Of course, as you may have guessed, I am drawn to unusual things, so I learned it."

"I bet that really gets on Lord Bath's wick," Raf murmured. "Good."

"Oh, it does, it *does*!" Dina chuckled. Cecily adored how irreverent Dina was, nothing like the boot-licking Snelling. "Whenever it crops up, he pretends that he can understand it, then he gets annoyed and insists I read it, then afterwards he says, *of course I knew that, I was just testing you!* Which is nonsense, of course."

"But he could read the scroll..." Raf murmured, furrowing his brow. "Or is that not in the same language?"

"It's in a more common style of Ancient Egyptian," Dina explained. "While the court used the magical language, as it was known, Menkare II, like Lord Bath, wasn't entirely at home with it. And so the scroll was written in the version of Ancient Egyptian that he understood."

"How funny that Menkare II and Lord Bath are so similar," Cecily said. "No wonder he's so keen to get into the tomb. Wouldn't it be scary if he opened the casket and found he was face to face with *himself*?" She was only joking, but Dina's smile in response seemed rather strained.

"They sound like they'd get on," Raf agreed. Then he frowned and said, "I wasn't sure what Lord Bath was up to tonight at first. He was pacing out the sand from the pyramid, and he had some blokes putting down string in a big grid, like they were marking out a building site. I watched them for a bit before it occurred to me."

Dina was thoughtful for a moment. Her expression was unreadable as she said, "Oh, and what occurred to you?"

Cecily had a feeling Dina knew what Lord Bath was up to, or had an idea, at least.

"The entrances to the pyramids aren't usually at ground level, in my limited experience." Raf shovelled up a forkful of food. "The sands only shifted so far. There's a lot more pyramid under the ground."

Dina nodded. "You are quite right. There is more to that pyramid than anyone can guess. At least, so I should imagine. How much deeper will Lord Bath dig, that's the question."

"He'll dig for miles!" Cecily said. "As long as he doesn't have to hold a spade."

"So the question is, how do we get in to lay Ido's spirit to rest?" Raf asked.

Dina shrugged. "I believe it is Ido who is keeping the pyramid closed. And do you know, that is a *good* thing. Because when a mummy falls under the control of a spell, as Ido seems to have done, sometimes there is nothing left of them. But if, as I *suspect*, Ido is keeping the door sealed, he is not entirely lost. Do you see?"

Raf nodded slowly. "Yeah..." he murmured. "We really need to help him, don't we?"

"Oh, poor chap, it must be terrible to be controlled by the whim of someone else," Cecily said. "And it's not even someone he knows. It's some English earl who's decided to pick up the reins."

"It is an awful fate," Dina replied, her expression soft with concern. "For a brave, good man such as he was in life to be treated as nothing more than a tool. No, it is not right at all. I wonder, now that it seems that Ido is holding the door closed, there are some spells I can perform to let him know he has friends, and not to be afraid to let go."

Raf smiled and nodded. "We'll need to choose our moment. We can't risk Lord Bath seeing us, but even *he'll* have to take the odd break."

Dina chuckled. "Yes, even him. And if necessary, I have the means at my disposal to ensure he enjoys a nap." She gestured to her many herbs, and Cecily giggled again at Dina's irreverence.

"A sleeping draft in his tea?" Cecily said. "Oh, Dina, you're naughty, but why not?"

"He's got security up there too," Raf told them. "But I'm not sure how keen they'll be to stick with the job if there really are lights in the sky and phantom wolves howling at the moon."

"So you didn't see any?" Cecily asked him, disappointed. "Does that mean they exaggerated?"

Raf shook his head and asked Dina, "Could it be because he hasn't summoned Ido tonight?"

Dina bit a spear of asparagus and chewed thoughtfully. After a moment she replied, "Yes, I think that might very well be the case. After all, summoning a long-dead spirit to do one's bidding sends things in the cosmos rather askew."

The Nile Priestess

"Good heavens, I hadn't thought of that," Cecily gasped. "But it makes sense — if you turn one thing one on its head, then others will follow."

"You'll put it back to how it should be," Raf told Dina. "And whatever help you and Bastet need from us, you just name it."

"I hope to," Dina told him. "Your protective spells will be important, but, Cecily, if you can sense Ido's spirit, perhaps you might be able to communicate with him too?"

Cecily laid her hand on Dina's arm. "I can certainly try. I'd be happy too. I haven't communicated with a mummy before. Is it dangerous?"

"I would be less than honest if I were to tell you there are no risks at all," Dina admitted. "But you have a gift, Cecily. And you will have the protection of Raf, and myself, and we have Bastet, too. Remember, Ido was not a bad man in life, and in death, I hope he is a good spirit."

"This sounds a bit crackpot, but is it worth making contact before we try to get in and do the job?" Raf asked. "Sort of let him know we're on our way and we're not looking for trouble or to pinch anything?"

"Oh, yes," Cecily agreed. "Rather like making a telephone call before you drop in on a friend."

Dina laughed at that. "Exactly, like a telephone call! Yes, we should try it. We only need to be *near* the pyramid, not inside it, to speak to Ido. I just hope there is enough of him left to be able to hear us."

"When should we do it?" He looked from Cecily to Dina.

"As soon as we can," Dina replied. "Can you come to the site tomorrow?"

Cecily knew why Dina spoke with urgency. They needed to act before more people were killed.

"Yes, I think we could," Cecily replied. "Raf, darling, do you mind going back to the pyramid tomorrow?'

"Evening, right?" Raf asked. "I'm guessing it'll be a bit busy in daylight."

Dina nodded. "Yes, evening is best. Just after sunset. Aside from midnight, it is the most potent time of day for magic."

Cecily smiled at Raf. He knew very well about the magic of the night.

"That sounds perfect," Cecily said. "And Raf won't have to worry about the sunshine."

He picked up a piece of pitta bread as he told Dina, "I've got sensitive skin." Raf bit into the bread with his fangs. "I inherited it from my mam."

Chapter Thirteen

It was late once Cecily and Raf got back to the Rosetta of the Nile, and the next day, they stayed in bed until midday. They went into Cairo for lunch, and as they ate, they overheard an American couple talking about the discovery of Menkare II's tomb. *Everyone* knew about it, it seemed.

And Cecily and Raf would be going back there that evening.

They spent the afternoon at the museum, Cecily trying her best not to tune in to any of the spirits who lingered there. She needed to conserve her energy for trying to reach Ido.

As afternoon turned into evening, Raf drove a hired car out to the site of Menkare II's pyramid, Cecily in the passenger seat, preparing herself for the evening ahead. She clutched a piece of rosemary, hoping that its link to remembrance would help Ido to recall his life before he was walled up alive in the pyramid. At her side Raf was silent, but Cecily could sense that he was preparing himself for whatever might come. When she saw his lips move, she knew that he was asking for protection for all of them, and probably for Ido too.

Cecily touched her *cocosul* charm as they crested the hill and headed down into the valley where Menkare II's enormous pyramid awaited them.

"Hello, Ido," Cecily whispered. "I hope you're around this evening. We wanted to come and say hello."

The arc lamps were switched on around the dig site, and there seemed to be a great deal of activity. Cecily could see Dina and Abasi with some of the workers standing on the edge of the pit. Others were busy unrolling something across the sand.

"What's that, Raf? Rope?" Cecily wondered. She had a sick feeling in her stomach, though. It didn't look like good news. "I can't quite see from here."

"Oh, bloody hell," Raf murmured. "It's a flipping fuse. He doesn't mean to dynamite his way in, the mad sod! Can you see Dina?"

Dina watched Lord Bath with disdain, her arms folded.

"Yes, she's over there, on the edge of the pit. She doesn't look happy." Cecily shook her head. "Can we stop him?"

"I guarantee you he's got all his precious permits," Raf said with a tight shake of his head. "And I don't know how well it'll go down if I punch his lights out."

"Erm…no, that might not be a good idea," Cecily agreed. "Ellenby would be after you in a second."

They watched as Snelling marched about with a megaphone, the workers scattering and leaving the area by the pyramid's door vacant.

"Won't dynamite damage the stone?" Cecily gasped, horrified at an ancient monument receiving such rough treatment. She felt anger, too, and as she watched through the windscreen, she suddenly realised something.

This anger isn't mine.

"This is what they used to do in the last bloody century," Raf told her. "They couldn't get in, so they blew their way in. He must really want what's inside. And there're the men from the ministry, of course!"

From Lord Bath's tent the earl emerged, followed by a small group of middle-aged white men in stiff, expensive suits. With their cigar smoke and their self-satisfied smiles, it looked like a scene from a gentleman's club in Whitehall. No wonder Lord Bath could get all the permits he wanted. Men like him always had friends in the right places.

The car came to a halt beside a large, sleek, black car. It looked like it came from the embassy, and had a Union Jack on the bonnet.

Cecily bit her lip, anxious as she watched the scene unfolding. They weren't going to stop, and the anger — someone *else's* anger — seemed to boil in her stomach.

"Raf, someone's angry. I can feel it," Cecily told him. "It's dreadful. They're furious, Raf!"

He turned off the engine and looked at her.

"A live someone, or a dead someone?"

Cecily closed her eyes. It was so dark. As dark as the grave. Keeping her eyes closed, she replied, "Dead. They're dead, and they have been for a very long time. And so angry... I can't tune in any further, Raf. I daren't with anger like this."

"Can you back off from it?" Raf took Cecily's hand and held it softly. "Shut it down?"

"I'll try." Cecily brought the rosemary up to her face and breathed in the scent. She thought of the garden at home, and she thought of the beach below. She saw herself and Raf skimming stones, the anger encased in each flat piece of rock, and bit by bit, the sensation ebbed until Cecily was able to open her eyes again. "Oh, I think that's cleared it. I feel different now… The anger's gone."

Raf lifted Cecily's hand and kissed it.

"Can you describe the anger?" he asked. "Was it malevolent, or d'you think it was something else?"

"It was a hurt sort of anger," Cecily replied, trying her best to describe it. "Not an evil sort of anger, hell-bent on destruction, but the anger of someone who suffered. Oh, Raf…you know, I wonder if I've managed to tune in to Ido?"

He nodded gently and said, "I think maybe you have."

"I wonder if it's his anger at Menkare II?" Cecily wondered. "Or if he's angry at Lord Bath? God knows, he's justified being angry at both of them."

"I want that bloke to find some peace with his girl," Raf admitted. "I think about me and you and that old bastard you were married to, and how he kept you shut away from the world and…I suppose I feel like he had you buried alive, in his way. And we found each other and fell in love, and we're happier than ever. So I want Ido and Selene to find each other, even if they have to do it in the next world."

Cecily leant across and hugged Raf. "And that's why I love you, because you're always concerned that everyone else should be happy. I know…the more I hear about Menkare II, the more he sounds like someone I used to know. But we'll do our best to reunite Ido and Selene. I really hope we can."

"I wonder what happened to Menkare when they weighed his heart," he murmured. "I bet it wasn't a happy ending for him. That's the risk you take when you're the sort of old bugger who bury folk alive and force women to marry you."

"Good," Cecily said. "Serves him right! Devoured and destroyed. And speaking of destroying... They really are going to do this, aren't they?"

Snelling strode over to Lord Bath and the dignitaries. He waved his hands about and there was some nodding then all eyes turned to a box with a red handle poking out of it. Cecily shuddered at the sight of it.

Raf nodded and asked, "Shall we get out? Dina might want some moral support from her mates."

"Yes, let's go and see her." Cecily gathered up her things and climbed out of the car. "Poor Dina, this must be so hard. But *we* know she doesn't want any part in dynamiting a pyramid."

Cecily waved towards Dina, and Dina turned and waved back.

She knew we were here...

But Cecily wasn't about to try to work out how Dina had known.

Raf came round to Cecily's side of the car and took his wife's hand. As they strolled across the sands towards the gathering, the sound of labouring engines announced the arrival of two charabancs from the hotel. Through their open windows Cecily could hear the excited chatter of the guests who truly believed they were the glitterati. To them this wasn't tomb robbing, nor the dynamiting of an ancient monument, it was simply entertainment. It was a thrilling story to share once one was back home in Belgravia or the Hamptons.

Cecily shook her head sadly. No wonder Ido was angry. He'd met a horrible end in life, and in death wasn't allowed to rest by anyone.

"Good evening," Dina said. "I'm so glad to see you both. I tried to tell him, I begged him, and I tried to persuade him." *With a spell?* "But nothing works. He's a peer of the realm, and he will do whatever he pleases."

Raf cast his eye over Lord Bath, who was positively preening as he addressed the diplomatic crowd. He was like an actor basking in his ill-deserved limelight.

"This isn't going to end well," Raf said. He glanced back towards the passengers pouring out of the charabancs. "What a bloody scene."

"Dynamite and ancient monuments…" Dina shivered. "It is horrifying to me. Nothing but horrifying."

"Make sure everyone keeps a safe distance," Lord Bath told Snelling. "We'll detonate in two minutes."

"Two minutes!" Snelling bellowed through his megaphone. "Get back, all of you, get back!" He held a cane and swished it about, sending the workers running and the hotel guests laughing.

Cecily clapped her hands over her ears. And as she did, she heard laughter. But it wasn't the guests, it was inside her head. A booming laugh.

It's Ido!

But along with the laugh, she heard something else. Another voice, speaking something she couldn't understand as the laugh went on. She looked over at the pyramid and sensed a presence there. And, she realised, there was another. It was fainter, but it was there.

"Raf, there's two presences in the pyramid!" Cecily whispered urgently to him.

Raf widened his eyes and asked, "*Two*?"

"One of them's laughing really loudly, and the other... I don't know what they're saying, but they're speaking really fast," Cecily told him. "I'm sure the one who's laughing is Ido. He's laughing at Lord Bath and his dynamite! But I don't know who the other one could be. There must be all kinds of people buried in there, servants and goodness knows who else."

But Raf's expression grew darker and he whispered, "Speaking fast? Are you getting any sense of what they feel?"

"They're very faint...let me see..." Cecily closed her eyes and opened herself up, trying to tune in. She started to hear the voice more loudly, and with it, she could pick up on their tone. It was so strange, with the booming laughter still going on, but the tone was unmistakable. "Raf...they sound *worried*."

"And I'm guessing we don't speak the language, right?"

Cecily shook her head as the laughter and the worrying went on. "I don't understand a word. Just his tone... Worried! And I can't even make it out clearly enough to repeat it to Dina, because otherwise we — "

"I said, get back!" Snelling roared again, even though he was closest to the pyramid of everyone. He was clearly enjoying his power.

"Snelling!" Lord Bath barked. "Are we ready to detonate?"

"Yes, My Lord, we're all ready!" Snelling bellowed again through the megaphone.

Cecily looked up at the night sky, hoping for something that would stop the explosion. But there were no signs of rain clouds covering the stars or the moon. Lord Bath would continue his folly unchecked.

Dina whispered something under her breath, and Cecily wondered if it was a spell. She nodded to Raf. Perhaps that was all they could do, protection spells to save the pyramid from being badly damaged.

Raf's lips were working too, his free hand worrying at the charms around his neck.

"Ladies and gentlemen!" Lord Bath stepped towards the detonator box. "Welcome to our firework display!"

The guests from the hotel clapped and cheered.

Oh, you silly fools! Don't you ever think?

Cecily placed her hands over her ears again as the detonation grew near. The laughter was still there, and the worried voice was now weeping. There was nothing Cecily could say or do. She leant against Raf, nervous of the dynamite going off. She'd never seen an explosion before, and had no idea what to expect.

"Let's start the count from ten!" Snelling said, still speaking through his megaphone. "Ready, My Lord?"

"Ready, Mr Snelling!" Lord Bath strode across to the detonator. "Let's hope Menkare II is, eh?"

"Ten!" Snelling yelled, and the hotel guests joined in as he carried on. "Nine!"

On and on it went, each number like a hammer blow to Cecily's head, until finally, Snelling bawled, "One — go!"

Every muscle in Cecily's body tensed as she prepared for the explosion. Raf held her hand tight, his lips still moving in an unheard enchantment until Lord

Bath, with all his strength, pushed down on the detonator.

For a moment, there was no sound at all. Even the racket in Cecily's head had stopped. It was as if everything had paused, frozen.

Then came the noise — a huge detonation that made everyone gasp, followed by a series of smaller ones. Then for a second, no sound, until a showering patter of sand began to fall.

Cecily opened her eyes carefully, but didn't look at the pyramid. She feared that it would show a huge hole in its side. "Oh, Raf, what's happened? I daren't look!"

"Bloody hell..." Raf whispered. From the hotel guests she could hear murmurs of disbelief and wonder. There were other murmurs too though, and some of them sounded not awestruck, but terrified. "There's not a scratch on it."

Raf wouldn't tease me about something like that, surely?

Cecily turned her head. But Raf was right. There really wasn't a scratch. It looked just as it had before. But the sand had been disturbed, and now there was a trench in the sand, showing more of the pyramid's wall.

"It's even bigger now!" Cecily gasped.

The laughter in her head sounded again, and she realised it was two people laughing. The worried voice had gone.

"They're both happy anyway," Cecily whispered to Raf. "They're *both* laughing now."

"That ruddy door!" Snelling roared into the megaphone, as if he could shout it down. He lowered the megaphone and kicked the sand in frustration.

Dina looked on, smiling to herself.

But Lord Bath was smiling too. In fact, he was positively beaming.

"The pyramid *does* go deeper!" he exclaimed. "Abasi, have the men dig down. I want to know how big it really is. We could have something that dwarfs the Great Pyramid itself." The earl turned to the crowd. "And somewhere beneath these sands, my friends, we should find the very courtiers who were buried beneath the desert. And the pharaoh's faithless wife too, still in her chains!"

The hotel guests clapped and cheered again. Cecily grimaced at the thought.

"Fancy being excited at the thought of finding lots of dead people…" she whispered to Raf.

Abasi gave his orders to the workers and they headed down to the pit, shouldering their spades and baskets. While some of them started to dig, others adjusted the arc lamps, spilling light into the new trench. Everyone craned forwards to see more, and the hotel guests clicked away with their cameras.

"I say, Lord Bath!" a posh hotel guest called. "Can you stop the workers for a while so we can get some snaps?"

"The photographs will be all the better if the workers are toiling away in them," he said benevolently. "The sweat of the brow, eh?"

"Oh, jolly good point, what?" the guest called. "Show them back in Blighty how the natives do it!"

Cecily groaned inwardly. The workers kept digging, Snelling following with his megaphone. He shouted at the workers, he shouted at Abasi, but it all seemed rather pointless.

"Keep going! Put some welly into it! We haven't got all day!"

Lord Bath left the trench and strode across the sand towards the Egyptian workers who had been laying out the wires and detonator when Raf and Cecily arrived. One of their number wore a collar and tie and it was to him that the earl began to speak, his gestures animated and expansive. There was no sense that he was a guest in this man's country, but instead he seemed to have planted a flag for little England here in the desert, regardless of whether he had any right to do so.

"He's going to have them blast the sand out," Raf observed. "You know what's strangest about all this? That Lord Vane-Stanhope sees nothing odd in a pyramid that's impervious to dynamite. He didn't even blink."

"No, he didn't, did he?" Cecily agreed. "He must know that he's got his work cut out there. That this is no ordinary pyramid, and it won't give up its secrets without a fight."

Although no sooner had the words left Cecily's mouth than she heard a terrible racket. She'd tuned out of the voices from inside the pyramid, but this was a very different sound, a seething, hissing, scratching noise which seemed to fill the air. She looked up and the stars were obscured. Was it a cloud? Maybe it would rain after all?

"Locusts!" Dina shouted, and just as she did, their insect bodies landed against Menkare II's pyramid.

Cecily crouched down with Raf, swatting them away as a few hurled themselves at the watching crowd. She peered down into the pit where there seemed to be some activity, despite the swarm.

Snelling had been leaning over to see something that a worker was pointing to with great excitement, then he stood and bellowed through his megaphone, fighting against the racket of the swarm, "Ladies and gentlemen, we've got a skeleton!"

Yet his excitement was drowned out by what sounded like a thousand hissing, whirring engines, and the darkness above descended towards the tomb. The tourists ran, their screams splitting the din, and Raf pulled Cecily down as the vast cloud of insects swept overhead, close enough for her to feel the vibration of their flight. When she looked up at the pyramid, Cecily saw that it was stone no longer. Every visible inch of the monolith was covered in the swarm, buzzing and shifting as the people on the sand ran for their vehicles. Yet the innumerable insects were impassive now, watching the scene beneath them.

Cecily fought back memories of the clouds of corpse flies that had accompanied a demon that she and Raf had done battle with. She felt nauseous at the thought. And the work still went on, the arc lamps catching something white in the sand.

A skeleton. A skeleton that's been lying there for thousands of years.

Dina crawled across the sand towards them. "Did *you* summon them?" she whispered.

"I wouldn't know where to start," Raf said. Behind them, the engines of the hotel charabancs chugged into life, but they didn't drive away. No doubt their passengers were torn between escape and missing out on a story with which to enthral their friends back home.

The workers kept digging, and more skeletons appeared. Cecily flinched away as she heard the echo of their screams, their last moments on earth as the sand covered them.

"I should go down and see what they're unearthing," Dina said. "Will you come too?"

As Raf opened his mouth to answer, the sound of a wolf's howl joined the buzzing of the locusts. Then came another and another until it was a cacophony of what sounded like hundreds of wolves, unseen but anything but unheard. With them came an eerie chuckle that grew in volume as a choir joined the call, the pitch of the spectral laughter rising into an ear-splitting wail.

"Hyenas," Raf told them. "What a bloody racket!"

"It's horrible! How can Lord Bath carry on?" Cecily gasped.

But even if he wanted to carry on, the workers who did all the back-breaking labour threw down their spades and ran, scrambling up the side of the pit. With a great rustling sound, the locusts covering the pyramid shifted, forming themselves into the shape of an enormous eye.

"The Eye of Horus!" Dina told them. Then she brought her hand out of her pocket to reveal Bastet, who was twitching on her palm.

"Get back here!" Snelling yelled, but then he glanced up and saw the eye too. His megaphone dropped from his hand. Even Lord Bath was still, gazing up at the pyramid that rose over them.

"My God..." Lord Bath gasped. He stumbled back from the trench, a sand-bleached bone still clutched in one thin hand. All at once the air was silent. The wolves no longer howled, the hyenas' laughter reached an abrupt end, and on the surface of Menkare II's tomb the Eye of Horus watched, not a sound disturbing the night from the locusts that had gathered on the pyramid.

And without warning the immense stone slab that had stood for millennia and withstood even the blast of dynamite suddenly plunged into the trench.

Chapter Fourteen

No one moved or spoke or made any sound for what felt like a long time. Cecily stared — they all did — at the hole in the side of the pyramid. And even she was aware of the stale smell that poured out of it.

A tunnel led off from it, heading into darkness. From where Cecily was standing, she could see carvings inside the tunnel. Just as she began to wonder what they said, there was commotion as the charabancs roared away, the hotel guests evidently deciding that wolves, locusts, hyenas and skeletons were too much for them. Even the idea of being the first people to see inside the pyramid wasn't enough for them to stay.

The workers, too, who had climbed out of the pit, had rushed to the tents and were packing away their things, then running out into the darkness of the desert. Abasi, who had been in the trench with them, had started to run, but he had stopped, frozen to the spot, staring down at the bones that gleamed silvery white under the moon.

At Cecily's side, Raf took out a bottle and dabbed its contents onto his handkerchief. Then he held it under his nostrils and grimaced. "That smells rotten. Bloody hell!"

"Snelling!" Lord Bath bellowed. "Bring the lanterns. I'm about to be the first living creature to set foot inside the tomb of Menkare II for three thousand years. My grandfather was right... This is no legend. And if the tomb is real, then think of the treasures it holds!"

Snelling appeared to be out of sorts. He still hadn't picked up his megaphone. He nodded slowly. "Of course, My Lord, let me fetch the lanterns. Although...might it not be better to do this in daylight?"

"Daylight?" Bath snapped. "Haven't I waited long enough, man? Lanterns! Now!"

"If I were you, I'd wait until daylight," Raf agreed. "Could be anything in there. Cobras, curses, anything at all."

Snelling flinched. "Yes, let's do it in daylight. May I suggest, My Lord, that we come back tomorrow with a doctor in tow? You never can be too careful. One might even get a scratch and end up with tetanus."

He's scared. So much for all his bellowing through his megaphone.

Dina stepped forwards and said, "Snelling is right, and so is Mr de Chastelaine. The night-time is when all manner of cursed creatures might come forth. It is their time."

"Lamps," the Earl of Bath spat. "*Now.*"

Raf gave a low whistle but said nothing.

Snelling started to walk towards the side of the pit, then he came back and picked up his megaphone. Not that there was anyone left for him to shout at. He climbed up the incline and out of the pit, then hurried into one of the tents, where he clattered about.

Then he emerged, weighed down with an array of hurricane lamps.

"I brought all the ones I could find," Snelling called as he skidded down the side of the pit to rejoin them.

"First thing in the morning, get me more workers." Lord Bath snatched one of the lamps from him. "I'll pay double this time. They said this expedition would ruin me, eh, Snelling? You heard them back in London!" Raf gave Cecily a slight nudge as Lord Bath assumed a mocking voice and sneered, "You'll be left without a penny, Vane-Stanhope! Not a penny! Your grandfather died for a fairy tale and it'll ruin you next!" He laughed and threw down the ancient bone. "Ruin me, will it? I'll be rich as Menkare himself!"

Abasi gestured to Dina, and they spoke together for a few moments. He looked anxiously at Lord Bath, then Dina took a step forwards.

"Lord Bath, we are missing a skeleton," Dina said. She didn't sound at all surprised. "Shackles have been uncovered, but without a skeleton to wear them."

"Selene?" Cecily whispered to Raf. "Where can she be?"

"This is the tip of the iceberg," Lord Bath assured them. "She'll be under the sand!"

Dina shook her head. "But they are *definitely* her manacles. There is a sigil on them, to stop her from using her magic. It didn't work, of course."

Dina smiled wryly at that, then she took the manacles from Abasi and brought them over to Lord Bath. They were barely rusted at all. "Do you see, the eagle feather?"

The earl peered at the manacles and said sharply, "Of course. A sigil, you say?"

"Yes," Dina said. "I know from my extensive research that this sigil was put on Selene's shackles. So these *must* be hers. But *she* isn't here."

"I really do think we should come back in daylight..." Snelling said. He jumped as the locusts scuttled across the pyramid so that the eye they had formed seemed to blink.

Lord Bath snatched the shackles from Dina. They were still fastened, and Cecily couldn't help but feel a terrible pang of sadness for the woman who had been forced into them.

"Her skeleton is under the sand." The earl handed the shackles back. "The chains merely fell from her once she was only bone."

Raf ruffled his hair and asked, "How's that then? Under twenty-odd foot of sand, her skeleton's somehow shifting about?" He shook his head. "I mean, I've seen some things, but that's a stretch even by my standards."

"It cannot be," Dina said. "If you look at the other skeletons, they are still wearing armour, and holding their spears and shields. There are still bracelets around their wrists. They are like the figures at Pompeii, found exactly how and where they fell. Selene's bones are not in the sand. I *know* they're not!"

Cecily inched closer, and saw a bony hand sticking up from the sand, still wearing a gold ring with a large red stone.

"We will know that when we excavate the sands with the men Snelling will hire tomorrow." With that, Lord Bath went down on one knee beside the fallen slab. He passed his lantern over the surface. He ran his hand across it as the light illuminated carved symbols, and in the flickering flame, gemstones glittered like diamonds in a night sky. "Miss Mansour, I have some more *sigils* for you."

Dina nodded and went over to look at the door. She crouched beside Lord Bath and whispered to herself as she ran her hand across the carved surface. Her hand came to rest on a sapphire set into the stone.

Then she said, "I am sorry, Lord Bath, but I cannot read them."

"You *cannot*?" He shook his head. "Nonsense. Translate, woman!"

"I cannot. I don't understand it." Dina brushed her hand over the hieroglyphics again. "There must have been another enchanted language at use in Menkare II's court that no one knew about."

Cecily heard a voice. The worried man was speaking again, but his tone had changed. He was coldly furious now, his voice getting louder and louder by the moment. Cecily put her hands over her ears but it made no difference.

But the other voice was silent, only Cecily *felt* something now. A wave of love went through her, so intense that Cecily nearly fell.

It must be Ido.

But who was the angry man? Cecily couldn't bear it but it wouldn't stop.

The look Lord Bath gave Dina was colder than the desert night and for a moment Cecily wondered if it was his anger that she was sensing, but she dismissed the thought. It wasn't mere passing wrath that she felt, but something deeper. It was a loathing so absolute that she'd scarce encountered such darkness before.

The Earl of Bath rose to his feet and told Abasi, "Stay here. Watch the slab." He began to climb the vast building blocks of the pyramid, each a step up towards the gaping darkness of the entrance. "And don't touch those gemstones!"

Abasi nodded. His gaze ran back and forth across the stone, but he gave up trying to read it and instead watched Lord Bath's ascent.

Snelling began to follow him, but he stumbled as he climbed. "Just a quick look, what? We're just going to have a little peek and come back tomorrow?"

"Go into Cairo, Snelling." Lord Bath turned and handed him a car key. "Find me some men to keep watch here tonight. Otherwise I might end up hiring this Romanian runt and his floozy!"

"If you talk about my wife in that way again," Raf warned with a breezy smile, "hyenas'll be the least of your worries, mate."

Cecily bristled, but Lord Bath's words hadn't surprised her. *What a rude man!*

Snelling took the key. He looked relieved that he had a reason not to go inside the pyramid.

"My Lord, perhaps Abasi can go inside the pyramid with you?" Snelling suggested as he retreated.

"And who will watch the slab in that case?" Lord Bath asked, but it was Raf who answered.

"Look, everyone's cleared right off except the locusts," he pointed out. "And you've already got six dead tomb robbers. If I were looking to pinch some grave treasures and I got here to see a million locusts giving it all *Eye of Horus* on the outside of the pyramid, I reckon I'd come back another time. Let Mr Snelling try and get the security, but I don't think he's going to have much joy."

"I'm happy to go to Cairo," Snelling said, sidling away.

"But everyone in Cairo will already know about all this," Dina told him. "No one will come! Not tonight. Certainly *not* tonight." And she was so certain that Cecily wondered if she had cast a spell around the pyramid. "Hire Mr and Mrs de Chastelaine, Lord Bath. You cannot, after *all* you have seen and heard, continue to insist that there is nothing unusual afoot."

Lord Bath shook his head and resumed his climb. As he reached the mouth of the tomb he turned and looked down at them, again surveying what was left of his court.

"Miss Mansour, Abasi, join me. Snelling, guard the slab, you yellow-bellied creature. Tomorrow though, at first light, I want you in Cairo drumming up labourers and guards." He settled his gaze on Raf and Cecily. "As for you two. If you've the blood for it, why not join us in the tomb of Menkare II?"

Cecily glanced at Raf, then up at Lord Bath. As scared as she was, with the growling of the angry man in her head, who knew what unseen mysteries ahead. She thought of Ido's love for Selene and knew that she and Raf had to go inside the pyramid.

"Of course," Cecily said. "Raf, darling, do you want to go inside, too?"

Snelling walked past them, his shoulders slumped as he took up his post by the fallen door. He jerked his finger towards the pyramid and Abasi seemed to understand the message, and began to make his way up the edifice with Dina.

Raf lowered his voice and asked Cecily in a whisper, "Are you sure, Sissy? I don't want you to do anything if you don't want to do it."

"We're the best people for the job," Cecily assured him. "We'll stop anything bad from happening, I know we will. I'm afraid, but...but at least that will make me cautious, won't it?"

Raf drew her into a hug. Cecily heard Lord Bath give a huff of disapproval, but if the peer thought that would stop her husband from embracing her, he was badly mistaken.

"No risks." Raf sounded worried. He kissed Cecily's cheek, then drew back a little and looked into her eyes. "Promise me? No risks."

"No risks at all," Cecily replied. She tapped the end of Raf's nose, trying to be playful in the face of her fear. "And that means you too, remember?"

"When do I ever?" Raf winked, then kissed her tenderly. "I promise."

From the tomb entrance, Lord Bath could be heard telling Dina and Abasi, "Stand back, the pair of you. This is *my* discovery. I go first."

His discovery in *their* country. A discovery that he wouldn't have made without Dina, not to mention the workers who had laboured at the site and all the fruitless digs before it.

Dina and Abasi stood aside for Lord Bath.

"Of course, Lord Bath," Dina said. "A man like you would not believe the superstitious stories told about the curse that falls on the first person to enter a tomb, I am sure."

At the distant sound of a hyena wailing into the night, Raf glanced upwards at the locusts. They hadn't moved, but stayed there on the face of the pyramid, waiting for the earl to make his decision.

"Curses kill the weak," he declared. "Those of us with real power know we have nothing to fear."

He took another step and the black mouth of the tomb seemed to swallow him whole.

Cecily's stomach lurched. She clung onto the rock as they climbed higher. Once they were near the door, she looked back and saw Snelling, alone under the bright arc lamps. Alone apart from the skeletons, at least.

Dina and Abasi reached down to help Cecily and Raf the last little distance.

"Thank you for agreeing to stay," Dina said.

The angry voice was even more furious now. Cecily winced.

"There's a very angry presence in the pyramid," Cecily told her. "And I don't mean Lord Bath. There's another that's very loving. But the angry presence won't stop!"

"Maybe it will when you're back in Cairo," Dina suggested. "And now we follow Lord Bath…"

Cecily lifted her lantern and the juddering flame illuminated the chamber that had lain concealed behind the door for so long. The stone was plain and unmarked, apart from one tablet, carved with hieroglyphics, on the wall. In the centre of the small chamber stood Julian Vane-Stanhope, third Earl of Bath, his lantern held high. Raf's gaze wasn't on the walls though, but on the pitch darkness at their feet. It wasn't as if he really needed a lantern to see, after all.

Despite that, Raf touched Cecily's hand and they paused on the threshold. He held his lantern close to the ground within the pyramid chamber and Cecily's heart skipped in fright at what she saw. There were the footprints of Lord Bath, and those of Abasi and Dina too, but there was another set of prints in the undisturbed sand. They looked like someone with stocking feet had walked across the chamber twice, once leaving the tomb, and once entering it. The prints of the mysterious stocking feet stopped at the wall on which the hieroglyphics were carved, as though their owner had passed straight through solid stone.

Stocking feet...or bandaged.

Cecily shuddered. She'd wanted to come to Egypt so much, but she had never dreamed that this could have happened. Here they were, in a pyramid, and somewhere on the other side of the stone was a mummy.

A mummy that had killed.

Cecily glanced at Dina. She was peering into her pocket, and Cecily suspected she was checking on Bastet. But she couldn't bring her out and lay her on her hand in case Lord Bath saw the gold figurine. Bastet had wanted to return to the pyramid, but now that she had, would she twitch around even more?

"We can go no further," Dina said, her voice echoing against the ancient stone. But if Lord Bath heard, he gave no indication. Instead he threw back his head and laughed, the sound more chilling than any of the howls and wails of the creatures of the desert.

Raf drew Cecily close. He put his arm around her shoulders as Lord Bath announced, "No further! No further, she says!"

"How do you intend to breach the chamber?" Dina asked him. "Dynamite will not work."

"Do you not understand, Madame?" Lord Bath asked. "Menkare II's kingdom was never conquered. His armies were never bettered. He ruled his lands as a god." He turned on his heel to address the little group. "He cost my grandfather his hand, his sanity and eventually his life. But *I* have conquered Menkare II's tomb. The wall of the citadel has fallen, has it not? *I* shall claim his treasures and drag his carcass back to London, and nobody will give a second thought to Carnarvon and Carter's bloody Egyptian sideshow!"

"Drag him back?" Abasi shook his head. "But, Lord Bath, Menkare II was a king. You cannot *drag* him about. He might not have been a very fair king, but I do not think he would like to be dragged about."

The angry man was even more angry. One of Menkare II's close advisors, perhaps, furious that his king's rest had been disturbed.

"Ah, but, Abasi, Lord Bath is merely hoping to show Menkare II the respect he showed people in life," Dina remarked. "Which is…none at all."

"Even his undead servant serves another master," Lord Bath said with a sly, almost wicked smile. It could be taken as a joke in bad taste, perhaps, a reference to the superstitions attached to the scroll, but Cecily knew better. Lord Bath was speaking the truth.

Dina shot Lord Bath an expression so stricken that Cecily wished she could do or say something to mend what her fellow countryman had done.

"Perhaps you ought to pass the reins to an Egyptian," Cecily suggested. "England didn't even exist when Ido was put into this place. It doesn't seem quite right that you should be controlling him."

"I've met a fair few people who think they're the ones in control of spirits, devils. Never a mummy before, but there's a first time for everything," Raf told the earl. "I'll tell you something, Vane-Stanhope. They're always wrong. Just like that cobra bit your granddad, this is going to bite you."

Lord Bath gave a shrug and said with a smile, "Oh well. One gets nowhere without taking the odd risk."

Then he turned back to the slab. "Miss Mansour, you must be able to translate, surely?"

Dina stepped across the chamber towards Lord Bath and the slab, mouthing something. It looked to Cecily as if she was reading the hieroglyphics that danced in the lanterns' flames, but Dina shook her head.

"I am sorry, Lord Bath," she said. "But I do not understand it. They have used the same secret, enchanted language that is on the inside of the door."

"Rubbish," Lord Bath spat. He rounded on Dina and snapped, "You will read this or find another expert who can, Miss Mansour. We'll return to this godforsaken chamber until you do one of those two things, because this expedition will not be stopped by locusts nor landslides nor a stone bloody wall! Do you understand?"

As Lord Bath finished his outburst, he suddenly coughed. No, not coughed, *choked*. He bent double, retching and choking, his eyes bulging in his skull as the sound echoed off the ancient walls.

Dina hurried to his side and walloped his back.

"He's choking! What's wrong with him?" she exclaimed.

Cecily stared, not sure what to do. Lord Bath was so obnoxious, but even then he was a human being. She couldn't just leave him there to choke. She ran across the sandy floor and joined Dina in hitting his back.

"What is it? What's wrong?" Cecily asked him urgently. Lord Bath couldn't speak, instead reached up and clutched his throat, giving one last almighty cough before *something* emerged from between his lips. It was a fat, long locust.

Cecily stepped back in horror. How had it got into his mouth? She turned to look out into the night, expecting to see the swarm invading. There was nothing. At least, not at first. Then she saw a line of locusts starting to trek their way into the chamber across the wall.

"I hope they don't plan to bring all their friends," Cecily said, pointing to the single file of insects. They were joined by another locust from Lord Bath's throat, and another and another until he had disgorged thirteen of the insects. Only then did it stop, leaving the nobleman gasping for air like a drowning man.

"Come on." Raf took his arm and walked him to the doorway of the tomb. "Deep breaths."

"Thirteen…" Dina whispered. "Bad luck."

"Because there were thirteen at the Last Supper?" Cecily asked her.

Dina shook her head. "Because when Osiris was chopped into fourteen pieces by his enemy, Isis could only find thirteen. His…well, his manhood was missing, so Isis made him a new one out of gold."

"Gold?" Cecily had a lot of questions about how a gold *manhood*, as Dina put it, would work. "That certainly *is* unlucky!"

She glanced up, and noticed that the line of locusts had stopped and were turning back towards the entrance. In fact, Cecily was fairly sure that they were following Lord Bath.

Cecily crossed the chamber to Raf. "How's Lord Bath?" she whispered to Raf, not sure Lord Bath could answer. His throat must've been rasping.

"I think he should come back to this in the morning." Raf patted Lord Bath's shoulder. "Sleep on it, mate. We'll make sure nobody sticks their nose in here, and that nobody comes out either."

"Miss Mansour, you're dismissed until tomorrow," the earl managed to croak, his voice rough as sandpaper. "Abasi, relieve Snelling on guard duty. He can stand down for the night."

Still issuing orders, even now...

"Let's get you to your tent first," Cecily suggested. Lord Bath really didn't look well. "Have you got some brandy? It might help your throat."

Lord Bath shrugged away Cecily and Raf and clicked his fingers towards Dina and Abasi.

"If I believe you've compromised this site, you'll be very sorry indeed," Lord Bath told Raf and Cecily. Then he turned to Abasi and snapped, "Relieve Snelling."

Then, without speaking another word, he began to descend from the tomb, leaving Cecily and Raf on guard duty.

With that, the earl made his way up the edge of the pit, towards his tent. As the nobleman walked, still coughing a hoarse cough now and then, the locusts followed. They came from inside the tomb and from its exterior walls, where the Eye of Horus rose into a swarm once more. It followed Lord Bath across the sand to his tent, where he disappeared inside without a glance back. As he did, the insects settled on the canvas, shrouding it from sight.

Abasi went down to speak to Snelling, who was crouched by the fallen door slab. Snelling struggled to his feet and on unsteady legs made his way out of the pit. Abasi didn't seem especially pleased about being left by the door, but made himself as comfortable as he could.

Dina turned to Cecily and Raf. "I am dismissed until tomorrow. So that means I'm on my own time now."

She smiled mischievously. "And it just so happens that I might know how to get into the pyramid after all."

"I don't suppose you've brought your scroll with you?" Raf teased, knowing full well that she wouldn't have. "But we can at least call this a dress rehearsal. We're probably not going to find the jackpot first time out."

Dina shook her head and sighed. "No, I don't have the scroll here. But if we can get in and look around — then it'll be much easier when I do come back with the scroll."

She turned to Abasi and they spoke quickly. Abasi didn't seem surprised.

Then she gestured to Cecily and Raf.

"Abasi will keep watch while we go inside," Dina explained.

Although Cecily was feeling rather nervous, she followed Dina with Raf, climbing up the outside of the pyramid to the newly revealed chamber. Then Dina led them over to the tablet on the wall. She ran her hand across the carvings, and seemed to go into a trance. She chanted, her words filling the chamber with a vibration that Cecily felt in every part of her.

And suddenly Cecily heard a scraping sound, like stone moving against stone.

She glanced at Raf. "Is this really happening? Is the pyramid opening?"

"So long as it isn't filled with one really, really big locust…" Raf put his arm around Cecily's shoulders. "What do you feel?"

"Nervous," Cecily replied. "So nervous, I haven't tuned in… Let me see." She concentrated on the voices inside the pyramid. The one voice was still filled with anger, and now the other voice was too. "They're furious, Raf! I don't think they want us to go in."

But still Dina chanted, and the stones ground against each other. And finally, Cecily saw a gap opening between the wall and the ceiling. The entire wall in front of them was slowly dropping, revealing darkness beyond.

Chapter Fifteen

"We don't know why that slab fell," Raf murmured. "I'm going to have a fly down that tunnel and do a recce. Nobody's heading into a pitch-black tomb before I've had a look."

Cecily blinked but her eyes wouldn't adjust. The dark was a viscous, moving thing, and she held Raf's hand tight. The air was stale and she wondered how badly it must smell for her husband.

Dina came out of her trance. "You are very brave, Raf. I hope very much that I will be able to thank you one day. I'm glad to find out that it still works, after all this time. That tablet of hieroglyphics you saw is like the riddle of the Sphinx. It poses questions, and all I had to do was answer them. And...the tunnel into the pyramid has opened."

Raf stared into the thick darkness. He would be able to see more than they could, Cecily knew, but when he let out a long sigh she realised that it might be impenetrable even to him.

"Can't see much," he admitted. "But I'd say it slopes down at the end. Right…let's go and have a look."

He kissed Cecily's cheek.

"Good luck, darling." Cecily kissed his cheek in return. "Don't be long! And be careful, there could be anything down there. The air's so stale. They wouldn't use poisoned gas, would they?"

"There were many traps put inside the pyramids," Dina replied. "But if Raf is *flying,* then he won't tread on any of the stones that would trigger them. He should be safe, I hope."

If Raf was surprised by her observation he didn't show it. Instead he said simply, "Sounds good to me." With that his clothes and charms fell to the floor and there was the little pipistrelle bat, visible for a moment in the lantern flames before he flitted into the darkness.

Cecily stared into the mouth of the tunnel, hoping with all her heart that Raf wouldn't come to any harm.

Dina took a step closer to Cecily. "You and your husband are very gifted people. I feel as if I am with kindred spirits when I am with you. He won't come to any harm, Cecily. He's brave, and he won't take any risks. And besides, we are protected."

Dina held up her hand, revealing Bastet on her palm, purring. Cecily stared at the figure.

"She's moved!" Cecily said. "Not just all that twitching she does, her limbs are in a different position. Unless it's a trick of the light?"

"Oh, no, not a trick of the light at all," Dina replied, smiling. "She has indeed moved."

And Cecily wasn't surprised one bit.

She waited with Dina, telling her more about her life with Raf in Yorkshire, and the cases they had worked on, but Dina, Cecily noticed, was very good at not saying very much about herself. She nodded, she smiled, and she seemed to contribute to the conversation, but Cecily realised that she still knew very little about her. Who were her family? Why did she live in that big old house on her own? And how come it felt so unlived-in? Cecily still didn't know, and she didn't feel she could ask. Not yet, anyway.

"Can you girls hear me?" Raf's voice was distant, echoing from within the depths of the tomb.

Cecily's heart leapt with joy.

He's all right!

At least he was speaking to them, even if she couldn't see him.

Cecily cupped her hands around her mouth and called, "Yes, we can hear you! Wherever are you, Raf? You sound very far away."

"This place is massive!" Raf called in reply. "I'm heading back up. You won't believe what I've found down here!"

"Oh, hurry back!" Cecily started to collect up Raf's discarded clothes and charms. "I can't wait to hear what you discovered."

Dina chuckled. "I'll look away, don't worry. I wonder what he's found down there. There were rumours of something quite amazing inside the pyramid, but the sources I've consulted were never very clear."

Cecily listened for the sound of Raf's return in the silence of the tomb and a minute or two later, she heard it. It was the soft sound of beating wings, growing louder and closer until the little bat flitted out of the darkness into the light of the lanterns. Dina was as good as her word, turning away as Cecily's husband returned to his human form.

Cecily held his things out to him and kissed his cheek. "I'm so glad you're back in one piece, darling!"

"Ta, Sissy." He kissed her then took his clothes and began to dress. Raf's eyes were glittering with excitement, and Cecily heard it in his voice too when he began to tell them what he had seen. "The tunnel is covered in paintings and chiselled hieroglyphics, and I mean *covered*. It looks like it's telling a story of some sort, probably Menkare's life, I'd guess."

Dina nodded, her back still to them. "Yes... Yes, I imagine it would. I can explain what's there, and... and..."

She was suddenly standing very still again, statue-like once more. Cecily nudged Raf. What happened to Dina when that change came over her? Where did she go?

"Dina, what is it?" Cecily asked her, patting her on the shoulder.

Dina stirred and laughed awkwardly. "I'm so sorry. This is very hard to do. I thought I was equal to it, but there is so much...so much..."

By now dressed, his bare feet leaving prints of their own besides those unexplained, bandaged footprints, Raf paused. Then he put his charms around his neck and told Dina softly, "You know you can trust us, Dina."

"I know I can, and yet... I'm so scared. You are my friends, and you might think I am mad!" Dina said.

"Raf's dressed now," Cecily told her gently. "And why would we think you're mad? We've seen so many things, I can assure you we won't. If I'd told you my husband could fly, what would you have thought?"

Dina turned then, and took Cecily's hand. "I have not been entirely honest with you. And I am sorry for that. But it is only a name, that's the thing. Just a name. You see, I am not Dina Mansour. I took the name, just as I have taken many others over the years."

Over the years? How many years?

"The name my parents gave to me was not Dina, but…Selene."

Cecily blinked at her. She tried to understand. Selene, Ido's lover and Menkare II's wife, who had died in the sandstorm her grief and rage had created. It was hard to believe at first, but Cecily thought of that strange, empty, old house that Dina lived in, and her affinity with the moonlight, which Cecily had seen on the ship. And the way that Dina avoided ever giving much away about herself.

Cecily believed her. Because there wasn't much else that made sense.

"Better three thousand years of wandering than getting stuck with that old bastard in the afterlife, right?" Raf suggested. Nothing ever seemed to faze him, and Cecily loved him for it. "It's good to meet you, Selene, and I'm sorry for what he put you through."

Dina — *Selene* — smiled at Raf.

"Selene! Oh, you cannot imagine how long it has been since I was called that name!" Selene seemed to have lit up from inside as she spoke now. "My mother was Greek, you see. She always said she had called upon Selene to give her a child, and I was born, so I was named after her. You are quite right, I did not want to die. Because if I did…" She gestured to the stone walls around them. "My husband would claim me for the afterlife. But you know, living for as long as I have… There are so many things I remember — languages that have long become extinct. But I couldn't find Menkare II's tomb. And it was my fault it was lost, as I had called down a sandstorm. Can you imagine…? And now I'm here, actually here, and I have to listen to that pompous Englishman telling everyone he discovered it. He has no idea, none at all. And if he did, I expect he'd sell me to a museum as a living artefact!"

"If it's any comfort, I don't think your husband ever made it to paradise," Raf admitted. "Me and Cec met when I had a case about a man like him. This one was in England and he was a judge, not a king, but they had plenty in common besides. He'd committed so many rotten acts in his lifetime that the older he got, the more worried he became. This old so-and-so was terrified that the door he'd be touching after death would be a hot one."

Selene laughed. "Oh, that is so funny, the way you put that! A hot door? Besides, your judge *does* sound like Menkare II, and yes, they both deserve to touch the hot door! You are right, though—not so much a hot door for Menkare II, but the belly of Ammit, devoured and destroyed."

Cecily thought over Raf's words.

Worried? The judge had been worried…

And what about the worried voice she had heard from inside the pyramid, which had turned angry?

"Oh, heck!" Cecily gasped. "Maybe Menkare II's not dead at all!"

"Wait." Raf furrowed his brow. "Is he out there somewhere, like Selene here? So who did they think they were burying—Ohh, I get you. Just like the old judge refused to pass over, you think Menkare's soul's still here?"

"Yes!" Cecily nodded. "Because there's two presences in the pyramid. And one of them was worried, then he turned angry once the slab fell. And I wondered why, and now I think, perhaps it's Menkare II, and his soul hasn't gone over. He's hanging on because he knows he'll be devoured. But imagine that… He's spent millennia in here!"

Selene shook her head. "I don't want to believe it. I want to believe he's gone. I don't want to face him again. But you could be right, Cecily. And I have to accept that. You could very well be right."

And what about Ido, his own soul trapped here for three millennia with the vengeful, terrified pharaoh? What had he endured in death as well as his final, frantic days? It was too much even to imagine it.

Raf clasped his hand around the scarab charm he wore as he told them, "I think it's time Menkare II continued on his way, don't you? Selene, that scroll of yours…it sends the soul where the soul's meant to be?" He glanced back towards the dark corridor. "If Menkare *is* here when you read it, as well as sending Ido to paradise, will it send Menkare II wherever he's bound for too?"

Selene nodded. "Yes, the scroll should achieve both. Ido will be at rest, and Menkare II will be devoured."

"So it's a happy ending," Cecily said, bouncing on her toes at the thought of the angry pharaoh finally getting his just desserts. "And I suppose we should go and have a look at the tunnel you found, Raf? So that Selene knows the route when she comes back with the scroll."

"But…what about you?" Raf asked Selene. "Was it your willpower alone that kept you going all these years? That's a hell of a magic you've got, you know."

Selene stared off into the dark tunnel, then she looked back at Raf. "Yes, it is my magic that has kept me alive. I wonder sometimes, when the goddess

Selene gave me to my mother, did she give me my powers? Or at least make me open to them. But yes, for three thousand years I have not grown old because I have not wanted to. I cast a spell of immortality, you see. And I have lived in the shadows, a few years here, a few years there. As soon as people joke that I don't seem to age, I know it is time to move on."

"What happens once you've done what you came to Egypt to do?" Raf's voice was soft. "Will you join Ido at last?"

"I might." Selene nodded. She looked from Raf to Cecily with an awkward look. "It could well break my immortality spell, because the strength needed to send Ido might sap my ability to maintain my life-spell. You have both been so kind, and invited me to visit your home, but I know in my heart that I might never see it."

Cecily hugged Dina. "Don't be sad! We have visits all the time from people who've passed on. And you're welcome to bring Ido's spirit with you when you call."

Yet Cecily couldn't help but feel sorry that she would lose her friend that she'd only just met, even if she did pop by in spirit. But it was selfish of her, Cecily knew, and she tried her best to be happy for Selene.

"You're always welcome in Acaster Garrow, don't you worry," Raf assured her. "So... You won't believe what I found in a buried pyramid in the middle of the desert. The corridor is an incline. Not too steep, but it goes down a long, long way and at the bottom... Go on, guess."

Oh, a mystery!

"A palace made of sand?" Cecily guessed. "Like a sandcastle on the beach, but big enough to live inside?"

"A burial chamber?" Selene suggested, evidently going for a scholarly suggestion.

"A lake," he told them. "And it's massive. I don't know what's on the other side, but there definitely *is* another side. I couldn't get any further though, because there's another tablet, and I can't answer ancient Egyptian riddles."

"A *lake*?" Selene exclaimed. "I remember… Menkare II's engineers spoke of this pyramid as it was being built, and I knew about the riddles, but there was something they would not speak of. I never found out what it was. But that must be it—a lake! My goodness…a lake, in the desert."

"How extraordinary!" Cecily remarked. As much as she'd hoped the huge sandcastle was real, the lake was just as exciting.

"I think perhaps we should go and look, don't you?" Selene said with a grin. She lifted her head and called, "We know your secret, Menkare II!"

Her voice echoed away down the tunnel.

They collected up the lanterns and began to head down towards to the lake.

"I will go first," Selene said. "Watch my feet and put yours on the same stones as I tread on. There is a pattern to it, otherwise the traps are set off."

Cecily followed Selene into the tunnel, her lantern casting a circle of light as she watched for the right stones to tread on. They had gone a few feet into the tunnel when Selene stopped and held up her lantern.

"Look at the carvings! Oh, just look!" Selene gasped.

Cecily stared at the lit-up section of the wall. The carvings were a mixture of hieroglyphics, with life-size depictions of a king on his throne, surrounded by soldiers and servants. They were ancient, yet looked so fresh, as if they had only been carved in the past week.

"Are you all right?" Raf asked her. "This must be bringing back some unwelcome memories."

Selene turned to Raf, careful not to move her feet. "Oh, yes, seeing his image there on the wall, it brings it back. He was seen as a god, you know. And he thought he was a god too. But he was as much a human being as me or you."

Selene shifted her lantern and the depiction of a woman appeared. She was almost the same height as the king, and had what looked like horns on her head and scratches on her face.

"Is that a demon?" Cecily whispered.

"No, not at all!" Selene laughed. "That's me! The goddess Selene is shown with a crescent moon on her head, and the tips look like little horns. They carved my image when I was married to Menkare II. When everything went wrong... Well, you can see the chisel marks across my face. They tried to obliterate me, but they could not."

"You can say that again." Raf chuckled. "Funny though, because here you are larger than life. The old bugger who tried to chisel you out of history though...forgotten. A legend to some, a *never heard of him, mate*, to others. King Tut he is not."

Selene grinned. "You know, you are right! All that power he *thought* he had, and yet he's spent the past three thousand years inside a pyramid under the sand while I have roamed the world. But come, you do not want to have to look through my old photograph album. Let's go on. It's cold. Perhaps it's the water down here?"

Raf steadied Cecily with a hand to her elbow as he told them, "The slope isn't steep, just take care and

173

watch your step. The last thing we want is anyone to break an ankle in here."

Cecily nodded, painstakingly following Selene's steps as they headed down the dark slope, farther into the pyramid. "I'll be careful. The sand makes it a bit slippery, though, doesn't it?"

Down and down they went, Cecily seeing only as far as the lanterns could throw their light. She caught sight of more carvings and wondered what tales they told, but no doubt they were merely paeans to Menkare II. More of his life-sized images followed, and Cecily flinched each time. She had stopped listening to his voice but the sight of his pictures reminded her that she was heading closer and closer to his tomb and the site of his earthly remains.

Chapter Sixteen

It seemed as if the tunnel would never end. But finally, Cecily heard a sound that was completely unexpected in the desert.

Water.

"We must be nearly at the lake!" Excited, Cecily tightened her hand around Raf's.

The water was rushing, chuckling, and it made Cecily think of the river back home in Acaster Garrow, as it ran through the woods and across the field and out into the sea. How different it was here, in the dark, and with only their lanterns to see —

And suddenly, Cecily was blinking, holding her hand in front of her eyes as bright light filled the — Not a tunnel, no.

"Where are we?" Cecily lowered her hand and saw that they were standing on the edge of a huge subterranean lake. Torches in large iron brackets had lit up around the walls. There were even some on the pillars that rose up from the water like tree trunks to support the roof.

"I did not light them!" Selene told them. "Someone must know we're here. Ido, my darling…" She whispered in a language Cecily didn't know, and yet Cecily still understood just what she was saying, a woman whispering to her long-lost lover.

Cecily blinked into the distance. The lake was so vast that she couldn't see to the other side. Maybe it went on forever.

Raf didn't seem to be seized by the same spirit of romance as Selene though. Instead he reached out and caught Cecily's arm, drawing her gently back to him. For a moment he was silent, his eyes glittering as they searched the darkness. Then he asked her, "Are you picking anything up?"

Cecily half-closed her eyes and lowered her defences. It was like switching on a radio, and the two presences inside the pyramid came through loud and clear.

"I feel love," Cecily whispered to Raf. "I can still hear the angry man, too, but the sensation of love has almost entirely drowned him out. But then, it's a love that's survived all these years — it must be ever so strong."

Raf nodded, saying nothing as he tipped his head back and drew in a long, deep breath.

"The air's…" He furrowed his brow, searching for the word. "Aromatic. In the entrance up top, it smelled bad. Here though…here it's almost sweet."

"Sweet?" Selene turned to Raf, her eyes glittering with interest. "Sweet like flowers?"

Raf nodded, his face settling into a contented smile at the very idea of it. "Like the garden," he replied.

Selene smiled dreamily. "Ido loved gardens."

Cecily sniffed the air. She wasn't sure she could smell a garden, though. How could Raf smell a garden down here? "Is it perfume? They always buried mummies with perfumes, didn't they? It can't be an actual garden down here. There's no sunlight."

And yet, there was a lake. Was it ridiculous that there could be a garden down here too?

"So... I've never heard of a lake in the desert. Or a sunken pyramid, but it's that sort of honeymoon." Raf looked to Selene. "Is a lake something old Menkare II would do? Does it feel like his style?"

Selene nodded vehemently. "Oh, yes. Because he believed he was a god. And a god could make water flow in the desert. And not only that, but keep it all to himself. Think of the good this water could have done, and think of the engineering this took to create. And it was all for a tomb." Selene crouched by the side of the lake and scooped up a handful of the water. It didn't look brackish at all. "An oasis for the dead."

"That water's fresh," Cecily observed. "Is it magic?"

"Perhaps a little," Selene said. "But it is also down to the work of the architects who Menkare II hired."

Raf dropped to one knee and scooped his hand through the water. He lifted it to his lips and tasted it before concluding, "Fresh as spring water too."

"Why would a tomb need fresh water?" Cecily wondered.

"Because it is the tomb of Menkare II," Selene replied bitterly. "It is a mark of his power, his wealth, his ambition. He wanted to take whatever he wanted."

Cecily stared around at the torches, and their reflections which rippled on the water. "Didn't do him much good, though, did it? An angry spirit, stuck inside a pyramid, and he can't even drink all this water."

And Ido, stuck there with him through the centuries, kept from his rest. But not for much longer, if they could help it. Soon Ido and Menkare II would both be moving on, and Lord Bath's scroll would be as powerless as the man who possessed it.

"How do you get to the burial chamber?" Cecily asked. "Is there another tunnel?"

Selene bit her lip. "I'm not sure. Usually, that was the way. The pyramid would be full of tunnels, and often they would be laid to confuse any would-be tomb robbers. But this pyramid…"

Selene's voice trailed off. Cecily heard a splash inside the vast space, and the water began to rush against…a boat?

Cecily blinked into the torchlight. Was she seeing things? Heading towards them over the glassy surface of the lake was a golden boat. It looked like something from a storybook, with a curled prow and a blue rectangular sail with the Eye of Horus decorating it in gold. Cecily blinked some more, assuming that there had to be sailors on the boat, but the deck appeared to be empty.

"Oh, heavens…" she whispered in awe.

"I don't know about this," Raf admitted. "Maybe you girls should wait here… If this is Menkare's idea of hospitality, there could be a nasty surprise waiting at the end of it."

Cecily planted her hands on her hips. "You know very well I won't let you go on your own. And besides, Selene's the expert. She has to come along too."

"I most certainly will!" Selene insisted as the boat drew nearer. It looked more splendid by the moment, the torchlight glinting from its hull. "This is Menkare II's royal barge. I remember sailing down the Nile on this. I am not at all surprised to see it here. But you know…" — she lowered her voice, as if Menkare II was eavesdropping — "Ido often sailed in it too. And so I wonder, it might not be Menkare II who has sent this. It might be Ido."

"It might be," Raf agreed after another moment spent peering into the darkness that seemed to stretch for miles, punctured only by the occasional distant light. "All right. We came in here together, so we'll stick together now we've come this far."

The boat glided towards them in near silence, then stopped at the bank. Golden cords at either end of the boat unravelled from perfect spools on deck and snaked to the bank, where they wrapped themselves around stone posts.

Selene held out her hand. Bastet was sitting on her palm, and the cat craned her neck towards the boat.

"Bastet seems to think we should board the boat too," Selene said. "But before we do — Raf, will you join me in casting a protection spell?"

"The more the merrier." Raf smiled, closing his hand around the scarab charm he wore around his neck. As he did, he reached out his free hand and caught Cecily's fingers. Then he closed his eyes and bowed his head.

Selene began to murmur, and Cecily recognised the rhythm of her words. It was an Ancient Egyptian spell, Cecily was sure. And as Selene murmured, Cecily felt Ido's love as a warmth surrounding them, even as Menkare's anger raged beyond it.

Selene lifted her head. "There, it is done. We are as protected as we can be."

As if on cue, a violent wave suddenly rippled across the placid surface of the lake, no doubt an expression of the pharaoh's fury. Yet in the face of the spells Selene and Raf had cast and the cushioning warmth of Ido's love, it was no more threatening than a child's tantrum. Yet Cecily knew from her experiences as one half of the de Chastelaine investigations team that such expressions were not to be entirely discounted. It was proof that Menkare II still possessed power, even in death.

"Someone isn't happy." Selene rolled her eyes. For all that she seemed to be downplaying her reaction to Menkare II's wave, Cecily noticed Selene's hands tremble. "Come, let us climb aboard. I ought to welcome you onto the ship, as the former queen, don't you think?"

"You certainly outlived the king." Raf smiled as he offered her his hand to help her aboard. "So in my book, that makes this *your* royal barge."

The vessel rocked slightly, but the wave that shook it had lost some of its predecessor's power.

Selene chuckled. "You know, you are right!" Once she was on board, Selene looked thoroughly at home, and glanced about at the luxurious silk cushions and couches on the deck. "Isn't it beautiful? I suppose it will be in a museum soon. *My* barge... Anyway, please, welcome aboard!"

"Lord Bath's eyes'll pop out of his head when he sees it," Cecily said, taking Raf's hand. He handed her onto the barge then followed, reaching to uncoil the mooring ropes before evidently thinking better of it.

"I'll leave that to Ido," he said with a smile.

The water lapped against the hull, almost chuckling, and Selene smiled.

It's Ido!

Cecily felt the strangeness of the moment, and yet it didn't feel odd at all. A long-dead mummy powering a golden barge didn't seem so peculiar once you were floating on a lake inside a long-lost pyramid.

With a susurration, the gold ropes moved again, loosening themselves from the stone posts and coiling back onto the deck far more neatly than they could have done if they'd been held by any human hand.

A breeze caught the sail, though Cecily hadn't noticed any draughts inside the pyramid, and the blue canvas began to fill, propelling the golden barge away from the bank and back across the lake.

Cecily had settled beside Raf on a silk-covered bench, opposite Selene on an identical couch.

"This is quite an interesting way to travel!" Cecily remarked. She could sense that Raf was still alert, but he seemed to have relaxed a little. Just like Cecily, he'd be able to intuit that things were mostly peaceful.

"The skeletons outside in the sand..." When Raf spoke, Cecily remembered again the bleached bones protruding from the desert, waiting for the likes of Julian Vane-Stanhope to pick them clean and claim their treasures as his own. "They're the pharaoh's court? And the priests too? The ones who died in the sandstorm."

Selene closed her eyes for a moment as if suppressing pain. Then she looked up at Raf and nodded, almost guiltily.

"Yes, they are," Selene replied. "And they are skeletons because of me."

"You mustn't blame yourself," Cecily told her. "*They* chose to be in the court of an evil man."

Raf nodded and asked, "When they stood outside the tomb with you in shackles, did they show you any mercy?" Cecily could already guess the answer to that. They had been Menkare II's disciples. They wouldn't know the meaning of the world. "Or did they just want to enjoy the show of Ido's punishment?"

Selene shook her head. "They did not show any mercy at all. Not one person moved to save Ido, for all that I pleaded with whoever would hear. I cast every spell that I could. I tried to save him, but there was nothing I could do in the face of all that self-serving hatred. They all did what the king wanted, because they knew that if the wind so much as changed, they would end up in shackles too. Or worse—buried alive like my poor Ido."

"I've been in a few tight spots, and being a bat's saved my life more times than I can count," Raf assured her. "But I hope you don't mind me asking…how *did* you get out of the shackles? When the sands came, why weren't you buried too?"

Selene leant back against the cushions, and Cecily thought of Cleopatra and the barge with the perfumed sails.

She was thoughtful for a moment, then replied, "I was buried alive by the sand. I don't know, but my protection spell must have helped to begin with. It was as if I was protected by a bubble. Around me, I heard the dreadful sounds of the death rattles of Menkare II's court. They cried out, then they suffocated. And I could not help them for it was all that I could do to preserve myself. I tried to fight my way out, but I could not— there was so much sand, and it was so heavy. And I wept for Ido and I wept for myself… Night fell eventually, and I had been sleeping, because I woke and blinked away the sand. I heard a scraping sound, and I heard a howl... It was a jackal. I thought of Anubis and I thought I must be dead. But still the scraping went on, and at last I found myself on the desert floor, a pack of jackals licking the sand off me. And I laughed—oh, how it tickled! And as I laughed, the shackles softened just as readily as if it were in a great furnace. And thank goodness they did. They became like putty and I pulled my hands free and...and I was free. There was no one else there, only me and the jackals. The pyramid had disappeared. I had no idea where I was. I heard a great swooping and there appeared before me an eagle. A huge beast, and she landed beside me, gently nudging me with her beak. I knew she was there to save me. I climbed onto her back and all the world fell away as we flew across the desert."

Cecily stared at her in amazement. Saved by jackals and a gigantic eagle. And by laughter. Cecily tried to picture it—shackles that melted at the sound of laughter. What a strange and marvellous world old Egypt had been.

"You've got an affinity with animals," Raf observed, as if he heard stories like this all the time. But since Cecily had been married to her Transylvanian Yorkshireman, they were becoming more common for her too. "How d'you get on with bats?"

"Oh, very well." Selene chuckled. "Aside from your good self, there are bats that roost in my attic. I like bats, I like how they are flipped over—they live in the air, not the ground. They fly by night, not day. And they sleep upside down!"

"Not always." Raf chuckled, squeezing Cecily's hand as the barge sailed on into the darkness. She felt it being tugged by the current, or perhaps it was invisible hands guiding the royal barge through the pyramid.

"The boat seems to know exactly where it wants to go," Cecily observed.

The water rushed against the side of the boat as it headed across the lake, turning just a little to avoid the columns that rose up from the bottom of the lake like trees in a forest made from brick and stone.

"Oh, now this is fun!" Cecily said.

"How're you feeling?" Raf asked Selene. "It must be odd, in its way. You've waited forever for one moment and soon…soon it'll be here. You know, if you want to come back with us to England afterwards for a holiday, we'd love you to."

"I think… I think I will only be able to visit in spirit," Selene replied, and Cecily felt that pang again, a sadness because as soon as she had made a friend, Cecily was losing her. Selene seemed to notice Cecily's sadness, and told her, "But don't feel sad for me. This has taken thousands of years. I have been alive for so long. It is right that soon my time will pass."

"Then we'll look forward to seeing you, even if it's only in spirit," Cecily said. "And Ido too, of course."

"Always," Raf told her with a smile. On and on the barge drifted, carrying them through vast vaulted caverns and along narrow tunnels, lit by the pale flames from unseen torches. On the few occasions that the path branched, the boat seemed to know which way to go and its unseen pilot steered the vessel on its route, deeper into the heart of the tomb.

Bastet had sat quite happily on Selene's palm, but suddenly she was twitching and sprang up, her back arching as she growled. Cecily gasped, wondering what Bastet had noticed, but before she could say anything, the barge began to rock violently from side to side. Cecily screamed and grabbed Raf, holding him tightly.

Maybe it was a mistake going into the pyramid after all. Maybe this really was Menkare II's trick, to lure them in, then drown them.

Chapter Seventeen

Raf held Cecily in return and she vaguely heard him whisper something in a language she didn't recognise before he asked Selene, "What's happening?"

"I—I don't know!" Selene clung on as Bastet leapt onto her shoulder, yowling in terror as the boat went on rocking.

Suddenly a noise tore through the tunnel like the roar of a furious lion at the zoo. But it was worse than that, like a shriek and a roar all at once, and Cecily clapped her hands over her ears. Water showered down on them and there in the torchlight Cecily saw the shiny scales of an enormous beast as it rose up from the water.

When it roared again, a huge blood-red mouth opened, revealing three rows of razor-sharp teeth and a sinuous tongue like a serpent.

"What on earth is it?" Cecily cried in terror. She scrabbled for purchase on the couch as the silk cushions tumbled to the deck.

"Bloody hell..." Raf gasped, looking up at the creature that towered above them. He held Cecily tight and addressed the creature as though he were placating an angry dog. "All right, mate? We're just passing through. We're not here to cause any problems."

"Leviathan..." Selene breathed. "He must have found the lake and decided to stay down here in the dark!"

Cecily blinked in amazement, but was terrified all over again as Leviathan roared.

"We need a harpoon!" Cecily said, though she didn't like the idea of that at all. But what could they do? The boat was rocking so violently now that water was collecting on the deck. "It'll sink the barge!"

Bastet howled and hissed at Leviathan, baring her teeth and claws like an alley cat sizing up an opponent in a fight. Selene stroked her arched back, whispering to her, and in moments Bastet was soothed, curling up on Selene's shoulder. But still Leviathan raged, and Cecily realised that these might be her last moments on this earth.

"If he does, he can give us a lift to shore...if he's solid enough," Raf observed and Cecily saw that there was something ephemeral about Leviathan, despite his fearsome roar and the whip of his tail. He shimmered like a dream or the phantoms she'd seen pottering happily in the gardens at home. The creature was certainly there before them, but he didn't seem to be quite flesh and bone. Raf rose to his feet and held out his hand towards the beast. When Raf spoke again, his voice was a gentle coo. "Come on, lad...who's a good boy?"

Leviathan roared again. Selene seemed to pick up on what Raf was attempting and held out her arm, clicking her fingers at the beast.

"What a lovely beastie you are!" Selene chirped. "Look at all those teeth you have, and your shiny scales!"

The boat was still rocking but with less energy now, and wasn't taking on any more water, Cecily noticed with relief.

"Or maybe you're not a good boy…but a good girl?" Raf chanced. He reached into his pocket and took out a little paper bag. "Do you like basbousa? You want to share some?"

Leviathan's tongue snaked towards them and Cecily flinched, terrified. She was convinced the tongue was coming for them and would either squeeze them like a boa constrictor or rasp off a layer of skin. But as the tongue flicked past her, Cecily realised that it was heading for Raf's basbousa.

"A little treat!" Selene said. Raf opened the bag and the sweet scent of confectionery filled the air.

"Come on then," he said brightly, holding the bag as high as he could. "Come on, girl, have a treat. This tastes much nicer than we would!"

The shimmering tongue, which wasn't quite real, swooped closer, and Cecily ducked as it reached the bag and in one go snatched it from Raf's hand. The bag vanished with the tongue as it withdrew into Leviathan's mouth. All was still for a moment, as if the creature was mulling over the taste of the treats it had just taken.

Then, instead of a roar, a deep rumbling vibrated from the beast, like the purr of an enormous cat.

"She loves it," Selene declared, chuckling. "Raf, you have tamed Leviathan with basbousa!"

"I'm not surprised. I can't get enough of the stuff either." Raf reached out until he was at full stretch, one hand gripping the side of the barge to prevent himself from toppling out. Very gently, he patted Leviathan's vast neck. Or would have, if his hand hadn't hovered somewhere between making contact and passing straight through. Still, the creature seemed to like it.

The rumbling grew louder and Leviathan half-closed her eyes as she twitched under Raf's hand. A fearsome beast no longer, it seemed. Cecily felt very guilty for contemplating a harpoon.

"How did you get down here?" Selene asked the creature, although Cecily had no idea how Leviathan could reply.

A splash some distance away attracted Cecily's attention. A shimmering tail floated out behind the creature, and Cecily felt a sensation of playfulness as the tail splashed again against the water.

Raf stroked Leviathan's neck. "Selene, I think she's been conjured here, maybe by Menkare? She's not quite here, but she almost is. Can you speak a language she might understand?"

Selene nodded slowly. "I believe I do. I have learned so many over the years, but...yes, I think I do. I'll ask her why she's here."

Bastet balanced on Selene's shoulder as the former priestess and erstwhile queen stepped across the barge to speak to the mythical creature. Selene spoke in a language Cecily had never heard before, a rapid flow of words spilling from Selene that Leviathan seemed to understand.

Then Leviathan croaked her reply, Selene nodding her on. They exchanged a few more words, and Selene reached forwards and patted Leviathan's nose before settling on her couch once more.

"That was very enlightening," Selene told them. "Leviathan says that a crocodile told her about a huge body of water that would be all hers in exchange for guarding the place. And she liked the idea of that, and before she knew what had happened, she was here. She said she woke up with a terrible headache—maybe from being conjured here—just as our barge came by, and that she'd like to apologise for being so rude to visitors."

"We've all been there with a headache." Raf narrowed his eyes then, thoughtful. "But would she like to stay here? I'm sort of assuming she can come and go as she pleases." He looked towards Cecily and explained, "It's that dimensional whatsitry. Flitting in and out and all that... Quicker than having to take the bus!"

Selene addressed some more questions to Leviathan, who replied, then splashed her tail again.

"She says it's very pleasant to swim here, and really rather peaceful," Selene translated. "And she can go if she likes. She says she wouldn't like to be stuck here forever, though—she would miss the sunlight and everything that goes on in the sea. Oh, and..."—Selene lowered her voice—"she says she can hear a very angry man inside the pyramid. I think we can guess who that is, can't we?"

Menkare II. What a charmer.

Raf gave another nod, then asked, "And if the pyramid is buried again? She can still leave?" He gave a bashful shrug. "I'll worry about her otherwise."

Selene translated for Leviathan and nodded as she gave her reply. "She says you don't have to worry. She arrived here while it was under sand and she can leave if it is buried under sand again."

"Gosh, being a mythical beast is ever so handy," Cecily said.

Raf chuckled, then stroked Leviathan's neck again as he said to Selene, "Can we just ask her one more thing? Behemoth and Ziz aren't knocking about too, are they?" He turned to Cecily and told her, "I've had a run-in with Behemoth before. He's grumpy as they come."

Selene asked Leviathan, who replied with what seemed to be a laugh.

"She says she's good friends with both of them," Selene translated. "And that she'll put in a good word for you with Behemoth. Give him some basbousa and he's like a little puppy, she says."

"I had no idea that mythical beasts enjoyed pastries," Cecily said.

Raf gave her shoulders an affectionate squeeze and whispered, "Not Medusa though. She wouldn't look twice at an iced bun." He lifted his head and addressed Leviathan again. "Is it safe to go on our way? There's no one else guarding the waters?"

Selene spoke, and Leviathan gave her answer.

"She says she hasn't met anyone else, other than some Nile perch, but they won't trouble you." Selene smiled mischievously. "She tells me that while Menkare II's magic brought her here, his powers are not strong and that she doubts very much he'd be able to bring more than one guard here at a time. Well, that is good to hear, don't you think?"

Cecily nodded. "Oh, it's smashing! He's not as powerful as he thinks." And that reminded her of her first husband, who had believed that he had complete control over Cecily.

How wrong he had been.

Raf bowed deeply to the creature, and Leviathan lowered her head in gracious acknowledgement. Then he stood up straight and told her, "We're indebted to you, madam. Safe journeys, and look us up if you're ever swimming off the Yorkshire coast. There'll always be a warm welcome."

Leviathan held out her scaly, iridescent paw to Raf, as if trying to shake his hand. She spoke, and Selene told him, "She says she sometimes swims past Yorkshire on her way to see her friend Nessie up in Scotland, and she'll definitely pop by next time."

"We'll make sure we've got some nice pastries for you," Cecily assured her. Raf reached out his hand in reply and touched it to Leviathan's paw. The immense limb dwarfed him, but for a few seconds they stood in silence, saying their farewells.

"We'll look forwards to your visit," Raf told her again. Then he put his palm beneath her paw and kissed it, a gesture that was rather more gentlemanly than the earthy Raf Cecily knew and loved. But Leviathan was a special guest, and she deserved to be received with due ceremony.

Leviathan seemed to giggle and looked almost shy for a moment. Then she slowly withdrew her paw. She shimmered more intensely, glittering now in the torchlight, then Cecily stared as the huge creature began to fade, bit by bit. For a moment, Leviathan was transparent, and Cecily could see the etchings in the wall behind her. Then it was all over and Leviathan was gone.

"I wonder where she's disappeared off to?" Cecily said in awe. Raf was silent for a few moments, a contented look on his face, before he kissed Cecily's cheek then addressed her and Selene as one.

"I've seen some things, but...that was special. Much more easy-going than Behemoth and sweeter smelling than Ziz." He drew in a deep breath of the lake air again. "I can still smell that garden, but there's something else with it." Raf grimaced. "That sweet smell you get when something's rotten. I reckon we're getting closer."

Selene nodded. "Something rotten... Like a burial chamber containing the dead?"

The barge began to move again, the sail filling with air as it glided across the water. Cecily hoped that Leviathan hadn't been mistaken when she'd told them there was nothing else in the water besides some Nile perch. She peered over the side and fancied she saw their shadows flit below the surface.

The three passengers settled back into the cushions, and the ornate royal vessel drifted into another wide cavern. As they moved across the surface of the water Cecily could make out the lights on a small stone jetty and it seemed as though the barge could too, because it turned a little, heading for the mooring point. In a matter of minutes they'd be back on dry land, ready to journey deeper into the subterranean tomb.

Chapter Eighteen

The barge arrived at the jetty and the golden cords whipped out once more and secured themselves around stone posts. The sealed mouth of a tunnel opened up a few feet from the jetty, flanked on either side by imposing stone cats. Bastet hopped down from Selene's shoulder and trotted over to the statues, then rubbed herself against them, purring.

"I hope she knows them," Cecily joked. "It could be rather embarrassing otherwise!"

"Bastet knows every cat there is to know," Selene assured her. Raf climbed out onto the jetty and offered his hands to Selene and Cecily, helping them from the barge. There in front of them was another sealed slab, decorated in hieroglyphics. The walls to either side were painted just as those in the corridors had been, and Cecily realised that she was looking at another celebration of the power of Menkare II, who was depicted on his throne again, a god amongst humans.

Selene sighed as she saw the panel. "More riddles, I expect. Don't worry, I'll solve them. If you've lived as long as I have, you know every riddle going."

She walked over to the slab and began to read, then was thoughtful for a few moments. She chuckled, and said a word out loud in what Cecily thought had to be an ancient language, and the sound of stone grinding against stone vibrated through the pyramid.

"The answer was a stone, but the riddle itself doesn't make much sense in translation," Selene explained. Bastet hopped back up onto her shoulder, and Cecily watched in amazement as the stone slab across the entrance slid aside, revealing a steep slope beyond.

"That's the problem with walking downhill," Raf surmised as they peered into the gloom, where torches flickered in welcome. "You have to go up again."

"We haven't come all this way to be defeated by a slope," Cecily said, peering into the tunnel beyond. There was no rope or banister that she could see. They'd just have to take their time and be careful not to slip.

"We must take care," Selene said. "One of the tricks they used was loose slabs. You'd be walking up the slope, then the slab would rock—like a see-saw—and fling you to the ground."

Bastet *miaowed*, her whiskers twitching. Cecily was amazed again. Since when had Bastet had whiskers? Or indeed claws and fur? And yet she was still fashioned from gold.

Raf winced as he realised, "Booby traps on the ground… Not much good for a bat to spot." He looked to the women. "Do you girls want to stay here?"

Cecily shook her head. *As if!* "No, we're coming too."

"I should be able to identify any hazards," Selene told them. "And Bastet too."

Bastet *miaowed* again, and seemed to be trying to hide behind Selene's neck.

"What is it, Bastet? Don't be afraid," Selene soothed.

"Should we be worrying if Bastet's unnerved?" Cecily asked.

"She's a little jumpy, don't worry," Selene said. She gestured towards the tunnel, which was lit with torches like the rest of the pyramid. It was as if someone wanted them to enter. "Come, let us see what lies at the top of this slope."

Raf led the way, which came as no surprise to Cecily. Not because he was the same sort of man as Lord Bath, who was only stopped by a literal belly full of locusts, but because he would face any danger before it had a chance to touch Cecily.

"More paintings," he observed.

They almost seemed to move in the dancing light cast by the torches. A huge white ship appeared in the carvings, and Selene began to translate the hieroglyphics that surrounded it.

"*From afar, there will come a ship*," she intoned.

"Does *afar* count for the barge we just arrived in?" Cecily wondered as she and Selene followed Raf up the slope. It was so steep that Cecily felt the pull on the backs of her legs. "It felt like we'd gone rather far, didn't it?"

Raf nodded. "It makes me wonder just how big this place is. And built by slaves, I'll bet."

"Oh, yes, it most certainly was," Selene replied. "I remember the crowds of people who built it, working under the heat of the sun. And the slave drivers told them, *You should be proud, you are building the tomb of a king and he shall live forever!"*

"That's not much to be pleased about," Cecily commented.

"Now, there is more..." Selene pointed to a group of figures, painted in white like the ship. *"And upon the ship there will come people as white as the clouds."*

"That sounds like you, Raf," Cecily said cheekily. "You can't afford to get a tan!"

"That *is* true." Raf patted his pocket, and through the pocket's cloth Cecily heard the tell-tale sound of his wedding ring against the little glass bottle of sun ointment that protected him. "Does it mention gorgeous girls called Sissy?"

Selene chuckled, shaking her head. "No, I'm afraid it doesn't. But this is very –" Selene looked down at the flagstones on the floor first before gingerly stepping across them to stand closer to the wall. "Look, look at that flat line with the little white figures standing on it. The hieroglyphics say, *After many days, they will think they are in an empty desert, but..."*

"But...?" Cecily followed Selene's gaze. Something didn't seem quite right. Selene seemed agitated, but she was reining it in.

"But the desert is full," Selene intoned, and gestured towards the next panel, where the little figures were dwarfed by an enormous pyramid.

"Oh, heck..." Cecily whispered. "This story's uncomfortably familiar."

Raf nodded as he murmured, "The desert is full..."

"I don't know how... I don't understand." Selene gasped as she ran her hands over the hieroglyphics "See the next picture! Oh, no! I have never seen that in Ancient Egyptian art before!"

Cecily turned her gaze to the next panel and couldn't believe what she was seeing. *Skeletons.*

"What...what does it say, Selene?" Cecily murmured. Her stomach had tied into a knot.

"*The skeletons of priests and soldiers appear from the sand,*" Selene read, then she turned to face Cecily and Raf. "None of this feels real. I don't...I don't..." Then she looked at the next picture and stifled a scream.

It showed another pyramid, with the figures standing below it. And across one side of the enormous edifice was the Eye of Horus, picked out in locusts.

"I wonder if they included the end of the story..." Raf murmured as he studied the paintings that seemed to prophesise the arrival of the de Chastelaines and the Earl of Bath. The paintings that had been beneath the desert sands for thousands of years.

Cecily peered at the next panel through her fingers. "I'm not sure I want to know what happens next!"

"Don't be afraid, Cecily," Selene counselled gently. "Look, there is the lake, and the barge."

Cecily dropped her hand and found herself staring at a representation of herself, Raf and Selene travelling through the tunnels of the pyramid. She followed the journey to the next panel, which showed them walking up a steep slope. Some of this panel had been chipped away so she couldn't make out all of it.

"This is the strangest thing... I've never been foretold before," Cecily said. "I feel as if the next panel will prophesy what we're having for breakfast. I rather fancy toast and—"

From somewhere inside the pyramid, a deep rumbling noise sounded. Cecily froze. It was as if the tunnel were shaking with the force of the noise. Dust and sand fell from the ceiling, and Bastet yowled in fright and scampered back down the slope.

"What's happening?" Cecily whispered. She glanced back at the foretelling of them on the slope. "What's been chipped off that panel?"

"Trouble," was Raf's considered opinion. Then he told them, "Run!"

At the top of the tunnel, a huge stone boulder dropped out of the ceiling with a crash that shook the ground. Cecily tore her stunned gaze from it and grabbed Raf's hand and Selene's. Then, with a yell of terror, she ran down the slope, praying that gravity would help their escape, even as it aided the boulder that was rolling down the tunnel after them.

I haven't come all this way to be crushed under a gigantic boulder!

The racket of the boulder on the stone was almost deafening, and it thundered towards them like the eye of a storm. Raf pulled his hand back from Cecily and told her, "You'll be quicker without me!"

"Raf!" Cecily screamed. But she knew he was right. His legs were shorter than hers. He couldn't keep up. But Cecily didn't care. She tried to reach behind for his hand but met only air as the gap between them grew. And as the boulder gained on them.

The mouth of the tunnel was only a few paces ahead. Selene yanked Cecily to the side, and they bumped against one of the huge cat statues in their haste.

The enormous boulder broke out of the tunnel's mouth barely a second later. It was travelling so fast that when it collided with one of the posts securing the barge, it was airborne for a moment before splashing down into the water. An enormous wave burst up from the canal and Cecily and Selene huddled together for cover as the cold water broke against them.

Shivering, Cecily glanced up at Selene. "What about Raf? Where is he?"

She turned, glancing this way and that, but there was no sign of her husband, and Cecily gasped.

I can't have lost him. Oh, no, I can't have!

Then, from within the tunnel, she heard a familiar, welcome sound. The sound of a bat's wings beating, but accompanied by something else. Something that sounded almost like wind chimes in a soft breeze.

Cecily braved herself to peer into the tunnel's mouth. She dreaded to see a small, crushed figure lying there, broken by the boulder. But there was no one there.

Apart from a familiar, tiny pipistrelle bat. And in his claws, he was holding his charms.

"Oh, Raf! You're safe! Thank heavens you're safe!" Cecily gasped, hurrying towards the bat, her arms outstretched. It wasn't easy to hug a bat, but Cecily had done it before and she did it now, pressing Raf in her embrace before he carefully deposited the charms in her hands. Then he flew back into the tunnel where his clothes were presumably waiting. Flattened, but waiting.

Cecily turned, giving him his privacy, and headed out of the tunnel. Bastet was in Selene's arms, purring.

"He turned into a bat," Cecily explained. "I honestly can't tell you what a useful talent that is."

"Useful and most unusual, too," Selene said, and brought Cecily into her hug with Bastet. "I'm so sorry… I should have realised when I saw that slope that they'd try the old boulder trick."

"It's not your fault," Cecily assured her.

"My clothes are still wrinkly!" Raf called a moment before he padded out on bare feet to join them beside the lake. And he was right. His clothes, despite being flattened by the enormous boulder, were as crumpled as ever.

Cecily laughed, with relief as well as mirth. "Oh, darling, don't ever change!"

Selene released Cecily from her arms, and Cecily hugged her husband.

"Sorry, we got rather wet from the splash!" she apologised. He didn't seem bothered though, and held her close. Cecily didn't want to think about how tight his squeak with the boulder had been, but she got the idea that it had been a very near thing indeed.

"I'm sorry I gave you a fright," he whispered against her ear. "Love you."

"I'm just glad you're in one piece," Cecily said. "You *are*, aren't you?"

Raf kissed her, then said, "All present and correct. If I hadn't let go, we'd all have been flattened."

Cecily nodded. She knew, and she knew too that Raf had almost sacrificed himself for them. Changing into a bat worked most of the time when he needed to, but any stress could knock out his ability.

"What do we do now?" Cecily asked.

"We try again," Selene said. "There can't be an endless number of boulders."

"I suppose we know what was chipped off that picture now," Cecily remarked.

"I'm not so sure as all that," Raf admitted. "Before I changed back into my dapper self, I took a gander at the rest of the paintings. You're going to love this, Sissy. They even knew I was going to turn into a bat and dodge that rock!"

"Really?" Cecily gasped. "This is so strange! How could they possibly know all this?"

"The priests and priestesses would take certain herbs and go into a trance," Selene explained. "And they would say prayers and they would stare into a flat metal dish and see the future. I tried it once, but it scared me so much I never attempted it again."

"Scrying. My grandma always said, *Be careful when you scry, because you might not like what you see*." Raf widened his eyes, then added, "And at the end of the hallway, there's another slab. And...that's it. The paintings stop with the knackered stone, so the last thing is us climbing the slope. Maybe the prophets expected us to be squashed into jam!"

"Ido held back the boulder as long as he could," Selene told them. "I'm sure of it. But he couldn't stop it completely. I don't know how much they would have seen from the scrying. Perhaps they saw nothing else. Or perhaps it was one of the last parts of the pyramid to be built and Menkare II died before the pictures could be finished."

"Oh, heck," Cecily said. "So there might be something even worse waiting for us?"

The three of them retraced their steps, this time with even more caution, yet as they reached the damaged panel where their story had ended, Raf stopped. He squinted into the darkness, where the torch flames flickered faintly, and murmured, "You're having me on..."

Cecily gasped again. Raf had said the paintings stopped with the damaged panel, but there was another now, showing the boulder, the women fleeing, a bat fluttering overhead. And another panel beside it depicted a Caucasian woman holding the charms out to a man, whilst Selene and Bastet looked on.

"You're sure those weren't there before?" Cecily asked him. But even as she spoke, the surface of the next blank panel began to emit a hissing noise, and Cecily blinked as dust whirled up from the stone.

Where there had been just a blank on the stone before, there was now a carved image of the three of them, with Bastet, back on the slope again, pointing to the pictures.

"Can't be easy carving a bat in stone," Raf commented. "Let's all watch our steps…just in case."

"I think Bastet sensed something," Selene said as they continued on their way. "She was afraid before we came up here, but she seems happy enough now."

Bastet hopped down from Selene's shoulder and seemed happy to trot along at her side as they carried on up the slope. At the top, they now knew that a corridor awaited them, and the slab that Raf had described, its surface decorated with yet more carvings. Another riddle, perhaps?

Cecily kept walking, but her legs suddenly gave way. She was overcome by the voices, which suddenly roared in her head in a cacophony.

"We're close… We're so close."

And as her eyes closed, she saw a darkened room. Figures skittered here and there, a huge stone sarcophagus standing in their midst.

"It's dark, so dark," Cecily moaned. "It's darker than ink! And it's swallowing…swallowing…"

She blinked and realised she was lying on her back on the slope, her head cushioned by something soft.

"You passed out," Selene said gently. Knelt beside Cecily, Raf stroked his hand over her forehead, tenderly soothing her. She could sense his concern, as welcome as the cushion beneath her head.

"You're all right," he said softly. "We've got you." He turned to Selene and asked, "Do you think the two of you should go back?"

"No." Cecily swallowed, her throat dry. "Raf, you can't go on your own."

"Ido is in there," Selene said. "I hope. And I will set him free at last."

Raf nodded and said with a smile, "I thought you might say that." He stroked Cecily's forehead again, all his attention on her once more.

Cecily pushed herself up. She could still see the darkness at the edge of her vision, but it wasn't coming any closer for now. "I'm perfectly fine, darling. And besides, I've always wanted to see inside a pharaoh's tomb."

"You're the bravest person I've ever met," he replied softly.

"Me, brave?" Cecily shook her head. She took Raf's hand as she recalled another time when Raf had said the same thing. Perhaps she *was* brave, in her own quiet way. "You risked getting crushed by that boulder for me. *That's* bravery, darling."

But Raf shook his head and placed a gentle kiss on her cheek. Then he looked towards Selene and asked, "How do you feel, Selene? Now you're so close."

"I wish I had thought to bring the scroll with me." Selene sighed. "He's near, I can feel it. So near...my love."

Cecily realised then what was holding back the darkness. It was love. And whether it was Ido's or Selene's, or maybe even Raf's and her own, she wasn't sure, but it stood in the way of Menkare II's ancient hatred.

"I don't suppose you can remember it?" Raf asked with the hint of a smile. "It's a hell of a journey to make again, isn't it?"

"It is…" Selene shrugged. "I am a fool, I should have brought it with me. I can't remember the words exactly, though I have read it again and again. There's no room for any mistakes. I daren't try it without the scroll to read."

Cecily knew what Raf was going to say even before he said it. He was the sort of man who never thought twice about helping those in need, and she knew that from personal experience. That was precisely what had brought them together, after all. It was how their friendship had started, and that friendship had blossomed into love.

"I could fly back to Cairo and fetch it?" Raf offered. "If you don't mind a bat going through your papers, that is."

"You would?" Selene blinked in surprise at him. "Oh, but I cannot expect you to fly all that way for me. You are so very kind to offer, though."

"If you change your mind, you just let me know." He smiled. "But…I'm in no hurry and I know Sis isn't. We'll miss you, Selene, if the scroll reading goes how you think it might."

Selene was quiet for a moment, then said, "I'll turn to dust. Just as if I had been dead all of these years. But don't be sad for me. I will be so happy with Ido. We will be free, for the first time since we came into being."

"Selene, let Raf go and get the scroll for you," Cecily said gently. It pained her to think that she was about to lose her new friend, but Cecily wanted Selene to be happy. "Your happiness is just within reach…"

Selene nodded slowly. "I am so close… I can't quite believe it. I have been alive such a long time, but now it feels like a mere blink of the eye."

Cecily thought then of Selene's peaceful house and the courtyard filled with blooms and exotic aromas. She thought of Sobek sunning himself on the wall, watching until Selene came home from her travels. And one day, maybe one night—maybe *this* night—she would never come home again.

"Would you like me to go?" Raf asked gently.

A tear ran down Selene's cheek as she replied, her voice cracking, "Yes…yes, please will you go for me? I can't repay you for your kindness, though. The scroll is in a silver box in my bedroom, on the dressing table."

Raf nodded. "Is there anything else you need? What about your home… Little Sobek?"

"Tomorrow morning, give a message to Maryam Hassan at the bakery at the top of my road," Selene said, another tear chasing down her cheek. "I told her my life is a dangerous one. I told her that I might not come back. She has been kind to me, and she is good to the street children. I leave my house and everything in it to her. She will do good things with it, I know she will. There is a document in my desk, in the top drawer, in a blue envelope. It is addressed to her."

"Maryam Hassan," Raf repeated. Then he smiled and said, "Selene, if Sissy doesn't mind sharing the honours…you're *also* the bravest woman I know. And I'm from Yorkshire, so that's saying something."

"I don't mind at all, Raf," Cecily replied. She smiled at Selene, the woman who was facing her mortality after such an impossibly long life. "Because it's true, you *are* brave."

Selene smiled bashfully at their compliments. "I don't know, but some people might think I am rather foolish."

"Not me," was Raf's reply. "If I was in your shoes and Cec was in Ido's, I'd do the same thing. He deserves his rest, and the two of you will move on together whilst that rotten old Menkare II gets his due. I don't have any doubts about that."

"I'm glad you think so," Selene said. "Just think, he's been hiding away here all these years, but tonight, with the words on that scroll, it comes to an end. At *last*."

Cecily took Raf's hand and squeezed it tight. "Safe travels, Raf. I'll see you back here very soon."

"I'll be back before you know it," Raf promised as he took off his tangled charms. He kissed her and added with a mischievous smile, "Just this once, stay put."

"All right," Cecily conceded as she kissed Raf back and carefully took his charms. "I'll stay here with Selene."

Selene half-closed her eyes and whispered a few words. "Another protection spell. I will keep it going while you are away, Raf."

"I'll be back." With that, Raf rose to his feet. He glanced along the corridor towards the slab, then set off back down the slope towards the lake, ready to start his journey to Cairo.

Cecily watched as all of a sudden his clothes dropped into a heap and a tiny bat wriggled free, then flew away.

Chapter Nineteen

Cecily waited with Selene and Bastet. She tried not to listen to the sigh of the desert night-breeze that whistled through the pyramid, and instead listened to Selene's stories. She had a great many to tell, but that came as no surprise considering how long Selene had been alive. It seemed a shame that even more stories would be left untold, lost as soon as Selene read the scroll and her earthly remains turned to dust.

"There is something I would like you to do for me," Selene said. "Will you and Raf look after Bastet?"

The golden cat was larger now, no longer a little statuette that had once fitted comfortably onto Selene's palm or in her pocket.

"Of course!" Cecily said. "As long as she won't mind exchanging Egypt for Yorkshire."

"She won't mind, I'm sure," Selene said. "Give her a cosy lap to curl up on and she will be happy anywhere."

Cecily chuckled as she glanced at her watch. "Raf must've been gone nearly an hour now. He should be back soon, I hope."

As soon as she said it, Cecily knew that her husband was near. The air positively crackled, like an approaching storm. She always knew when Raf was getting closer, she could sense him.

"I'm back!" Raf called from the sloping tunnel. "Getting dressed!"

Selene giggled and covered her eyes. She was so playful sometimes and Cecily swallowed down her disappointment again, that she would lose her friend so soon.

"Did you find the scroll?" Cecily called. She almost wanted him to say that he hadn't, so that Selene would stay.

A few beats of silence passed before Raf admitted, "I found it." She could hear his footsteps drawing closer. "And we've got company. Some welcome, some not so much."

Selene rose to her feet. "Who is here?"

Cecily blinked. She knew at once, a sensation deep in her belly. "Lord Bath. He wasn't as incapacitated by those locusts as we'd thought."

"Lord Bath," Raf confirmed as he crested the top of the slope and greeted his wife with a smile. In his hand he was carrying a papyrus scroll and on his shoulder, to Cecily's surprise, there was a little lizard perched.

Sobek?

"Sobek!" Selene said affectionately. "My little friend. Thank you for bringing him, Raf. I have the chance now to say goodbye to him." Then her smile wilted, "Lord Bath. He cannot bear to wait a moment, can he? Did he see you? How far away is he?"

Catherine Curzon & Eleanor Harkstead

Raf circled his shoulder, though Sobek didn't look unduly disturbed.

"Sobek's not such a little bloke when you're only the size of a pipistrelle." Raf winced. Then he glanced back towards the sloping hallway. "He's on the lake, and there's no sign of Leviathan. He's got Abasi with him… Vane-Stanhope's got a gun pointed at him, forcing him to row."

Selene spoke angrily. Cecily didn't understand her words, but she guessed that she was uttering some choice Egyptian swear words.

"How dare he treat Abasi like that." Selene clenched her fists. "We could get back onto the barge and confront him."

"But if Bath's got a gun, he could turn it on *us*," Cecily said. "I'm sorry, I sound like a wimp. I'd try to rescue Abasi, but I don't know how."

"We play for time," was Raf's advice, and Raf had probably encountered more than a few men like Lord Bath in his day. "There're four of us, plus Bastet and Sobek here, and one Julian Vane-Stanhope. So long as we don't let him read that scroll of his again, because I don't fancy having Menkare II coming after me. He smells bad enough from out here."

Cecily wrinkled up her nose. "Rotten in life, and even more rotten in death. You're right. There's more of us than there are of him. We better get inside the tomb."

Cecily was surprised at how confident her words sounded. On the one hand, she *did* feel brave, not to mention intrigued and excited. But her excitement was tempered by her fear of the furious dead pharaoh who was lying in wait for them.

210

They had barely taken a few steps before there was a soft hiss and the stones began to etch themselves again. This time they showed a small boat containing two men, and though the etched gun one of them held to the other was hardly detailed, it came as no surprise to Cecily to see it. The pyramid was writing its own history.

But does it already know how the story ends?

Who would Bath turn his gun on next?

"The entrance to the chamber must be at the top of the slope," Selene said. "We are so close now… Oh, Ido." And, as she continued her way along the steep tunnel, Selene called out to her lover in a long-lost language.

Cecily glanced at Raf, then took his hand. "Let's hope we can get into the tomb before Lord Bath turns up with his gun."

"I can hear you!" Lord Bath's voice suddenly echoed around the stone. "Chanting spells in your heathen bloody language! Don't think I can't hear you! How many of you are up there?"

"Chanting spells?" Raf whispered, furrowing his brow. "It's not just me, is it? Nobody else can hear that?"

Cecily let down her guard a little, tuning in to the spirits in the burial chamber. She didn't understand the words, but the rhythm was clear. The angry presence which she was certain was Menkare II was chanting.

"It's Menkare II," Cecily whispered. "He's chanting something. Is he trying to keep everyone out? Is he going to unleash another trap?"

"He was never very powerful in life," Selene told her. "Perhaps in death his powers have increased, but I hope not. We have our protection spells—we must hope they are enough."

"I have your friend Abasi and I have a loaded revolver!" Bath bellowed from somewhere behind them. "Unless you want me to put a bullet through his heathen brain, you will all go no farther!"

Selene closed her eyes and sighed. "We must wait. We cannot let Abasi die."

Cecily felt Selene's disappointment and frustration in grey, sullen waves. The presence of Lord Bath in the burial chamber could stop her plans to release Ido and herself.

"Don't worry," Cecily whispered urgently to her. "Once we're inside the chamber, Raf and I will keep Lord Bath busy, and that'll give you enough time to read your scroll."

"Should I let him know we'll wait?" Raf asked, looking to the women.

"Yes, or he'll shoot," Selene replied. "I'll tell him."

She cupped her hands around her mouth and called, "We shall go no farther, Lord Bath. Only don't harm Abasi!"

"We'll have to see about that, won't we?" Bath shouted in response. Then the silence fell again, but not to Cecily. In her head, Menkare II chanted on and on, by turns angry and intense, a storm crashing first overhead, then on a distant shore.

It felt hot and close inside the pyramid, and Cecily wished they hadn't come inside. But she and Raf had wanted to help Selene, and now Selene looked stricken. The former priestess and queen leaned with one hand against the carved panel that depicted Raf as a bat. She was speaking under her breath, her gaze dropped from Cecily.

Was Selene weakening?

Cecily shone her an encouraging smile, but she wasn't sure that Selene saw it.

Raf held out the papyrus scroll to her and said gently, "We won't let him stop you. We've handled scarier things than Lord Bath." Then he touched the tip of his finger to Sobek's nose and asked the lizard, "Isn't that right?"

The lizard seemed to nod in reply. Selene forced herself to smile as she came forwards and took the scroll from Raf.

"To be so close..." Selene murmured. Then a hint of mischief appeared in her eyes as she hid the scroll down the front of her blouse. "He won't take this from me. He won't stop me from freeing my love."

There were footsteps in the distance now, drawing closer. Two sets of approaching feet, marking the arrival of Abasi and the Earl of Bath. There was another noise too though, a faint, buzzing hum that Cecily struggled to place. She had heard it before though, and recently.

The locusts.

They had settled on Bath's tent and now it seemed that they were following him into the pyramid, a swarm of locusts as a living shadow of a peer of the realm.

"Does he not feel even slightly disturbed that he's got a personal swarm?" Cecily whispered. She scratched at her arm, the sound of the locusts making her skin crawl.

"I don't reckon he's thinking about it too much," Raf admitted. "He's not right sharp just now, if he ever has been. Two generations of one bloody family chasing a lunatic's tomb…doesn't seem like the best use of their time to me."

"No, it doesn't," Cecily agreed. She scratched again, then forced herself not to. "It's as if he's possessed by the very idea of it."

"Once you let a spirit like Menkare II in, even a little," Selene told them, "then he will settle there and slowly take over."

The footsteps were coming closer, but so too was the buzzing and scraping of the locusts. Raf reached out and took Cecily's hand. When their gazes met, he gave her a small smile to buoy her along, but she knew what he was thinking. They'd known a man like Lord Bath before, a man who was so wicked and so weak that he was easy prey for the spirit of a monster. Cecily had been married to that man once upon a time, and in the Earl of Bath, she saw her husband's likeness.

"Go on, don't dawdle!" Bath's voice snapped at his captive from the bottom of the steep slope. They emerged from the shadows into the torchlight and Cecily saw the revolver in Bath's hand. Its barrel was pressed to Abasi's back, right between his shoulder blades. "Keep moving!"

Abasi held his hands above his head. He looked so tired and resigned that he didn't seem to have the energy to be scared.

He thinks he's going to die, Cecily realised with a shiver. *Will we all?*

"It is steep, Lord Bath," Abasi said as he began to walk up the slope. In reply Bath jabbed him with the gun barrel and the pair of them continued their climb. Behind them the walls and floor seemed to be moving as thousands of locusts crawled and flew in their wake.

"Here we all are!" Bath announced as he and Abasi approached the top of the slope. "What a happy little gathering. Thank you so much for opening the slabs, Miss Mansour. You're not just a pretty face and a terrible attitude, are you?"

Selene narrowed his eyes at him. "I did not open them for you," she replied. Then her gaze fell on the gun and a change came over her as she ironed out her frown. "But for the good of humankind, to discover the wonders of this long-lost tomb, I mean."

"This place is booby-trapped," Raf began, but Lord Bath wasn't listening. Instead he was gazing at the walls with wide eyes, taking in the images telling the story of their arrival. He said nothing, and Cecily couldn't read his expression at all. She saw her husband there again, his face a blank, dark eyes black as night.

"I will go ahead and open the slab," Selene said. "I believe it may be the last barrier between ourselves and the burial chamber of Menkare II."

"You will *not!*" the nobleman bellowed, stabbing the gun barrel so hard into Abasi's back that the young man stumbled forwards. "My grandfather devoted himself to uncovering this tomb and from as far back as I can remember, it has been the purpose of my life too. I have led this expedition from the start, and *I* will be the first to lay my hand on the door to Menkare II's burial chamber!"

Selene glanced sorrowfully at Abasi, then she nodded. "Of course, Lord Bath. I apologise for my presumption."

Cecily recognised Selene's sudden change. It reminded her of the way she had had to live under her tyrant husband. She recognised the annoyance in Raf's face too when he heard how Lord Bath addressed

Selene, the woman to whom he owed a clear path to the burial chamber he had so long sought. Raf squared his shoulders and on one of them Sobek lifted his head and snapped his jaws like a tiny crocodile.

"You wouldn't have got this bloody far without Miss Mansour," Raf told Lord Bath. "You can put your hands all over that slab, but you won't be able to open it. Why is it so tough to admit that you need her?"

But Bath pushed past them and stalked towards the slab, the etched walls showing his progress even as he passed them. The locusts scuttled and buzzed in a cloud just inches from the rest of the party, but they seemed content to hang back and let the earl progress alone. He laid the palm of his free hand against the surface and murmured, "A king, eh? A king who was forgotten."

The slab stayed stubbornly closed.

I am brave, I am brave, Cecily reminded herself.

"Lord Bath, surely you need Miss Mansour to translate and solve the riddle," Cecily said. Unless Lord Bath thought he could shoot his way in. Nothing would surprise her now. She glanced at Abasi, who was still holding his arms aloft. "I don't suppose you'd mind if Abasi dropped his hands?"

"If he must," Bath said. Then he gestured towards Selene with the gun. "Come along, woman. Open the slab."

Abasi looked relieved as he dropped his arms, but only for a moment. His unease returned as Selene strode towards Lord Bath, her head held high. She was still every inch a queen. Bastet hung back and wrapped herself around Cecily's legs.

Selene ran her gaze across the slab and was thoughtful for a moment. "This is the toughest riddle of them all. Even I am not too sure what the answer is. And if I am wrong…" She drew their attention to a particular section of the text. "It says that a great fire will engulf us. I must — we *all* must — take great care."

Her words appeared to be aimed at Lord Bath. But he didn't seem to be the sort of man to take great care in anything, once his goal was in sight.

Bath had the gun pointed at Selene now and his voice was cold when he said, "What does the riddle say, woman? How difficult can such a thing be?"

"It is very ancient and based on wordplay that only exists if you understand a rare tongue," Selene replied. Her gaze moved between the gun and the hieroglyphics. "The words for *king* and *death* sounded like other words — and that is what the riddle is based on. Let me think… Let me think… Oh, that is it… I remember now."

Selene began to chant in a language unknown to Cecily and there was that grinding sound again, of stones moving after so long. But it was louder this time, much louder, as if more stone than just the slab ahead of them was opening.

With a cry of "Look out!", Raf yanked Cecily's hand hard, pulling her against him as the stone floor of the corridor fell away. Where she had been standing there was nothing but a chasm, cut deep into the foundations. From the bottom of the chasm rose row after row of gleaming spikes, tall as a person and sharp as a razor. There was no way back now.

Chapter Twenty

Cecily was wondering how they'd ever get out when she smelt an overpowering stench of mustiness and rot. She wrenched her attention from the spike-filled chasm, only to be confronted by the entrance that was appearing as the slab dropped into the floor.

The sight was extraordinary. Hanging from the ceiling and sticking out from the walls were a mass of carved stone snakes with red, jewelled eyes.

Bastet yowled fearsomely at them, and Cecily had the strangest impression that the snakes were twitching.

But it can only be a trick of the light, surely?

"The burial chamber lies beyond," Selene told them. "And that riddle was very clever — because *king* and *death* sound like *spike* and *snake*."

"Spike and snake?" Lord Bath scoffed. He glanced towards the wall, where the last etching was appearing. It showed the slab dropping to reveal the burial chamber, and the spikes behind it. Above the pit was a cloud of buzzing locusts and as Cecily looked back, she saw that dark swarm for a few seconds until it turned tail and disappeared, moving as one into the darkness of the tomb.

Even the locusts are leaving.

But there was no more story to tell, it seemed, because the space on the stone had run out. All that lay before them now was the burial chamber.

Lord Bath snatched one of the torches from its wall bracket and held it aloft. He took a step forwards, shoving Selene roughly aside as he edged closer to the heart of the pyramid.

"My God..." the earl murmured in awe. "Such treasures..."

Beyond the snakes, gold glittered in the torchlight. Cecily forgot her fear for a moment and peered in fascination, before she felt something brush against her hair. She took a step back in fright, nearly losing her balance on the edge of the spike pit, and looked up to see that the stone snakes had come alive, writhing and hissing, swiping out at them.

One of the snakes began to coil itself around Lord Bath's wrist, while Selene tried to swat away another that appeared to be heading for her neck. Abasi grabbed a torch and swung it at the snakes, but three of them went for him, wrapping themselves around his arms and his waist, holding him still.

Snakes or spikes. It's not much of a choice.

The snakes writhed and twisted, holding Abasi, Selene and the Earl of Bath in place. One of them lashed at the earl's wrist and sent the revolver skittering away as he shouted, "Help us, for God's sake! They'll throttle us!"

Bastet rose up on her hind legs and hissed, swishing her paws at the snake who was trying to strangle Selene.

Cecily glanced at Raf. "What do we do? Use the torches?" She was already reaching for a nearby torch that hung on the wall over the chasm. "I think I can just about reach it if I stretch my arm just a little bit more!"

But Raf caught her arm and drew it back.

"I'm not having you fall in there. And I'm not risking batting in case one of those bastards snaps me right out of the air," he said. He approached the doorway and the nest of snakes, their bodies moving just slightly as they began to tighten their grips. Very carefully, murmuring to himself all the time, he flattened his back against the wall and extended his hand into the tangle before he instructed Lord Bath, "Let go of the torch."

"Not a bloody chance!" was the furious reply, though the earl's voice was breathless. "You'll leave us to them and take the treasure!"

"My husband's trying to rescue you!" Cecily protested. "We don't want to take the accursed treasure!"

"Listen to them, Lord Bath, please!" Abasi pleaded, his voice choked as the snake around his waist tightened. "Give Mr Chastelaine your torch! Take mine, please!"

"Give me the bloody torch!" Raf snapped as he took Abasi's and passed it back to Cecily. "Or we'll all die in here anyway!"

With a gasp of throttled annoyance, Bath relinquished the torch to Raf.

Cecily clasped her torch in both hands and held it up to the snake that was now wrapped snugly around Selene's neck. The snake hissed at her, its forked tongue as bright red as its glowing ruby eyes. Cecily didn't recoil but kept the torch steady, and the snake began to slacken its hold.

Selene panted with relief as Cecily watched the snake uncoil, and Selene ducked out of the way as the snake withdrew, hissing in defeat. Then Cecily turned her torch towards poor Abasi, whose eyelids had dropped.

"Don't give up, Abasi, you'll be free soon," Selene told him, her voice hoarse, as Cecily went first for the snake around his waist. It widened its jaws at Cecily, but she wasn't afraid.

"Let him go, you legless stone pillock!" Cecily yelled. Raf held his torch alongside Cecily's, jabbing it at the snakes that still held Abasi and Lord Bath. The serpents snapped their jaws, bobbing and weaving in their attempts to bite or seize their assailants, but the more they flailed towards Raf and Cecily, the looser their grips on the two men became.

"Abasi, Stanhope," Raf addressed them. "Try and pull free into the burial chamber. There's not space on this side for all of us without risking those spikes!"

Abasi nodded. Despite looking exhausted, he found reserves of energy from somewhere to jerk sideways, away from the snakes and into the chamber. The snakes tried to reach after him, but they were still attached to the walls and the ceiling and couldn't pursue him.

"I'm inside!" Abasi called. "Oh, it is the most amazing place! I cannot begin to tell you!"

"Don't touch a thing!" Bath warned as he pulled himself free of the snakes and plunged into the burial chamber beside Abasi. "Don't you dare, you damned heathen!"

Raf narrowed his eyes and murmured, "No need to thank us." Then he gave a decisive nod and turned to Selene and Cecily. "When I say go, heads down and throw yourself through into the burial chamber. It's the only place we can go."

Cecily nodded. "Gotcha, Raf!" she said, trying to dismiss all the questions in her mind about how they'd ever get out of the place.

"Of course," Selene said, picking up Bastet, who was still trying to scratch at the snakes. Raf took Sobek in his free hand and held him against his chest, sheltering the little lizard from the reptiles. On the other side of the nest, both Lord Bath and Abasi now had torches of their own, distracting the snakes by jabbing the flames towards them. Cecily had no illusions why the earl was helping them though… There might be hieroglyphics in the burial chamber that he couldn't interpret without the help of Selene.

"Ready…" Raf took a deep breath, then gave a nod. "Go!"

Cecily lowered her head, plunging through the snake-filled doorway. She felt them in her hair and brushing against her limbs, but she was too fast for them and in a moment she had passed to the other side.

She turned to watch Selene follow, Bastet seeing off the snakes with her sharp claws. Raf was the last one through, with Sobek snapping his tiny jaws towards the snakes as they passed the flailing serpents.

But they'd all made it. And somehow, they were alive.

Cecily chuckled with relief. "We did it! We're in! And we're all in one piece, too!"

And what a place it was. Cecily stared about in fascination at the chamber. The walls were richly carved in hieroglyphics, and with images of figures depicting, she supposed, Menkare II and his court. And the chamber was filled with treasures. Cecily couldn't quite take it all in, but everything a pharaoh could need in his next life was there, from ceramic and metal pots to weapons, and even what appeared to be an enormous gold chariot complete with a ceramic horse.

And the pharaoh himself was there. Cecily sensed Menkare II's dark pull and she turned to look at the painted sarcophagus that stood in the centre of the room on a plinth. An elaborate oil lamp hung above it on a chain, and as Cecily stared, it lit up all by itself.

Selene stared about, and Cecily saw that she had noticed the other sarcophagi in the room. Not so grand as Menkare II's, Cecily realised that one of them must contain Ido. Cecily reached out for Selene's hand and held it, trying to comfort her.

Even with Menkare II's lurking presence, Cecily sensed the warmth of Ido's love around Selene and it made her smile.

"Look at it…" Lord Bath murmured again. He fell to his knees beside the chariot, scrutinising it. "My God…"

But Raf looked anything but awestruck. Instead his gaze was flitting from left to right and after a moment he said with a grimace, "It smells like death. If I was you, Vane-Stanhope, I wouldn't take anything out of here. And not just because you've no right to."

"If you were me?" Lord Bath sneered, scrambling to his feet. He had retrieved the gun, but it hung at his side for now. When he spoke again, his voice went on rising in pitch and volume. "If *you* were *me*? You could never be me, you bloody foreign oik! And I am *not* Vane-

Stanhope to you, or anybody! You will address me as *My Lord*! Do you understand? Do you all understand?"

Selene nodded sheepishly. Cecily did too. After all, he had a gun. She'd call him whatever he wanted to be called, as long as it stopped him from shooting anyone.

Even so…

"Maybe we should just have a quick look around and then…then you could come back with cameras?" Cecily suggested. "And leave everything where it is."

But there was so much treasure. Candelabras and chairs and tables, a couch, even a rowing boat. All made from gold.

"Leave everything?" Bath scoffed. "Why on earth would I want to do that?"

"Because this is a grave," Raf spat. "Of a man who should be forgotten!"

Selene gripped Cecily's hand tighter and heaved for breath.

"It's all right," Cecily whispered, even though she knew it wasn't really. She glanced over at Lord Bath. Her idea of keeping him distracted had seemed like a good one to start with, but now she wasn't sure how they'd do it. The moment he saw Selene holding a scroll, wouldn't he demand to see it and know what it was? But then, perhaps they could get Selene to read it out first, at which point the scroll would do its work and Lord Bath wouldn't be able to stop her.

It was then that she saw Lord Bath's lips moving. She couldn't hear his words, but it looked like a spellcasting. And the air was growing thicker.

Selene turned to look at him. "What are you doing, Lord Bath?" she asked hoarsely. "What's that you're saying?"

Cecily glanced around the chamber. Nothing had moved, at least, she didn't think it had. And yet, she had the impression of motion from somewhere in the room. It wasn't only the torchlight dancing on the surface of the gold.

"Who are you summoning?" Cecily whispered. Her stomach was tied into a knot of fear.

"There is only one king here." Lord Bath's voice was low. As he fell silent the slab thundered into place, sealing the burial chamber once more. With them inside it. "And the so-called *pharaoh* is my servant now."

"What have you done?" Selene gasped. "This is not your choice to make! You cannot take these people's lives!"

"These four people are grave robbers," he announced to some unseen audience. "Kill them as you killed the men who tried to defile your tomb!"

"He's summoned a mummy!" Cecily yelled, swishing her torch this way and that as if the mummy were there before her. How would they ever get out, sealed alive in a burial chamber with the undead man who had dispatched the tomb robbers, snapping them like reeds in the wind?

Selene began to chant quickly under her breath, her arm extended as if she was pushing something back. But for all Selene's strength, Cecily had no idea if she could withstand the spell from Lord Bath's scroll.

"Kill the defilers!" Lord Bath demanded. From his pocket he produced the scroll, which he unfurled with one hand. Then he began to read again, with more confidence this time.

As Bath spoke, the sound of stone grinding against stone filled the chamber. The stench of dust and rot was overpowering as the great sarcophagus of Menkare II began to open. Raf started towards the earl but he raised the gun with a steady, white-knuckled hand, still reciting from the scroll.

Selene cringed, but she was still chanting, still trying to hold Menkare II back. Cecily had a small insight into how she must feel. If her own dead husband were rising from the grave before her, Cecily would've wanted to do nothing more than run away as fast as she could. And yet they were all trapped, sealed into the burial chamber.

"Stop, Lord Bath!" Cecily shouted. "Stop it! Look what you're doing!"

Abasi lunged for the scroll. "Stop it, you mad Englishman!"

The gunshot was deafening when it came, but thankfully Lord Bath's bullet went wide as Abasi sidestepped his effort. The last words of the scroll fell from the earl's lips and the fingers of a bandaged hand appeared from inside the sarcophagus like the legs of a monstrous spider. They tightened on the ornate lid and on the bandages Cecily saw the dark stains of blood, no doubt from the tomb robbers. From within the bandages came a low, guttural growl and the lid shifted farther, revealing the ancient mummy of Menkare II within. Upon his head was a nemes, not of cloth, but of solid gold and vivid, rich blue. From the centre of it rose a bejewelled uraeus, the golden cobra's ruby eyes glittering in the torchlight.

"Kill those who would defile your tomb," the Earl of Bath commanded. "All of them."

Cecily froze in terror as still Selene chanted, but it seemed to make no difference.

And Cecily realised they'd blamed the wrong mummy. They'd thought it was Ido who'd been escaping from the tomb at Bath's command to wreak havoc, and yet it had been Menkare II all along. A king at the beck and call of a scroll.

Raf was murmuring, but the words did nothing to stop Menkare II, who lumbered from his sarcophagus and stood before them. Then his bandaged feet began to move again, padding across the chamber towards the group.

Cecily flinched in fear and held out her torch. Maybe the dry bandages and desiccated corpse within would catch fire? But it didn't seem to make any difference.

From the other side of the tomb, there came a scraping sound. Cecily couldn't bear to think what could be coming next, but another sarcophagus was opening and struggling out of it was another mummy. It wore no gold or jewels and it moaned as it climbed out of its resting place and the stone lid of its sarcophagus fell to the floor with a crash.

Cecily couldn't quite believe it when she saw the mummy pick up a gold spear. What on earth could they do against *two* mummies?

"Call them off, reverse the chant!" Abasi urged Lord Bath desperately, as he plunged his torch at the mummy of Menkare II.

"Two of them… Let the fools in London laugh at me now! Just let them mock my grandfather and me!" Lord Bath looked almost delighted with the discovery, but his smile began to fade as Menkare II shambled past the group of four as though he hadn't even seen them. Instead, the pharaoh was heading for the Earl of Bath.

The man who had defiled the tomb.

Cecily dared to smile. So Lord Bath would get his just desserts after all.

And the other mummy was getting closer, too, following in the shuffling footsteps of Menkare II. The spear gleamed in its bandaged hand, and as he moved, something — a piece of metal, it seemed — fell out from the bandages and clattered to the floor.

Selene dived forwards and swept it up in her hand. "It's Isis. I — I've seen this before. It's the same as the figure I asked to have put in his wrappings, along with the tiny golden Bastet. It was to protect him. Wait — this is Ido!"

She stared at Ido as he moaned, treading heavily from side to side as he made his way across the burial chamber.

Menkare II came to a halt in front of Lord Bath. The nobleman was silent now, his jaw slack with terror for a few seconds before he stammered, "N-not me! I freed you! I'm your friend!"

The gun was shaking uncontrollably when the Earl of Bath raised it and fired, point blank, into the pharaoh's chest. Clouds of dust puffed out of the bandaged bullet holes but still the monarch stood. Then he tilted his head to one side, as though scrutinising a creature beneath a microscope.

"You might not want to do that," Cecily said to Lord Bath. "Because you might just have made him even more annoyed."

And that couldn't be good news for any of them, trapped there with an unstoppable mummy.

With a long moan, Ido raised his spear and aimed it at Lord Bath. The point was still sharp, despite the uncountable years it had spent in the desert.

"Step back slowly," Raf instructed Lord Bath. "He might still—"

A hiss from the golden snake that projected from Menkare II's headdress silenced Raf's words. Then the cobra, inanimate and bejewelled, suddenly lashed out and stuck its teeth into the centre of Lord Bath's forehead.

Blood spurted out and spattered against Menkare II's already filthy bandages. And there was a crunch— Cecily watched through her fingers, convinced that the cobra had bitten through Lord Bath's skull. She was repulsed at the sight, and her stomach roiled, but she couldn't look away.

The man who'd been so determined to find the tomb, and all he had discovered inside it was his own death. And at the hands of the mummy he'd thought he controlled.

Julian Vane-Stanhope, third Earl of Bath, stood for only a few more seconds before the life went out of him. His last utterance was a rattle deep in his throat, then he crumpled to his knees and fell onto the stone floor. The earl's sightless eyes stared into the empty sarcophagus as from his lips, a single locust emerged. It took flight almost immediately, disappearing into the darkness at the apex of the burial chamber.

"He's gone..." Abasi said, crouching down beside the body. "He's gone, but..." He looked up at the two lumbering mummies. Ido was still holding his spear.

"It's time." Selene pulled the scroll from inside her blouse. "Abasi, I can't explain now, but maybe Cecily and Raf will do the honours."

Abasi frowned in confusion as Selene unrolled the scroll.

Her voice still hoarse to begin with, Selene began to read from her scroll. But as she went on, her voice became stronger. The two mummies turned to her as she read, and Cecily realised that the contents of the scroll must have been having an effect on them. Ido dropped the spear and held his arms out to her, but Selene looked down and kept reading.

Cecily took a step away from her, giving Selene space, and Bastet jumped down from her arms, then sat neatly, looking up at her as she read. Menkare II moved suddenly, letting out an immense roar of fury as he lumbered stiffly towards Selene, but Raf was faster. He got between the king and his unwilling queen, thrusting the flaming torch towards the mummified sovereign.

"Keep reading!" Raf shouted, ducking and weaving to avoid Menkare II's blows and the darting cobra that reared out of his headdress. Despite his speed, the mummy struck him a glancing blow to the side of the head, but Raf didn't let it stop him.

Selene read faster, tears running down her cheeks as her voice filled the burial chamber. Abasi swung his torch at Menkare II as well, trying to help keep him back. He had no idea, Cecily was sure, that Menkare II was confronting his long-lost wife.

Finally she reached the end of the scroll. She lowered it and stared at the two figures in front of her. Ido groaned and his legs gave way beneath him. He slumped to the floor.

Cecily stared at Selene. How long would it take for her to turn to dust? Was it already happening? And yet Cecily couldn't see any change. Had the scroll not worked?

Cecily's answer came when the monstrous snake upon Menkare II's headdress clattered to the floor, a creature of gold again. Seconds later, the king's mummy followed in a cloud of dust and rotten bandages, crumbling and folding in upon itself until all that remained were the wrappings and atop them, the golden headdress he had worn for centuries. Cecily felt something fall upon her then and for a moment she thought it was raining, because what else could it be that was falling from above? Raf held out his hand and murmured, "Sand..."

"He's gone," Cecily murmured.

"He has. And yet...and yet, I'm still here!" Selene gasped. She held out her hands and stared at them, turning them this way and that. "You can all still see me, can't you?"

"Of course we can," Abasi replied. "Why wouldn't we? It's not as if you're a—wait. Oh, wait. Miss Mansour, is there something you haven't told me?"

"I don't know how to even begin," Selene said. Then she glanced over at the other mummy. Ido had not dissolved into dust and sand as Menkare II had, and she hurried over to his side. "We should put him back into his sarcophagus."

"There's sand coming in," Raf said, with more urgency this time. The great pyramid seemed to be rumbling, as though an earthquake was shifting the earth itself, and Raf lifted his torch to illuminate the wall above the sarcophagus. There, etched into the wall, was the painting that told this part of the story just as they had told the others. The pyramid was being swallowed by the desert once more.

"You have to get out, now," Selene said. "Leave me. I'll follow if I can, but I can't bear to think of Ido being left like this, on the floor."

Ido moaned. He tugged at the bandages that covered his face, and they began to unravel. Cecily couldn't bear to look. She'd seen photographs of an unwrapped mummy once, and the ancient bodies were all wrinkled like prunes. But as the bandages fell, Cecily couldn't believe her eyes.

Under the bandages, Ido wasn't shrivelled at all. He was alive. Dazed, but alive. A flesh and blood, living man, as young as Selene, and handsome. He smiled up at Selene and in a creaking voice spoke to her in the old tongue that Cecily had heard Selene speak so often. Selene held him to her. Her scroll had worked in ways that Selene hadn't expected. By sending everyone off to where they belonged, she had condemned Menkare II to oblivion, and herself and Ido to life.

"We've all got to get out now," Cecily said. "Come on!"

But how could they? They were sealed into the chamber by the stone slab and beyond it, the snakes and spikes blocked their way.

"There's got to be a way out…" Raf looked this way and that as Sobek hopped down onto the floor and scurried into the shadows, defying Raf's efforts to capture him. "There has to be."

Chapter Twenty-One

"Where's Sobek gone?" Cecily gasped, glancing about. "We haven't time to go looking for him now! Bastet, where is he?"

Bastet *miaowed* forlornly as more sand fell in on them. Cecily felt just as lost. They were going to die, trapped inside a pyramid under a mountain of sand. How long would it take? There was water in the lake, and perch, but they couldn't live on that forever, could they? And no one would be coming to rescue them, Cecily was sure. Once the sand covered the pyramid again, maybe it would block the water off, and they'd be done for.

"Sobek! Come here, you little tinker!" Raf called as the lizard emerged from the shadows and scampered up the side of Menkare II's empty pyramid. He teetered on the top of the stone casket then leapt up onto the lantern. It dipped a little and on the far side of the tomb, a slab began to rise. Beyond it was darkness, no torches to illuminate the way this time.

"It's a tunnel… Sobek's a smart lad," Raf told them, squinting into the unbroken blackness. Sobek sprang down into Raf's waiting hands. "Let's go. It's our only chance."

Selene and Abasi had got Ido to his feet. Cecily picked up Bastet, who climbed onto her shoulder, and Cecily gripped her torch. They made for the entrance that had opened up. Ahead of them stretched another tunnel, unadorned by carvings or hieroglyphics.

"I hope there's no traps," Cecily said as she took her first few steps into the tunnel. But that was the risk they had to take, as there was no other way out.

"This must be the way the builders took," Raf mused. The rumble grew louder and behind them, the slab slammed shut. "Is Ido managing back there, Selene?"

"Just about," Selene replied. Ido shuffled between Selene and Abasi. He kept speaking to Selene, and she explained, "He keeps asking me how many years he's been dead. He can't believe it's been as long as it has! I've told him he's got to hurry, or he'll be dead again before he knows it."

"Dead end!" And Raf was right. There in front of them was…nothing. A blank, stone wall in a sea of darkness. "There's got to be a release. A switch! Everyone start feeling around… It has to be here!"

Cecily groped about in desperation. There had to be a way, there just had to be. But she was so confused by the circuitous route they'd taken to reach the burial chamber that she had no idea where the tunnel would come out, even if they *could* find an exit.

Ido spoke, and Selene translated. "Ido says he knows the way out. He says this is the way Menkare II used when he killed the tomb robbers. He followed him and tried to stop him."

Ido nearly tripped on his bandages as he walked slowly towards the slab that sealed the tunnel. He pushed a stone in the wall just beside it, and it slid in. Then he pushed in another just below it, and that slid in too. He reached inside it and Cecily heard a clicking noise like a crank being pulled, and the huge stone began to move.

More sand rained down on them and the pyramid shook as the slab scraped open. Cecily rested her cheek against Raf's shoulder as she watched the slab move, far too slowly for her liking.

"I love you, Raf. We've had a marvellous time, haven't we?" Cecily said to him.

"And there are loads of marvellous times in front of us too." He wrapped his arm around Cecily and kissed her. "You just wait and see."

Beyond the slab was darkness. But not just any darkness.

The air changed and was suddenly fresher, and the darkness beyond was twinkling, full of precious stones.

No, they're not precious stones! They're stars!

"We're free!" Cecily cried. "Look, look, it's the sky!"

"Ido, you're a bloody treasure!" Raf exclaimed. "It's a couple of steps down then run for it. We've got to beat the sand and it's coming in at a hell of a whack." Raf stood back to let them all go. He would never be the first out. Cecily could have predicted that.

As Ido was still unsteady on his feet, Cecily stood aside for him and Selene and Abasi helping him. Then once they'd begun to make their way down, Cecily turned to Raf and kissed his cheek before starting her descent. The sand rasped against her skin and she could barely see against the onslaught. They still weren't safe, that much was obvious.

Ido, Selene and Abasi reached the sand, then hurried as best they could with Ido trailing his bandages. Their footsteps vanished as soon as the sand whirled across them, and Cecily gasped in dismay as the strong wind blowing in the sand nearly extinguished her torch. But she finally reached the desert floor, which was rising by the second, and stopped for Raf, who was still climbing down.

"Darling, we're nearly safe!" she called. Raf dropped to the sand and reached for Cecily's outstretched hand. Then the two of them made a run for it, with Sobek clinging onto Raf's shoulder for dear life.

The pit that the enormous pyramid had been standing in since it had appeared in the desert only days before was rapidly disappearing as the sand swept in. The tents in the camp were mercilessly blown about by the wind, pans and firewood rolling and clattering about. As Cecily and Raf reached the edge of the pit with their animal charges, she noticed a car approaching.

Not just any car. Wasn't it Lord Bath's?

It pulled up by the tents, and whoever was driving climbed out, leaving the lights on.

"What the devil is happening?" Snelling called into the sandstorm.

"The excavation's over," Raf shouted in reply. "Turns out he didn't have the right permits after all. Can we cadge a lift back to Cairo?"

"Of course!" Snelling replied. He strode over to Bath's tent and peered inside. "Where *is* Lord Bath?"

"Snelling, he's dead," Selene told him, without ceremony.

Snelling emerged from the tent and blinked at Selene. "*Dead?* He's *dead?* And who on earth is *this?* Was there a fancy-dress party out here?" he asked, pointing to Ido.

Raf pulled open the door on the car and began bundling people inside.

"He's an expert in Egyptiana," was his only explanation. "Now let's get out of here."

Epilogue

A year later

Cecily folded up the letter from Selene and Ido and replaced it in its envelope. It had been lovely to hear from them. Ido was doing well learning Egyptian Arabic, and he and Selene had both been hired by the university in Cairo as experts in ancient and obscure Egyptian languages.

Cecily put the photo of Selene and Ido, and their pets Bastet and Sobek, on the mantelpiece. She hoped she'd see that courtyard in Cairo again one day. And how wonderful it would be to visit Egypt without Lord Bath and Menkare II getting in the way.

It was twilight, and the French window was open into the garden, letting in the warm summer breeze. Cecily wandered out onto the veranda and gazed up at the starlit sky. A little bat swooped overhead, with another following quickly in its wake.

The two bats soared lower, the larger of the two tipping its wing towards Cecily in acknowledgement and greeting. They came lower still until, in the blink of an eye, Raf was standing there beside her. He lifted his arms and called, "C'mon, Sandy, time for bed, son!"

The pipistrelle landed on Cecily's shoulder, then hopped down into Cecily's arms. And there, the bat transformed into their six-month old baby, who was giggling for all he was worth.

"You enjoyed your flight, didn't you?" Cecily said, gently stroking their son's cheek. She turned and kissed Raf. "And what a wonderful teacher you have."

Raf returned her kiss before he said, "He's taken to it like Leviathan to water." Then he bent to kiss Sandy's forehead. "But we can't fly all night. Well, we *can*, but it's past your bedtime already."

A few months earlier Leviathan had, true to her word, called in on them on her way to Loch Ness. At least, Cecily had sensed her in the sea nearby and she and Raf had gone out onto the clifftop to wave at her as she shimmered by.

"To your crib, youngest de Chastelaine," Cecily said to her little boy. But she wanted to linger there in the twilight just a little longer, as the stars blinked against the soft summer cloud, and the sea sighed against the beach below.

There had been a time when she had thought she would never know happiness, when all of her family had disappeared. But now she had a *new* family, all of her own, and a happiness that she could never have imagined. Here on the Yorkshire coast, with her husband and their little baby dhampir, Cecily was enjoying the happiest adventure she had ever known.

Want to see more from these authors? Here's a taster for you to enjoy!

The Colour of Mermaids
Catherine Curzon & Eleanor Harkstead

Excerpt

Of course Eva wasn't going to turn down her invitation to the private viewing at the Hawley Gallery. Daniel Scott, *enfant terrible* of the international art world, was exhibiting in Brighton of all places.

She arrived fifteen minutes early, but the gallery was almost full. It seemed as if everyone who was anyone on the Brighton art scene had turned up for vast amounts of free drink and air-kissing. Eva waved to people she knew, and finally spotted her friend Lyndsey on the other side of the room in front of one of Daniel Scott's canvases. Somehow, a glass of Prosecco had appeared in her hand by the time she had squeezed through the crowd to reach Lyndsey.

"Hello, gorgeous!" Lyndsey put her hand on Eva's arm and leaned in to dart her lips to her cheek. As she did, she dropped her voice and whispered, "Not many laughs on these walls tonight!"

"Hello, darling!" Eva kissed Lyndsey back, her friend's summery floral scent enveloping them both like a cloud. "No, his work's not a laugh a minute, is it?

But it's so exciting that the exhibition's *here*. And thanks so much for sorting me out with an invite."

"I don't actually understand what it *is*. I don't think I like it." Lyndsey peered up at the canvas before her. From it, *something* vaguely human glowered down, a twisted, misshapen silhouette of a human face in a mist of fog. She cocked her head to one side then the other and shrugged. Then she smiled and murmured, "It needs a kitten or two, then we'll talk."

Eva laughed. "Like the ones on tea trays that grannies used to have? You do crack me up! I love his paintings... I'm always drawing *things* in my illustrations. It must be so freeing to paint emotion."

"I haven't met him yet, but Rupert says he's *super* intense." Lyndsey took a glass of Prosecco from the tray of a passing waiter. "He wouldn't let us so much as hang a single work until he'd been through the space a dozen times. We've had some tricky artistic types through, but *nothing* like this. Rupert'd let him paint the place neon green if he wanted, though, for the exposure we're getting."

"I can't say I'm surprised that he's intense. I mean, to produce art like this." Eva recalled the photos she'd seen of him in newspapers and magazines, dark eyes like coals that seemed to burn through the paper. "Then again, I bet he's been really spoiled over the years. Don't you think? Mr Rockstar Artist!"

"I just want another lovely sculptress to come and give us all biccies like that one from Cornwall." Lyndsey pouted. "She was so nice, like the perfect mum! I mean, nobody came to see her work but...that meant biccies for the office!"

"Sorry about that, Lynds... I was busy." Eva hadn't been, of course, but at the time she hadn't wanted to go out and her own studio had been her sanctuary. "She sounds lovely, though. No biscuits from Mr Scott, I take it?"

"No, nothing from Mr Scott other than shirty emails from his people about the quality of the light and the spacing between the works." She took a sip from her glass. "You know none of them are for sale, and we've had offers on every single one?" Lyndsey dropped her voice again and confided, "I can't tell you how much because Rupert won't tell me. He just says think of an insane number and then add at least one zero. Mr Man-in-Black apparently *might* let some go once the exhibition closes. Personally, I can't think who'd want one! Would you want these things above your bed?"

"Possibly not!" Eva looked up again at the canvas. She had trouble turning away from it. She'd seen his paintings reproduced in books and everywhere else, but actually seeing his artwork up close — close enough to see each individual brush mark — made the emotion it represented all the more intense. "But imagine it in the lounge, it'd be quite the conversation piece at parties!"

"The problem is, to buy this you'd have to sell your house, so you'd have no lounge to hang it in!"

"That's true!" Eva laughed. "Thing is, don't you think he should, I dunno, up his game a little? Develop his style a bit? It is exciting seeing all these works up close, but it's as if he's painting to a tried-and-tested formula. The Daniel Scott Method!"

"Are you accusing our *enfant terrible* of painting by numbers?" Lyndsey affected mock outrage. "Tell me more, Ms da Vinci!"

Eva gestured towards the painting while she sipped a mouthful of Prosecco. "Well, I do paint myself, as you know, and I try to...do different things. I mean, imagine if he broke from type and did a landscape.

Although I suppose if you get to be as famous as him you're trapped in one style, because everyone expects to see a Daniel Scott, and this is what they want."

"Oh, don't stop there," a male voice said from behind the two women. "I'm enjoying learning from a master."

Eva didn't recognise the voice, although it seemed familiar. Some annoying hanger-on, no doubt, who thought they were an expert. But when she turned, her eyebrow already raised in scornful retort, she was facing Daniel Scott himself.

His coal-black eyes held Eva fixed to the spot. "I...erm... My God, Mr Scott. If I'd known you were stood right behind me, I really wouldn't have said all that. Sorry. Erm..." She swallowed, then held out her hand to him, an awkward grin on her lips. "Eva Catesby. I am actually an artist, before you ask! Not just an opinionated bystander."

"Eva Catesby." He took her hand very briefly and narrowed his eyes as though trying to recall her name. "Did I see you exhibited at the Met last season? Or was it the Tate Modern? You'll have to remind me, I seem to have forgotten."

Because, of course, he has to be an egomaniac.

Eva rolled her eyes. "How unfortunate that you can't remember. By the way, you also appear to have forgotten your sunglasses. We *are* indoors." She indicated his Ray-Bans, which were perched on his dark hair.

"Eva!" Lyndsey whispered urgently, no doubt seeing her job as PA to Rupert Hawley flashing before her eyes.

"That's why they're not on my face," he replied, deadpan. "As you correctly say, everybody wants to see Daniel Scott and they'd be disappointed if I didn't have my sunglasses. I've always been a people pleaser."

"Is that so?" Eva arched her eyebrow again. He was dressed entirely in black. His suit, his shirt. Was it an act, and at home he tooled about in flip-flops and Bermuda shorts? "Of course, some people are much harder to please than others. And I'm one of those people, I'm afraid. What can I say? I'm sure you're not all that fussed by the views of a provincial artist you've never heard of."

"Mr Scott." Rupert Hawley was suddenly beside them, as if conjured from nowhere. He was almost bowing, Eva realised, his hand extending to shake Daniel's. "I was hoping to announce you, you managed to evade me!"

"I was meeting the locals," Daniel told him. He subtly turned from Eva, angling his body away from her a little. "Tough crowd."

Rupert glanced to the two women for just a moment, but word of the artist's presence seemed to have spread and an interested crowd was gathering. Everyone was eager to meet the star in their midst and none of them, Eva knew, would tell him that he needed to try something just a *little* different next time he put brush to canvas.

"That's Brighton for you." Rupert managed to force a smile to accompany his words. He moved to put his hand on Daniel's back as though to steer him away, but it hovered there before falling. *He can't touch the icon, can he?* All he could do was wring his hands and say, "Let me introduce you to some people. Excuse us, ladies."

"Ms Catesby," Daniel addressed Eva, the hint of a smile chilling on his lips, "thank you for the notes. I'll keep them in mind."

"Oh my God," Lyndsey groaned as they departed in a crowd of excited chatter. "Oh my God, oh my God. Why did you do have to do that? You didn't have to do that!"

"Do what?" Eva sipped her drink as she watched Daniel walk away. *Cocky sod.* Although, she had to admit it, a very good-looking sod, which was probably part of the problem. A man who had lucked out thanks to the universe granting him both a handsome face and talent. "I was merely expressing an opinion. That's the point of a private viewing, isn't it? I mean, I know everyone *really* just comes out for the free booze and schmoozing, but there are paintings on the walls, and we're allowed to comment on them. It's not my fault he was eavesdropping. His work is great, but I just think... Bloody hell, if he pushed himself, it could be amazing."

"It's *Daniel Scott*," Lyndsey reminded her. "His last exhibition was at the Pompidou and when he came back to England he didn't go to the Tate or the National, he came to our humble little gallery. You were really rude to him, Eva, that wasn't on. It costs nothing to be nice, you know."

"I did apologise, but then he came out with all that egotistical bollocks, and I saw red." Eva adopted a snooty tone. "*I've exhibited at the Met, I've exhibited at the Tate Modern, I'm a great big poser with my sunglasses on my head, I dress in black because I want everyone to think I'm a badass, I still sleep with my teddy.*"

"It was rude," Lyndsey told her again. "And you were saying you loved his work, why didn't you tell him that?"

"Because that's all he ever hears!" Eva watched his progress through the room, handshaking with some of the most annoying people in Brighton. Everyone was smiling and fawning over the man. "Look, when I do outreach with those kids, I don't just say *well done* to everything they paint. I'll say, *well done*. And next time, what if you do *this* a bit differently. There's nothing wrong with pushing people. As long as it's a gentle shove."

"He's going to complain about you." As Lyndsey spoke, Daniel glanced over his shoulder at them for a moment. Eva flashed him a sarcastic grin and momentarily raised her glass. He raised his own in turn, the red wine catching the light before he turned away again. "And Rupert will blame me for inviting you and I'll lose my job. You know how moody Rupe can be. You'll have to go out for drinks with him again and save my job!"

"Oh God, Rupe and his lacklustre snog." Eva wrinkled her nose and giggled like a gossipy schoolgirl. "There's someone I won't be going on a date with again. Ewww!"

"Bless his socks, give him another chance." Lyndsey laughed. "You know, in three years of working with him, he's never had a girlfriend for more than a couple of months. You looked so cute together, and he still likes you!"

"He's a nice bloke, but really…" Eva shook her head. "He's not for me."

Whereas Daniel Scott…

What a thing to think. But he *had* been a bit flirty with her, although he was probably like that with everyone. Eva watched as Daniel lowered his head to speak to a woman who fashioned genitalia in colourful pottery. She was giggling at him. *Giggling.* Eva looked back up at the painting again. Something in it which she hadn't seen before, which she wouldn't have been able to describe even had she attempted it, made her come out in goosebumps.

"Do you want to see the rest of them?" Lyndsey touched her arm. "And maybe accidentally bump into Mr Scott and grovel at his feet? Tell him he's amazing and how sorry you are? *Pweese*?"

"I'd love to see the rest of them, but speaking to him depends on how likely he is to keep talking to that woman about her pottery pudenda." Eva snorted with laughter. "Am I mean? It's just...my foundation art course was bulging with them, and *she* somehow makes a living from crockery cocks!"

"She's probably not being rude to him." Lyndsey slipped her arm though Eva's. "Come on, talk me through these scenes of horror, it's not a world I often inhabit!"

"After that show last year of the comedy seagull photos, I'm not surprised you find them a bit" — Eva glanced at her friend's benign face, then up at a canvas of swollen, dark paint, which seemed to throb before her eyes — "unfathomable. You could see that one, for example, as...a bruise. An emotional bruise. We all have them. I suppose that's what frustrates me. He's putting all this emotion on canvas, and it could be dark and disturbing, but I feel almost as if he's cranking them out to order. Do you see?"

"I liked the seagulls," Lyndsey smiled nostalgically. Then she glanced over her shoulder, satisfied that Daniel was at a safe distance, still surrounded by acolytes. "But when I look at this... It's like there's something wrong with him. What's going on in his head?"

"Who knows? Does *he*?" Eva tipped her head to one side, to see the painting from another angle. "But don't you think that's the point of art, really? I look at this and it makes me think of...well...splitting up with Miles. An emotional bruise, which faded. And everyone else looking at it thinks of something painful that happened to them. And maybe — *maybe* — he does it on purpose, but in his production line way, stirring those feelings up, forcing people to *look* at that pain inside them. Or maybe horrible things *are* going on in that handsome head, and he spills it out in paint." Eva sighed. "Maybe it's a cross of the two."

"Oh God, he's looking at us," Lyndsey whispered, quickly turning her attention to the painting. Years in gallery administration had left her with the talent for looking both interested and appreciative even when she wasn't, a skill that Eva knew her friend was justifiably rather proud of. A skill that had saved her career on more than one occasion. "You've *really* upset him, Eva, so you'd better hope what's in his head *isn't* as horrible as his pictures."

Eva met his glance as she combed her fingers through her long hair with a careless swish. He was doing a very good job of not looking upset at all, despite what Lyndsey seemed to think.

"He's smiling, Lyndsey. He doesn't look upset to me."

"I'm not going to look at him. He might put me in a painting if I do!"

Eva nudged her, laughing. "Don't be silly, you'd *love* it if he did that!"

"Only if I could have bunnies," Lyndsey told her cheerily. "But if he painted bunnies, he'd probably paint them with...I don't know, horns or something. Horny bunnies, can you imagine?"

"Horny bunnies?" Eva laughed loudly and hid her mouth behind her hand. "Is this a new *ladies' toy* that's just hit the market?"

"I wouldn't know." Her friend laughed. "Go on, show me another Daniel Scott masterpiece, before he asks us what we're talking about. I'm a teeny bit terrified of him!"

They went on to the next painting, but all the while Eva was aware of someone's gaze following her. She glanced over her shoulder, only to see Daniel again, assured and confident as he toured the room, watching her. Had she got under his skin?

Good. Because he's got under mine.

"This one... It looks like a scream, doesn't it? Not that you can see a mouth, as such, but it *feels* like a scream. There's tension in it. You can almost hear, can't you?" Eva gestured towards it, her silver bangles jangling on her wrist.

"I wouldn't want it in my loo! It'd scare my little Pears Soap children witless. They'd run out of their frames."

"At least you don't have a crocheted crinoline lady on your toilet roll, or she'd faint!" Eva laughed. "But this sort of art, it's not meant to be background noise. It's not meant to be lift muzak. It's supposed to challenge you. And it does..."

Lyndsey nodded, her lips pursed as she considered the canvas. Then she admitted, "I think I sort of fancy him, though. Isn't that awful?"

"He's a handsome sod, there's no getting around it. He knows it too... But are you sure you find it attractive, all that intensely intense business?" With a return of her schoolgirlish mischief, Eva giggled. "I do hope he wears black underpants, though. Or perhaps none at all! If you found out he wore ones with cartoon characters on, it'd be pretty disappointing, wouldn't it?"

"Or horrid grey y-fronts." Lyndsey gestured to a waiter and took two more glasses, handing one to Eva. "Or silky lady's knickers! He's too intense for me. I like someone a bit more…you know. A boy who'll wine and dine me, not one with things like that in his head!"

Eva took the glass. He was watching again, she knew, and the thought of it made her burn inside. He was playing with her, though—of course he was. The man could have anyone he wanted. And, if rumour was to be believed, he regularly did. But it was exciting to think that Daniel Scott, of all people, was flirting with her. As she sipped her drink, she caught his glance again, so she ran the tip of her tongue across her lip. "Oh, I don't know, I think he'd be rather fun."

He lifted his hand and brushed it through his dark hair, catching his sunglasses in his fingers as he did so. Still holding her gaze, he slipped them into his jacket and raised one eyebrow, as though to ask, *happy now?*

"I bet he's really dirty." Lyndsey giggled. "In the bedroom, I mean."

Eva raised her hand casually to her hair but shielded her face from Lyndsey as she gave Daniel a wink in response that her friend couldn't see.

Then she turned her back on him. "Dirty as in covered in paint?" She laughed. "Oh, but I know what you mean. I bet a man like him would be incredibly naughty!"

"You fancy him!" She took a sip of Prosecco then whispered through giggles, "Eva and scary artist sitting in a tree, k-i-s-s-i-n-g!"

Eva blushed as red as her satin dress. "Well? And so what if I do? Tons of other people do as well. He's hardly going to be interested in me, is he? Especially not after my terrible review of his paintings!"

Lyndsey glanced at her watch and pouted. "I have to leave you alone and round up the punters. Rupes wants to do a little talk and pay homage to the great man in our midst. Promise me that you won't insult anybody while I'm gone?"

Eva patted Lyndsey's arm. "Worry not, I'm on my best behaviour."

"I was going to say enjoy the artworks, but" — Lyndsey gave a theatrical shudder — "maybe not!"

The she trotted away on her ballet flats, quietly ushering the patrons towards the centre of the gallery space. Lyndsey Davis was perfectly suited to this sort of schmoozing, petite and smiling and neatly turned out in her rose-patterned sundress, a red cardigan over her shoulders. She gave her boss and his guest a wide berth, concentrating instead on the great and the good who had been invited to this monumental occasion in the history of the gallery. Of course she would leave the guest of honour to Rupert's care, because nobody loved the limelight like Rupert Hawley.

Eva stood in the crowd of dinner-jacketed men and women in their evening gowns, of artists so dedicated to the cause that they had turned up in ripped jeans and raggedy knitwear, of reporters tapping notes on their phones. But she didn't pay any attention to them. Her entire focus was absorbed by Daniel Scott. *The handsome sod.*

She fanned herself with the exhibition programme that she hadn't got round to looking at and waited.

Rupert moved to stand beneath the largest painting, a canvas drenched in reds of every imaginable hue, thickly coated with streaks of paint, the textures leaping from the surface as though it were an alien landscape.

Blood by numbers.

Daniel stood ten feet or so to the side, his arms folded across his chest, his face unreadable because, for reasons best known to him, he was wearing the Wayfarers that had been nestled in his hair.

Indoors. Because of course, he was Daniel Scott, who had made art the new rock 'n' roll. Allegedly.

He wouldn't be giving a speech — Eva knew enough about him to know that. She also knew enough about Rupert to know that he would have more than enough to say to make up for Daniel's avoidance of the limelight. He was just that sort of man.

"Ladies and gentlemen." Rupert clapped his hands and glanced back at Daniel, as though seeking some approval. He didn't receive it, Eva noted, as Daniel merely waited, arms folded, his mouth set in a tight, serious line.

"Ladies and gentleman," Rupert began again, not at all deterred. "Please join me in welcoming Daniel Scott not only back to the UK, but to Brighton and the Hawley Gallery."

He turned to Daniel again and applauded, joined by the enthusiastic audience. Every eye in the place fell on the bad boy of English art and he rewarded them with the briefest, most cursory tip of the head that Eva had ever seen.

'Was it the Met or the Tate Modern?'

But the applause just went on. And Eva didn't join in.

It was too warm in the gallery, too many overdressed people packed in together. Too much free booze. And far, far too much sycophantic twaddle. Eva made for the French windows at the back of the room and headed out onto the terrace. A cool breeze came in from the sea and fluttered the pages of her programme open on a moody photo of Daniel. A gushing blurb, doubtless penned by Rupert, filled the opposite page. Eva read it under her breath.

"Autodidact... Self-taught genius... No formal training. Raised in care. Visceral...controversial... Cocking a snoot at the Art Establishment...the Met...Tate Modern...Pompidou...BBC 4 documentary...household name."

It told her nothing new about the man. These were merely the same facts that were always trotted off about him with the ease of myth. The man who had upset the art establishment apple cart, then been taken for a lap of honour in it.

Eva took her time leafing through the programme. The photos really didn't do justice to Daniel's paintings. They had to be seen in person, to stand under them and take in their size. But if only... *If only he'd push himself.*

Inside, she could hear the steady drone of Rupert's speech, the occasional burst of polite laughter or applause, but out here, all was calm. The sun was setting over the ocean, reflecting red on the surface as the heat of the day bowed to a sultry night. Eva took a deep breath of fresh air, her only companion a distant yacht sailing a peaceful horizon.

There was another rustle of applause from inside, this one going on longer, signalling the end of the speech. Tribute had been paid to the man who wore sunglasses indoors and was, she imagined, being adored by his public even now. Standing beneath his paintings and silently preening, the quintessential man in black.

She vaguely heard the sound of a cigarette lighter igniting close by but didn't pay her fellow escapee any attention. She wasn't in the mood for sharing platitudes about how marvellous it was to welcome Daniel Scott to Brighton. Besides, Lyndsey would be back with more Prosecco soon enough — all she had to do was wait.

"I've wracked my brains," she heard a man say. "Was it the Moscow Modern?"

Daniel Scott himself.

Eva slipped the programme into her handbag. "Yes. And MOMA in Glasgow." She raised her eyebrow at him. "And my most famous work, the border of dancing cakes on every page of a bestselling cookbook."

"That was *you*?" Daniel took a long drag on his cigarette. His eyes were still hidden behind the lenses of his Wayfarers, but she sensed his gaze was on her. "You must be due a retrospective?"

"Put it in your diary, you won't want to miss it, it's next month at the South Bank Centre." *You infuriating, good-looking bastard.* "You're not annoying me, you know. You *are* outside now, so I won't complain about the sunglasses. Although once the sun's set, they should really come off again."

"Call it the *Daniel Scott Method*," he suggested, repeating Eva's own words back to her. "Should I include a sunset in my landscape? *The Haywain, with Sunset and Dancing Cakes.*"

"Don't you even want to try?" Eva's gaze drifted down from the sunglasses, which only showed her reflection, to the triangle of exposed skin peeping out from his unbuttoned shirt. The man radiated sex, and standing out here on the terrace with him — and only him — Eva was deeply aware of her attraction to him, of every reaction in her body at his closeness. She was at risk of making a fool of herself, she knew, but…she wanted him.

"Do you think I should?" He held out the cigarette to her. "It's a genuine question."

About the Authors

Catherine Curzon

Catherine Curzon is a royal historian who writes on all matters of 18th century. Her work has been featured on many platforms and Catherine has also spoken at various venues including the Royal Pavilion, Brighton, and Dr Johnson's House.

Catherine holds a Master's degree in Film and when not dodging the furies of the guillotine, writes fiction set deep in the underbelly of Georgian London.

She lives in Yorkshire atop a ludicrously steep hill.

Eleanor Harkstead

Eleanor Harkstead often dashes about in nineteenth-century costume, in bonnet or cravat as the mood takes her. She can occasionally be found wandering old graveyards, and is especially fond of the ones in Edinburgh. Eleanor is very fond of chocolate, wine, tweed waistcoats and nice pens. She has a large collection of vintage hats, and once played guitar in a band. Originally from the south-east, Eleanor now lives somewhere in the Midlands with a large ginger cat who resembles a Viking.

Sign up to receive their newsletter at
https://curzonharkstead.co.uk/newsletter/

Catherine and Eleanor love to hear from readers. You can find their contact information, website and author biographies at https://www.totallybound.com.

Home of Erotic Romance

Sign up for our newsletter and find out about all our romance book releases, eBook sales and promotions, sneak peeks and FREE romance books!